Absolute Power

Absolute Power

Zari

www.urbanbooks.net

Urban Books, LLC
300 Farmingdale Road, N.Y.-Route 109
Farmingdale, NY 11735

Absolute Power

ISBN 13: 978-1-64556-346-4
ISBN 10: 1-64556-346-4

First Trade Paperback Printing July 2022
Printed in the United States of America

10 9 8 7 6 5 4 3 2 1

*This is a work of fiction. Any references or similarities
to actual events, real people, living or dead, or to real
locales are intended to give the novel a sense of reality.
Any similarity in other names, characters, places, and
incidents is entirely coincidental.*

Distributed by Kensington Publishing Corp.
Submit Orders to:
Customer Service
400 Hahn Road
Westminster, MD 21157-4627
Phone: 1-800-733-3000
Fax: 1-800-659-2436

Absolute Power

by

Zari

Chapter One

Imani Mosley got out of bed, picked up her robe from the accent bench, and stepped out on the balcony of her beachfront condo in Jacksonville Beach. As she put on her robe, Imani took a deep breath and inhaled the fresh air. She leaned against the rail and looked out at the full moon hanging over the Atlantic Ocean. Ever since she was a little girl enjoying walks with her grandparents, she had loved the beach—the sight and smells of the ocean, the gentle breeze. So even though she lived at her father, Orpheus Mosley's house, this condo was Imani's own personal retreat.

She would go there at times when she needed space or wanted to clear her head from the pressure of everything that was going on in her world, and on those days when her younger brother, Hareem, seemed to do a dance all over her last nerve.

"Which is damn near every day," she said aloud and laughed, because on this day, it was all three.

Since moving to Jacksonville, Imani had been working to rebuild the family's legitimate business, Luxury Private Charters, and return it to the unparalleled customer-focused private aviation and transportation service that it was before they had got run out of Miami three years ago. This day had definitely not been a good day in terms of the effort to improve the business's quality of service.

During the day, Hareem had come to her at the office to complain about Benjamin Cameron, a dealer who worked for a woman who called herself Diamond. She was Hareem's main competition for control of the Jacksonville drug market. He wanted either to push her out of the market or get her to buy from him.

"Problem is I don't know who she is or how to get with her," Hareem had told Imani when she was trying to deal with ten other things at once. "She's like a ghost in them streets."

Imani looked up from what she was doing. "Then don't you think finding her should be your first priority?"

"Yeah, I guess you're right."

"Forget about Cameron. He's the small fish and a waste of your time. I'll put Lucius on finding Diamond, okay?"

Hareem nodded his head. "Cool," he said. Even though he didn't like Lucius Cunningham and thought that he was an asshole, Lucius did know people in Jacksonville, and he got results.

"Now get out. I have work to do," Imani said, and Hareem left her office.

That was how most of her day had gone. She'd put out one fire and moved on to the next. And then Imani had had a date that evening, so this had been one of those days that had ended with her needing some space.

And on top of all that, the following day was an important one for her father. It was the day that weapons trafficker Brock Whitehall was getting out of federal prison in Atlanta after serving every day of a ten-year sentence for the unlawful possession of firearms and transporting assault weapons. Ten years that he had done for her father. So Imani not only wanted but truly needed to clear her head before tomorrow.

Part of her day had been spent arranging for a limousine to pick Brock up once he was released and take him to the airport. And when he arrived in Jacksonville, another limousine would pick him up from the airport and bring him to the house. Imani had even included a little something extra to occupy him while he waited for his flight to depart from Atlanta. Her father was excited that the day had finally come, and he was really looking forward to seeing Brock.

It is the only thing that went right today, she thought. "You ain't fooling nobody," she said aloud and laughed. "You're just as excited about seeing Brock again as Daddy is."

Imani was excited because before Brock went to prison, she'd had what she called a schoolgirl crush on him. It had developed the very day he started working for her father. By the time she'd met him when she was fifteen, Imani had had a grown woman's body, complete with full breasts and a small waist, and she'd had an ass that men would follow and pay homage to. But despite all that body she'd carried, Brock had barely noticed her, and when he finally did, he'd treated her like the little girl that she was. By the time he'd gone to jail when she was seventeen, Brock Whitehall was the star of her fantasy life.

It was that tall, muscular body, that deep brown skin, and those penetrating eyes that had made her want him. But it was his deep baritone voice that she had sat on the steps and listened to while she'd run her finger up and down the seam of her jeans until her legs would shake. Imani used to imagine Brock sneaking into her bedroom when nobody was home. Then she would show him just how much of a woman, and not a little girl, she was. She would wrap her long legs around him while he dicked her down long and hard. Just the thought of it all these years later still had an effect on her.

She heard the sliding door behind her open, and soon she felt D'Mario's arms around her waist. He nuzzled her neck and then kissed Imani on the cheek.

"Are you coming back to bed?" D'Mario asked as he glided his hands down Imani's body. He was about to ease between her thighs when she turned in his arms and kissed him on the cheek.

"I am, but you're not." She kissed him on the other cheek and freed herself from his embrace. He had done what she needed him to do. "It's time for you to go."

Chapter Two

"Stand up! Count!" the guard yelled, and the men on the block slowly began coming out of their cells to be counted.

Brock Whitehall got up from his bunk and stood for the count one last time. He was getting out that day, so he hadn't really slept all night. He'd been out of bed and pacing back and forth since five in the morning.

"You might as well sit your ass down. Guard ain't gonna open that door no sooner just 'cause you getting out today," his cellmate told him.

"You're right."

So Brock sat down to wait, but sitting didn't make him any less anxious. He had done his time, and now it was time to go.

"Morning, short-timer," the guard said to Brock as he opened the door to the cell. Brock stepped into the corridor, and the guard passed by to continue his count.

"What you gonna do when you get out, Brock?" asked an inmate from the next cell.

"I'll tell you what he gonna do!" an older inmate yelled out. "He's gonna get a drink of fine liquor, fuck a couple a fine-ass bitches, kill him a couple a niggas, and come right back home."

"That's *your* plan, old man." Brock laughed. "You're institutionalized," he added, and then he went back in his cell to wait to be released.

He lay down on his bunk and stared up at the bunk above him and asked himself the question. It was the same question he'd been asking himself for the past few years. Ever since his release date had begun getting closer and getting out had actually started to feel like something real, something he could actually feel and hold on to, Brock had been asking himself what he was going to do when he got out.

What he usually came up with was a list of things that he didn't want to do and a list of reasons why he didn't want to do those things when he got free. Brock had served ten years for the unlawful possession of firearms and for transporting assault weapons, so the one thing that he was absolutely sure of was that he didn't want to do that or chance anything else that might lead to him getting locked up again.

"No more penitentiary-type chances," were the words Brock said aloud as he got up from his bunk for the very last time. It was the promise that he'd made to himself, and he had every intention of keeping it. All that was left now was to be processed out, and Brock Whitehall would be a free man.

It was a little after nine that morning when the limousine that Imani had ordered for Brock parked in the parking lot at the United States Penitentiary in Atlanta. The driver wasn't at all sure what time they were going to release Brock, but the flight to Jacksonville wasn't until that afternoon, so he was prepared to wait. It was a little over an hour later when a man came out of the main building. The driver looked at the picture he had been given, got out of the limousine, and opened the back door.

"Brock Whitehall?"

"Yes," Brock said, surprised but happy with the reception.

"My name is Anthony. Mr. Orpheus Mosley sends his regards and hopes that you'll be comfortable on your ride to the airport."

"Thank you, Anthony. I'm sure it will be a smooth ride," Brock said and got in the limo, knowing that it didn't matter if it was smooth or not as long as he was free.

As they pulled out of the prison parking lot, Brock noticed that there was a large envelope on the seat next to him. He picked it up and saw that it was addressed to him.

"What's this, Anthony?" he asked, holding the envelope up and feeling the weight of it.

"I'm not sure, sir. It's addressed to you."

"I noticed," Brock said. He opened it slowly and looked inside. He took the note from the envelope and looked at the picture attached to it. He smiled at the picture, and then he read the note.

A little something you might be interested in doing while you wait for your flight to depart.

The note had an address on it, and it was signed M.

Brock recognized the man in the picture and knew that he had a decision to make. He thought about the two promises that he had made to himself at different times in his life.

No more penitentiary-type chances, Brock thought and took a deep breath. That was the second promise.

"I need to make a quick stop, Anthony. It won't take but a minute," Brock said as he looked at the other items that were in the envelope.

"Not a problem, Mr. Whitehall. Where to?"

"Stone Mountain. And take your time, Anthony. I want to see the world."

"Yes, sir. Surface streets and cruise, just the way I like it. You sit back, Mr. Whitehall, relax, and watch the honeys walk by. This the ATL. We thick with honeys walking the street, looking for something to get into," Anthony said as he headed toward Memorial Drive.

As he enjoyed the sights on the forty-five-minute ride to Stone Mountain and marveled at how much the city had changed since he had last been there, Brock thought more about those two promises and tried to reconcile them. He decided that the earlier promise, the one that a younger man had made to himself, was unfinished business. Therefore, this promise had nothing to do with his more recent "No more penitentiary-type chances" promise to himself.

"Some promises have to be kept. Especially the ones you make to yourself," Brock said softly as Anthony turned into a strip mall on Memorial Drive and parked in front of a barbershop. "I'll be right back, Anthony. This will take only a minute."

"Take your time, Mr. Whitehall. I'll be right here," Anthony said as Brock got out of the limo with the envelope in hand.

As he walked toward the barbershop, Brock took the gloves from the envelope and put them on. Then he stopped at the barbershop door, took the gun from the envelope, and then went inside. The shop wasn't crowded: just a couple of guys waiting and one in the chair, getting a cut.

"Come in and have a seat," the barber said without looking at Brock, as he was totally focused on cutting the perfect line.

"What's up, Sonny?"

The barber looked up and saw Brock with his gun raised. "Oh shit," he said resolutely and prepared to die.

"I thought you were dead," Brock said and pulled the trigger.

His first shot struck Sonny in the head, and once his body hit the floor, Brock stepped up and shot him twice more before he turned and left the barbershop. He dropped the gun in the trash can outside of the barbershop, walked calmly to the limo, and got in.

"That didn't take long," Anthony said and pulled off.

"No. In and out, like a robbery."

Sonny was the reason that Brock had lost ten years of his life, so he had to die.

"Just needed to keep a promise that I made to myself," he added and then relaxed for the ride to the airport. He would get rid of the picture, the gloves, the note, and the envelope when he got there.

Chapter Three

It was about that time that Orpheus Mosley, or Mr. O, as he was called, stood looking out the dining room window of his six-bedroom Ponte Vedra Beach home and thinking about the past. His father, Hughbert Mosley, had come to America from the island of Antigua in the early 1950s and had settled in New Orleans. He had got hired on to work on a fishing boat and had saved his money until he was able to buy a small boat of his own. He had just begun offering fishing charters when he met Lois Johnson, a very beautiful woman from Miami. She had come to New Orleans to visit with friends, and a charming young man her invited her on his boat. The two fell in love, and it wasn't long before Hughbert moved his business to Miami, and soon after, they were married.

By the mid-1960s, Hughbert and Lois had three children, a boy, Orpheus, and two girls. At the time Hughbert was working as a janitor while trying to expand his fishing charter business. But he was working at a disadvantage, because not only was he limited to offering his charter services on the weekends, but potential clients often passed up his older, smaller boat in favor of the newer boats. And in those days, just being a black man came with disadvantages of its own.

"Good morning, Daddy," Imani said when she came into the room.

"Morning, Imani. How are you today?" he asked as she walked up to him and kissed him on the cheek.

"I'm fine," she said and then went to help herself to some eggplant hummus and bacon-asparagus crescent spirals from the buffet that their housekeeper, Kimberly, had arranged for the family and anyone who came to the house. There was also a cheesy ham, egg, and potato breakfast casserole; eggs Benedict; ham, mushroom, and cheese quiche; and Amish pancakes.

"What's on your agenda today?" Mr. O asked.

You mean other than seeing Brock? "I have a meeting with the new company that I'm looking at to do maintenance on the air fleet, and then I need to see what I can do to resolve an issue that Hareem is having," she said and sat down at the table. She looked up at him. "You're not eating?"

"I'm not that hungry this morning. I'll grab something later," he said. He poured a cup of coffee before coming to sit down at the table with Imani. "What kind of problem is he having?"

"He's still on this Diamond thing."

Mr. O chuckled. "Does he know who she is yet?"

"That's the problem. I told him that discovering her identity should be his first priority, and I put Lucius on finding her." She put down her fork and reached for her father's hand. "Why don't you want to eat? Are you feeling all right, Daddy?" Imani asked. He was a diabetic, and he'd had a stroke years earlier, so she was worried about his health.

"You worry too much, Imani. I'm fine. Stronger than a whale." He flexed his arm, but the truth was that he had been feeling a little tired lately. "I'm just not hungry, and I got a lot on my mind." And he thought that was the reason for the mild heartburn he'd been suffering lately.

"Like what?" Imani giggled. "Other than Brock getting out today, I mean."

"Just thinking about all this. What this family built, what we're trying to do here." He sipped his coffee. "Thinking about the future."

"We certainly have come a long way from Granddaddy and that one little boat," Imani said, and then she thought briefly about the times that she had got to spend with her grandparents when she was young. She could sit for hours with them, fascinated by the stories that they used to tell her. She loved to hear Grandma Lois tell the story of how she and her grandfather had met at the dock.

"Chile, let me tell you, your granddaddy was a fine, handsome man," she would say as she began the story. She would tell her granddaughter that she didn't even fish; in fact, the smell of fish made her nauseated. But she fell in love with Hughbert the night he took her for a romantic evening out on the water.

But Imani's favorite stories were the ones that her grandfather used to tell her about how they had got started in the weapon-smuggling business. Her grand-mother hadn't approved of him telling young Imani those stories, but he had felt that it was a part of her heritage and she needed to know who she was and where she came from.

He had told Imani of one hot, muggy, overcast day in particular, when he'd sat on the deck of his boat, taking a nap. It had been a slow day, even for the white boys, as overcast days tended to be, so Hughbert had been surprised when a man kicked the bow of his boat.

"I want to charter a boat. You available?"

"I sure am," Hughbert said, springing to his feet. "You ain't worried about the weather turning bad on you?" he asked as he got the boat ready to shove off.

"I think it's better fishing in cloudy weather. On days like this," the man said as he came aboard. "Fish are more active in reduced sunlight, and that makes them much easier to catch."

Eventually, the man introduced himself as Saulo Lorencio, and they set out to sea and spent the afternoon fishing for grouper. By the end of the day, when Hughbert was getting ready to head back to the dock, Saulo asked him to have a beer with him.

"I don't drink when I'm working, sir."

"Saulo. Please call me Saulo." He pointed. "That's a wise practice, my friend. But you do drink?"

"Yes, sir. I can hold my own, just not while I'm working."

"Then you're fired," Saulo said and took out the money he owed for the day. He handed it to Hughbert. "Now you're not working. I'll pay you the same amount to take me back to the dock after we have a drink together."

"Fair enough," Hughbert said and broke out the beer.

As they talked over their beer, Hughbert told Saulo about his family and the goals that he'd set for himself. After that first beer, Saulo asked if Hughbert had anything stronger. Hughbert broke out the Scotch, and they drained the bottle before they headed back.

Early the following morning, Saulo was back with a full bottle of Scotch.

"Back again?" Hughbert said, smiling, because Saulo had already made this the best weekend he'd ever had, and now he was back.

"Yes, my friend, and I want to show you one of my favorite fishing spots. I promise you that you'll have the biggest haul that you have ever seen," Saulo said and poked Hughbert in the chest. "You are ready to change your life, aren't you?"

Hughbert laughed. "I sure am," he said, and once Saulo was aboard, they set out to sea, with Hughbert thinking that it must be one hell of a spot if it was going to change his life.

When they got to Saulo's life-changing spot, Hughbert dropped anchor and broke out the fishing tackle. For the rest of the day, the two drank Scotch and engaged in good conversation but did not catch many fish. It was later in the day, as the sun began to go down, that Hughbert saw another boat approaching.

"Don't worry. I've been expecting them," Saulo said, standing up to wave the boat over.

Soon four crates were being loaded aboard Hughbert's boat. Hughbert didn't ask any questions; he just helped get the heavy crates aboard. After Saulo talked with the men on the other boat, he told Hughbert to head back to the dock.

"Guess you want to know what's in the crates," Saulo said as the two men stood over them as the boat skimmed the water.

"I don't know. Do I?"

"Remember I said this was life changing?"

"I do."

"Then you want to know what's in here if you want to change your life," Saulo said, and Hughbert nodded. "Got a crowbar?"

After Hughbert handed Saulo a crowbar, he opened up one of the crates.

"Guns," Hughbert said as he looked into the open crate.

"This time." Saulo handed Hughbert a fat envelope. "Next time it might be something else. Marijuana, cocaine. Might even be people. You got a problem with that?" Saulo paused. "If you do, once we reach the dock, you help me unload my cargo, and we never have to see each other again. Or!" Saulo raised a finger to empathize his point. "Or we can shake hands . . . I see you next week . . . and your life changes forever."

Hughbert looked in the envelope and then held out his hand. "See you next week, Saulo." He and Saulo shook hands, and with that, the Mosley family was in the smuggling business.

"Morning," Hareem said and went straight to the buffet and filled his plate with the cheesy casserole, slices of quiche, and Amish pancakes. He rarely stayed at the house; most nights Hareem stayed with his girlfriend, Cynthia Miles. She was the daughter of Alexander Miles, who owned the largest black real estate firm in North Florida. But he came to eat at the family home every morning, because Kimberly could cook her ass off.

"Morning, son," Mr. O said and sipped his coffee as Hareem sat down.

Hareem shoved some food in his mouth. "What's the matter with you?" he asked Imani.

"What makes you think something's the matter with me?"

"'Cause you got that 'Shit's fucked up' look on your face."

"No. Nothing is wrong. I was just thinking about your problem, which really isn't a problem, but I think the solution is not to find her but to make her come to you."

"Smart," Mr. O said, and Imani nodded.

"Okay. How do I do that?" Hareem asked, and both Imani and Mr. O looked at him.

"Do I have to tell you how to do everything?" Imani asked, but she knew that the answer was yes. Her half brother was a doer, not a planner.

"Get in her pocket. That will draw her out, and if you do it right, she will come to you," Mr. O said, thinking that the way to do that was with good quality and the right price. "We'll talk about ways that you can do that later."

"Okay, Daddy," Hareem said just as his phone rang. He pulled it out of his pocket, looked at the display, and got up from the table before he answered. "What she say?" he asked as he walked out of the dining room.

"Be patient with your brother."

"I am being patient, Daddy. I'm just not as patient as you are. If he's gonna run that side of the business, then he needs to run it and not keep running to me for everything."

"You're right, Imani. He should. And one day he will. But in the meantime, I expect you to help your brother, and if that means that you make every decision for him and make him think it's his idea, then that's what you have to do. We're a family, Imani."

"It's our strength," Imani said before he could.

"That's right. Family. That's what your grandfather built this business on."

With the influx of capital from working with Saulo, Hughbert had been able to expand his charter fishing business during the closing years of the sixties, and by the early seventies, at Saulo's urging, Hughbert bought his first airplane. It was an Aero Commander 100 that had been built in 1967. It needed a lot of work, but it could fly. And for the remainder of the decade, both men's charter and smuggling businesses flourished. By the eighties, Hughbert had five boats and two planes. But it was Miami in the eighties, a time of drugs, guns, and money. And Hughbert's son, Orpheus, or Big O, as he was called in the streets, took the business to the next level.

"I thought *you* built this business on guns and cocaine?" Hareem said as he came back into the dining room.

"I did," Mr. O said proudly. "But it was the foundation that I inherited from your grandfather, the understanding of the importance of family being at the center of everything we did, that made this family what it was."

"And what it will be again," Hareem said. "Wait. You'll see. We gonna be bigger than we were in Miami." He looked at Imani. "If I have anything to say about it, that is."

"You?" Imani questioned. "You think *you* can do it better . . . and smarter than Daddy and Granddad?"

"I never met the old man," Hareem said bitterly. "And no, I don't think I'm better or smarter than Daddy." He pointed at her. "That's you. I'm learning from the best." He pointed at his father. "So just like Daddy took the old man's program to the next level, I'm gonna do the same."

Hareem was right. It hadn't taken young Orpheus long to realize that he had access to what everybody wanted. He saw how much more money he could make with a few minor changes to the way his father did business. With his father's blessing, Orpheus met with Saulo, who, once he'd asked if Orpheus was sure that this was what he wanted to do, introduced him to an associate. Arrangements were made, money was exchanged, and solemn promises of loyalty and discretion were spoken, and Orpheus made his move into the very lucrative Miami gun and drug market.

With two products that were in high demand, Big O was a force to be reckoned with throughout the eighties and the nineties. It was during those years that Orpheus began running the family's legitimate business, changing the name from Mosley Charter Service to Luxury Private Charters. He had grown up in this business and had plenty of ideas for expansion. His vision included private and group air charters, boat rentals, yacht charters, and river cruises. At the same time, Big O got deeper into the drug and gun trade.

But by the turn of the twenty-first century, things began to change. New players that didn't play by the same
rules entered the picture, and Big O, a man in his fifties,
who was now called Mr. O as a sign of respect, was forced
to change with the times. It was during those years that
he met and took under his wing a twenty-year-old banger
named Brock Whitehall, who was trying to buy guns.

Chapter Four

"Ladies and gentlemen, Delta Airlines welcomes you to Jacksonville. The local time is seven minutes after four in the afternoon. Please remain seated with your seat belt fastened until the captain has turned off the FASTEN SEAT BELT sign," the flight attendant announced.

After the plane taxied to the gate and the captain turned the seat belt sign off, Brock remained in his seat in the first-class section as the passengers in coach rushed into the aisle to retrieve their items from the overhead compartments, only to wait for first-class passengers to exit the plane. When the flight attendant opened the front door of the plane, Brock stood up and quickly got off the plane. Even though he had no luggage, he headed for the baggage claim.

It was the first time he had been to Jacksonville, so he was looking forward to seeing the city, and if he liked it, he just might stay. As he got closer to baggage carousel for his flight, Brock noticed a very pretty woman with great legs. She was dressed in a white shirt and tie, a black jacket, and a skirt that her hips filled nicely and was carrying a sign that said WHITEHALL, so he walked up to her.

"I believe you're looking for me," he told her.

"If you're Brock Whitehall, I most certainly am. My name is Ginger, and I'll be seeing to your comfort and safe arrival today. Please, follow me."

"With pleasure," he said, and then he followed Ginger to the limousine for the forty-minute ride to the Mosleys' home on Palm Forest Place in Ponte Vedra Beach, a beachfront community southeast of the city.

"Wow," Brock said when Ginger turned off Palm Forest Place onto a long driveway that led to a fabulous seven-bedroom, fifteen-thousand-square-foot house. "I could get with this," he added as she rounded the circle with a water fountain that was surrounded by palm trees.

When Ginger parked and opened the limousine door for him, Brock got out and looked around.

"Yeah, I could definitely get with all this."

"I hope that you enjoyed the ride," Ginger said and closed the door.

"I did. Thank you," he said, still marveling at the house and the grounds.

"Welcome to Jacksonville, Mr. Whitehall," she said and held out her hand. "I'm sure we'll see each other again."

Brock shook her hand. "I certainly hope so."

He got one last look at her legs as Ginger walked around the car. Then he walked to the front door and rang the bell. Kimberly opened the door several seconds later.

"Good afternoon. Brock Whitehall to see Mr. O."

"Please come in, Mr. Whitehall." When Kimberly stepped aside, Brock stepped into the foyer.

"Thank you."

"Mr. O has been expecting you."

From where he stood in the foyer, Brock gazed at the spiral staircase with a marble railing that led to the second level. His eyes were then drawn to the Crystal Rain chandelier that hung over the spiral design in the granite floor just in front of the staircase.

This is amazing, he thought. The foyer was three times the size of the cell he'd spent the past ten years in.

"Right this way, Mr. Whitehall," Kimberly said.

As Brock followed Kimberly through the spacious house, he examined the elaborate decor and thought about what he had missed the past ten years and how well this family had done for itself. When he heard the sound of Bob Marley's "Guiltiness" playing, he smiled.

The boss loves him some Bob.

It was Mr. O who had turned him on to reggae. Bob Marley's singing caused him to think that everything important he'd learned in life, he'd learned from Mr. O. Brock remembered spending hours riding around with him, listening to Bob, while Mr. O taught him the business. Brock never did get involved in the drug game, though. It just wasn't his thing. Smuggling and the weapons business, that was how he'd made his money.

"There he is!" Mr. O said as Kimberly led Brock into the large game room, which featured a pool table, Napa black leather furniture, and rich mahogany walls. Off the game room was an expansive back deck. "How the hell are you, Brock?"

"I'm fine. Thank you, sir," he said and shook the other man's hand. He looked out the floor-to-ceiling windows at the huge pool outside. *Is that a fuckin' waterfall?*

"Can I get you a drink?" Mr. O asked as he stepped over to the bar.

"Whatever you're drinking is fine," Brock said as he followed behind.

"I bet it is." Mr. O laughed. "I'm sure a real drink of anything would be fine with you."

"No shit. Anything aged over a week would be fine with me." Brock laughed as Mr. O poured his drink.

"How was your flight?"

"It was good," Brock replied, and Mr. O handed him the glass. "What's this?"

"Do you care?" Mr. O asked, motioning for Brock to drink up.

Brock shot back the drink and closed his eyes. "That's smooth."

"That's Jack Daniel's No. 27 Gold you're drinking," Mr. O said and poured Brock another and one for himself.

"You never know how much you miss drinking good liquor until you drink good liquor," Brock noted. He shot back his drink, and Mr. O refilled his glass once more.

"Anything else you miss?"

Brock chuckled. "I managed to get through all ten years without getting violated, and I didn't violate anybody, if that's what you're asking, so I am very hungry."

"We'll see what we can do about that when we roll out later tonight." He laughed. "But that was too much information."

"You asked," Brock said and looked around the room. "So what's all this?"

"You mean the house?"

"Yeah, the house. It's a fuckin' mansion."

"It's not a mansion."

"It don't seem like your kind of house," Brock said and shrugged his shoulders.

"That's 'cause it ain't. You know me. I like a low-profile spot up in the hood. I bought this house as an investment for Imani and Hareem."

"That his name?"

"Yeah. Hareem Jaleel." Mr. O refilled their glasses. "His girlfriend's people own a real estate firm. It was one of their agents, Alexis Fox, with her sexy fuckin' ass, that sold us the house. But you know all this shit." He shook his head. "You know this ain't me."

"Damn sure ain't." Brock pointed. "There's a fuckin' waterfall out there."

"Ain't that some shit?" Mr. O cleared his throat. "It's an artificial waterfall, and it's called a grotto," he said, trying to sound proper.

"Whatever you say, boss."

Both men laughed. "Damn, it's good to see you," Mr. O said.

"It's damn good to see you too, boss."

"While we're out tonight, I'll show you my spot."

"A low-profile spot up in the hood?"

"You know this." Mr. O picked up the bottle again, and Brock covered his glass with his hand.

"I'm good."

Mr. O put down the bottle and decided to stop wasting time and ask him the question that had been on his mind a lot lately. "You thought about what you want to do now that you're a free man?" he asked, because he had plans for Brock.

"I knew that we'd get around to you asking me that. I hoped by now I'd be able to answer you"—he tapped the bar—"and say, 'Bang, this is what I want to do.'" He tapped the bar again. "This is how I want to do it. But I can't." Brock sipped his drink. "All I know right now is that I don't want to go back to doing what I was doing."

"I can understand that." Although he could understand, he was disappointed. "Ten years is a long time to have to sit around and think of what you did to get there." Mr. O thought about the reason that Brock did that time. "We got plenty of time to figure all that out," he said, and then he paused. "Unless you're just passing through, come to get what's yours and move on. I can understand that too. And if that's what you want, we can take care of all that in the morning," he added, but he'd be let down if that was Brock's plan. "But I was hoping you'd stick around for a while."

Mr. O had always had plans for Brock; his going to jail had just postponed them for a while.

"Ain't no rush, boss. I ain't got nowhere I need to be no time soon." Brock finished his drink. "At least until I figure out what I want to do with the rest of my life."

Mr. O smiled and poured them both another drink. "Well, if that's the case, while you figure things out, Imani says I need somebody to drive for me."

"It'll be like old times." Brock laughed. Mr. O raised his glass, and they drank to it. "I remember the first time you tossed me the keys." He shook his head. "I was so excited to drive that Lexus—"

"That you damn near wrecked my Lexus," Mr. O laughed.

"I was too busy trying to look cool driving." Brock sipped his drink, drifted away from the bar, and leaned against the pool table. "So, Jacksonville, huh?"

"Yeah, Jacksonville." Mr. O shot back his drink. "Jaxport is nothing like the port of Miami, but it is perfect for what we do, and it doesn't come with that Miami heat."

"Believe me, I get it. It makes sense," Brock said, and then there was an uncomfortable silence between them. Mr. O had a feeling he knew why.

"Go ahead and ask me what you want to ask me," he said to get the issue out of the way.

"I heard you got run out of Miami. Is that true?"

Mr. O nodded. "True. I don't like the way it sounds. I like to think of it as more of a wise business decision, but yeah, we got run out of Miami."

"What happened?"

"Exactly what you said was gonna happen ten years ago."

Chapter Five

Miami, Florida
Ten years ago . . .

"New players in the game these days." Mr. O said as he smoked a blunt.

The sound of Bob's "Burnin' and Lootin'" pumped out of the speakers of the Ford Explorer that Mr. O had bought earlier that day. That night, Brock was driving them to meet Teon Fleming and Arturo Vargas to oversee the sale of M16 rifles for use in their guerilla war in Central America. There was nothing that he could really point to, but Brock had a feeling that something wasn't right, and he couldn't shake it. He didn't trust Arturo. He was too close to Warwick Vance, and Brock had a feeling that was where their guns would go.

Mr. O went on. "They don't play by the same rules. There used to be a time when all that killing was on the streets. Not anymore. Guys like Roberto, Joaquin Herminio, and Warwick Vance don't have respect for shit. Acting like a bunch of corner boys, shooting each other over bullshit. There used to be a time when you could sit down, work out your problems, and everybody went back to making money." He hit the blunt and then passed it to Brock. "Not happening. These muthafuckas nowadays only know one way to solve problems."

"Shoot first. Fuck asking questions."

"Questions?" Mr. O laughed. "No questions getting asked, no discussion being had. You might fuck around and learn something, reach an understanding." He shook his head. "Just kill them."

"Maybe we should think seriously about stepping back from the dope game and just focus on the guns. Safer. Attracts less attention from the local cops. Better to get out before they push you out or put you out of the game permanently," Brock said.

Mr. O said nothing, but deep inside, he knew that Brock was right.

The truth was Mr. O had gotten old in the game, and his health wasn't what it used to be. He wasn't the angry young man with something to prove to his father that he had been in the eighties. And he had less and less heart for all the violence and killing. But those years in the game had taught him that there were times when resorting to violence and killing was not only the best option but also the only option.

"Turn that up," Mr. O said when "Kinky Reggae" came on.

Brock turned up the song because he liked it too, but he stayed on him. "And I still don't think you need to be there tonight."

"Everything is going to be fine," Mr. O assured a skeptical Brock. "I got Laran and Kimble on the lookout outside. And my guy in vice says we're good. You worry too much."

"Even so, why you gotta be here? It's Sonny's deal. Let him handle it," Brock said, because something just didn't feel right to him. "There is no reason for you to be here."

Brock had always trusted his instincts, and they hadn't failed him yet. He glanced over at Mr. O. He had been a player in the game for years, long before Brock was even born. So if he said there was nothing to worry about, then there was nothing to worry about.

Right?

But Brock still wasn't convinced.

"With things being the way they are, I need to show everybody who still has the power and who still runs things," Mr. O revealed.

Brock looked at his boss and paused before he said, "You're planning on killing Arturo, aren't you?"

Brock got no answer. But now he understood why he'd been feeling like something wasn't right. Because it wasn't. Mr. O didn't trust Arturo, either. Arturo and Vance went back years, so Mr. O shared Brock's concern that this was where their guns were going.

"This truck, Sherwin, Rashaan, and Darnel, I knew something was up." Brock shook his head, because they were Mr. O's drug enforcers. Brock had asked about the changes and had been told that it was "just a show of force."

"And that's what this is. A show of force," Mr. O finally said.

"You could have told me."

"What would you have said?"

"I got you. That's what I would have said. I got you, boss, just like I always do," Brock said and turned into the warehouse parking lot.

Mr. O nodded. "I know that. Honestly." He smiled. "I didn't want to hear you try to talk me out of it."

"Because you know I'm right. Like I said, we need to push all the way back from the table and go back to doing things the way your old man used to do them."

"Maybe you're right. Maybe the only one I'm trying to prove shit to is myself," Mr. O replied, thinking that he was about to do exactly what he had just complained about. Instead of talking to Vance, he was going to kill Arturo to send a message.

Brock drove into the warehouse where the cargo van with their weapons was parked. Teon and Arturo stood on one side of a table, with their men and a van behind them. When Brock got out of the Explorer, he saw that Sonny and another man, whom he had never seen before, were standing at the table too, waiting for Mr. O to get there so they could get started.

Brock leaned back in the truck. "Wait here," he told Mr. O in a low voice.

"What's wrong?"

"You know that guy?" Brock pointed.

"He's one of Sonny's guys," Mr. O said, but he didn't know anything about him. "I've seen him with Sonny a couple of times," was all that he could say for sure.

"Still . . . wait here," Brock said and closed the door to the truck.

Sonny looked at Brock for the go-ahead to get started. Brock looked at the man with Sonny and then at Mr. O before nodding his head. Sonny pointed at Sherwin, and Sherwin and Rashaan opened up the back of the cargo van with the weapons.

"Go ahead. Have a look," Sonny said as Teon and Arturo moved toward the van to inspect the merchandise.

Meanwhile, outside Laran and Kimble were watching the warehouse and had noticed that there was a van parked across the street. Knowing that they needed to check it out, they left their post. As they were approaching the van, they saw a woman get out. They stopped in their tracks when she looked over at them as she walked to the building that she had parked in front of. Then she looked straight ahead and went inside the building. Thinking it was nothing, Laran and Kimble relaxed. It was then that the side door of the van opened and two men jumped out with weapons drawn.

"ATF!" they both shouted.

Laran and Kimble didn't put up a fight and were swiftly taken into custody. As they were being handcuffed, the rear doors to the van swung open, and then more men jumped out and ran toward the warehouse.

Back inside, Teon and Arturo were moving toward the cargo van to inspect the merchandise when ATF agents ran into the warehouse.

"ATF!" one agent yelled as more armed agents appeared. Sonny drew his gun and fired at one of the agents. The agent returned fire and hit Sonny in the chest.

Brock looked at Mr. O and hit the hood of the Explorer. "Go!"

As quickly as he could, Mr. O got in the driver's seat, slammed the gear into reverse, and stepped on the gas. He sped backward out of the warehouse, almost hitting the two agents that were running inside. He backed into the street, slammed on the brakes, put the truck in drive, and zoomed down the street.

When Brock saw the last two agents enter the warehouse, he immediately dropped his gun, kicked it away, and put up his hands.

"Get down on the ground!" one of the agents yelled.

Brock got on the ground and surrendered, and the agents handcuffed him. Since they were there to kill Arturo and Teon, Sherwin and Rashaan opened fire. Their first shots hit Teon as Arturo covered his head and ran. Hearing the shooting, Darnel came out from his position as planned and began firing at the agents with a semiautomatic weapon, expecting Laran and Kimble to back him up.

Another of the agents fired and hit Sherwin in the shoulder, and he went down from the impact. When Rashaan saw him go down, he tried to run, but he didn't get far before he was taken into custody. Darnel kept firing until an agent took aim and got him in his sights. He went down from a shot to the head.

When the shooting stopped, Mr. O was long gone, but Arturo, Rashaan, Laran, and Kimble were all taken into custody, along with Brock. Teon, Darnel, Sherwin, and Sonny were dead.

At least that was what everybody thought.

Chapter Six

"I thought Sonny was dead," Brock said.

"We all did," Imani said as she came into the game room.

Brock snapped his head around to look at her. *Who is that?* he wondered. He had to know immediately. He was mesmerized by the elegant and yet sexy way she walked by, looking at him.

"There she is," Mr. O said.

And there he is, Imani thought as she gazed at Brock. It had been ten years since she had last seen him, but he still looked good. *Even better, if that's possible.* The way that Brock was staring at her let Imani know that he no longer saw her as a little girl. His look screamed, *I want you.*

Both men stood still as Imani went over and kissed her father on the cheek. "Hi, Daddy," she said, and then she turned to Brock. She stepped closer to him and looked up into his eyes. "Welcome to Jacksonville, Brock."

"Imani?" he questioned and took all of her in.

That was the look that Imani had wanted when she chose the fitted black midi dress that kissed her curves, the mock turtleneck with a dramatic front cutout that teased her cleavage, and the leather slingback pumps and side slit that made her legs pop. She wanted him to want her.

"Yes." Imani smiled and politely held out her hand. She felt goose bumps appear on her arms as she stood that close to him. And the way that he was looking at her made Imani's insides tremble.

"I don't remember you being this . . . this tall," Brock said to her, instead of telling her that he didn't remember her being this fine.

"It's the pumps," she said, and that gave Brock an excuse to run his eyes slowly down her body until he reached her shoes. "I used to wear a lot of sweatshirts, jeans, and Nikes in those days."

"I see," he said and took his time running his eyes back up her body before he made eye contact with her.

"I'm not a little girl anymore," Imani said, then stepped away from him and sat down.

Mr. O sat down as well, but not Brock. He stood captivated as she crossed her legs. That was exactly the effect that Imani wanted to have on him. Finally, he averted his gaze and sat down opposite Mr. O.

"We all thought that Sonny was dead, because that's what the Feds wanted us to believe," Mr. O explained. "But he was in witness protection the entire time."

"The man who was with him that you didn't recognize," Imani interjected, "was an undercover ATF agent. Sonny got busted for possession by the Miami-Dade PD, and when he said he wanted to deal, they turned him over to the ATF."

Brock looked confused. "If he had a deal with the ATF, why didn't the affidavit they kept bringing up at my trial implicate the boss?"

"Because he couldn't be sure that Daddy would be there, he just told them that his source would be there, and they planned to arrest him on the spot with the merchandise," Imani explained.

"Me," Brock said, his voice low.

"That's why you were able to take the weight for me. But I was definitely the target," Mr. O said.

"Anyway, I appreciated the gift," Brock said, looking at Mr. O. But Imani was the one smiling.

"What gift?" Mr. O asked.

"Sonny."

"What about Sonny?" Mr. O asked.

"That was me," Imani finally said. "I remembered you saying that you would kill him if he wasn't already dead."

Brock nodded and smiled at her. "Thank you."

"Okay, what are you two talking about?" Mr. O asked and then noticed the way that Brock and Imani were looking at each other.

"I found out that the witness protection program had set Sonny up in Atlanta, and he was working as a barber. So I sent Brock the address and the means to take care of him."

"Did you take care of him?"

"Termination with extreme prejudice," Brock said.

"Good man," Mr. O said and raised a glass to Brock, who hadn't turned away from Imani.

Brock shot back his drink. "I owe you one," he said, staring into Imani's eyes. He wanted her. And the way that she was looking at him told Brock that Imani just might want him too. He looked at Mr. O and felt a little funny about wanting to fuck his daughter.

"No, Brock, I'm sorry, but you don't owe me anything. This family owes you a debt that we can never pay. So thank you for what you did," Imani responded.

"She's right. You willingly gave up ten years of your life for me. That is a debt that can't be paid with money. But we took care of you, so you're a rich man now, just like I promised," Mr. O said. His phone rang. He looked at the display. "Excuse me." He stood up. "I need to take this." He headed out of the game room. "Hey, Stacy," he began as he went.

Alone at last, Imani thought, and then she tried to speak, but Brock's intense stare had the words stuck in her throat.

"I know that you just got out, but have you thought about what you want to do now that you're a free man?" "Bend you over and dick you down," was what Imani thought he should say.

"I haven't decided yet. But the one thing that I do know is that I don't want to go back to doing what I was doing that got me locked up."

"You know he's gonna be disappointed. He has big plans for you." Plans that he hadn't chosen to share with her.

"I kinda got that impression when I told him. But I said that I would drive for him until I figure things out."

"He'll like that. You know you're the son he never had." Imani paused. "Until he found out he had one."

Brock smiled. "How is your mother?"

"She's good. Still in Miami. She said to tell you hello and that if you know what's good for you, you will get as far away from Daddy as possible." It was the same advice that she offered Imani each time they spoke.

"Tell Ms. Julia that I said hello and I promise to get down there to see her soon."

"You know she loves you like a son too."

"Ms. Julia was always good to me," Brock said, and then there was a few seconds of silence while each of them searched for something to keep the conversation going. But he couldn't stop looking into her eyes. It was as if her eyes were saying, *Take me, Brock*.

"I see the clothes I sent fit you nicely," Imani said as she sized up the single-breasted olive wool suit by Haitian fashion designer Davidson Petit-Frère he was wearing.

"They do. Thank you." Brock tugged lightly on the lapel. "How did you know my size?"

"I was the one Daddy sent to pack up your things and put them in storage when you went away." Imani stood up and walked over to the bar.

Brock's hands shook a bit, and he almost spilled his drink at the sight of her.

"All of it is here in Jacksonville, in storage." He stood up, and Imani watched him walk toward the bar. *Damn, he looks good in that suit.* "But I'm thinking that the clothes might be a little out of style now," she added and picked up a bottle of Rémy Martin. "Can I get you one?"

"Sure."

"What were you drinking?"

"Jack." He leaned on the bar next to her and looked into her eyes. "But whatever you're drinking is fine," he told her and then watched Imani pour and hand him the glass.

"I got you some more clothes. They're in a bedroom upstairs. I didn't know if you had a place to stay or not, so I had Kimberly get the room ready for you. You're welcome to stay as long as you want."

"No, I don't have a place to stay, so thank you, Imani," Brock said and raised his glass to her. "You think of everything."

"That's what I do around here. I take care of everything." Imani turned toward Brock and put the glass to her lips. "And everybody," she said very sexily before taking a sip.

"Well, thank you again, Imani. I really appreciate what you've done for me," Brock told her. He was about to say something flirtatious when Mr. O came back into the room.

"Come on. Let's get out of here. We got places to go and people to see," he said excitedly, because Brock was back. He walked to the door without noticing the disappointed looks on Imani's and Brock's faces.

Just when it was starting to get interesting, Brock thought. "I guess I'll see you later," he said to Imani and started for the door behind Mr. O.

Imani followed them out of the game room. "You two have a good time and enjoy yourselves, and I'll see you in the morning." She looked up at Brock when they got to the front door. "You're a free man now."

"Good night, Imani," Brock said, and once again they stood looking into each other's eyes.

Mr. O chuckled. "Come on, Brock."

And after one last long look at Imani, Brock left the house with Mr. O.

Chapter Seven

Hareem Mosley was parked in front of a house whose current occupant was named Gianna Jennings. She was the girlfriend of drug dealer, Benjamin Cameron. Although Hareem controlled a huge chunk of the local drug market, which extended as far south as Daytona Beach and as far north as Savannah, he had competition. Benjamin Cameron and Kevin Hedrick were the other major players in the city. Both of them worked for a woman who called herself Diamond, and they were both loyal to her, if not afraid of her.

Hareem had heard that a couple of her other dealers had robbed her. The word on the street was that when Diamond had found out about it, she had had them kidnapped and drugged. When they regained consciousness early the following morning, just before sunrise, they discovered that they were buried up to their necks in sand on a remote section of Fernandina Beach, and Diamond was standing over them. She promised to dig them out before high tide rolled in if they told her where they had hidden the money they stole from her.

Fearing for their lives and not wanting to die by drowning, both men quickly told Diamond what she wanted to hear. Once she had verified what she had been told, instead of having Hedrick and Cameron dig the two men out, Diamond waited there with them, explaining the folly in fucking with her money, until the tide rolled in and was just inches from their faces.

"And that is why you're gonna die here today," Diamond announced, and then she left them there to die by suffocation.

"See you in hell!" one of the dealers shouted as she walked away, and those were his last words before the tide rolled in farther and submerged him.

So even though Hareem had no idea who Diamond was, he had to respect her gangster. If he could get her on board or out of the landscape altogether, then he would finally prove to his father and Imani that he could handle bigger things. His first thought had been to kill Cameron and Hedrick, thinking that with two of her soldiers dead, Diamond would have to make her presence known, and then he would have her. But when he'd told Imani his plan, she'd told him it was a bad idea, but what did she know about the dope game?

If she knew anything about the dope game, we wouldn't have gotten run out of Miami, Hareem had thought. So he'd gone to his father, and Mr. O had lost his mind.

"Why the fuck do you think starting a war is the way you increase business?" And then Mr. O had explained all the reasons why going to war with Diamond was a bad idea.

"That's what I told him," Ms. Know-It-All Imani had said with that superior, "I'm better than you" scowl on her face. It was those looks that sometimes made Hareem feel like he didn't belong, like he had to prove himself worthy of being her sister. He'd felt that way ever since the day he came to live with the family after his mother died.

Unlike his father and his sister, he had thought the move to Jacksonville was the best thing that could have happened to him. Whereas Mr. O had seen the move as him getting run out of Miami and Imani had seen it as a loss of power, prestige, and position, Hareem had seen it as his opportunity to step into the void when they decided to get out of the retail end of the game and go back to their core business: distribution and weapons trafficking.

When his father had relented and decided to go along with Hareem's plan, Hareem had called his boys up from Miami, had broken into the Jacksonville market, and they'd gone major. Whereas he and his crew had been strictly small-timers in Miami, making just enough money to flash and play the role, in Jacksonville they were the Miami Boys, and they had come in hot and hard with a high-quality product. And like his father in his younger days, Hareem had the firepower to back himself up.

But on this night, as he sat in his car in front of Gianna Jennings's house, his mind wasn't only on business. Hareem's mind was also on fucking Gianna. He had met her at a party that some friends had thrown at the Hilton Hotel on the Riverfront. She had first got his attention when she'd drawn a crowd while she danced. He had found out later that she used to dance in clubs before she got hooked up with Cameron.

The story goes that Gianna had had her thick thighs wrapped around a pole and was hanging upside down, shaking her titties, when Cameron came into the club. He had stood at the foot of the stage, tossing twenties at her, until Gianna slid down the pole to collect her money.

"Thank you, baby," Gianna said as she picked up the money.

"There's more where that came from," Cameron said, and that was her last night dancing.

But what had drawn Hareem to her was her bragging to her girls at the party at the Hilton about being with Cameron and then her saying that she knew Diamond. That was all that Hareem had needed to hear. After he'd learned that, he had spent the rest of the evening talking up on Gianna. And that night, they'd left the party together and got a room of their own.

For the next couple of weeks, Hareem had worked her and had soon found out that Gianna didn't actually *know* Diamond. She had met her only twice, when Diamond had come to Cameron's house. If Gianna had chosen to be honest, she would have had to admit that the only conversation that she'd had with Diamond was when Diamond said to her in passing, "Girl, where'd you get those shoes?"

But Gianna had good pussy, and her head game was the truth, so Hareem had decided that he would fuck her one more time and be done with her. Hareem had called her earlier that day and had said he'd stop by that evening, and she had told him what time to come over. But when he was almost there, Gianna had called and said that Cameron had dropped by unexpectedly. She'd said that he probably wouldn't be there long and that she'd call when he left.

"The nigga just need to get the fuck up outta there," Hareem muttered aloud. Then he sat there thinking that since Cameron didn't have anybody with him, he could just pop him when he came out of Gianna's house. This would be the perfect opportunity to take him out. But then Hareem decided he would wait to hear what his father had to say about offing Cameron before he did anything.

Just then Hareem felt his phone vibrating in his pocket. He pulled it out, looked down out the screen, and took the call. "What's up, Marty-mar?"

"Where you at?" his boy Martel asked.

He was Hareem's right- and left-hand man. They had known each other since they were kids. They had started out in the game together, selling what little bit of dope that Hareem could steal from his father until they had made enough money to buy weight for themselves.

"I'm about to get into something. Why?"

"You remember me telling you about these three niggas that took a shot at Jamarcus and them?"

"Yeah, I remember. What about them?"

"I just saw them go into a house over on Forty-Fifth Street."

"Those are Cameron's people, right?"

"Yup. Sitting right here in that house, waiting to get taken."

Hareem thought about it. Killing Cameron might be bad for business, but fucking with him would serve its purpose in more ways than one.

"Take them out. Let me know when it's done," Hareem said, thinking that it would get Cameron up outta Gianna's place in a hurry.

"What he say?" Jamarcus asked when Martel had ended the call.

"He said take them out. Let him know when it's done," Martel said, and then he sent his men to the store on the corner.

When they returned, they had four forty-ounce bottles of beer, some dish towels, and a container of gasoline. Martel took all the bottles, unscrewed the tops, poured out the contents, and filled the bottles with gas as he knelt next to his car. Then he stuck a dish towel soaked with gas in each one. When he had given each man a bottle, Martel carried the gas container up the driveway and poured what gas was left around the outside of the house.

Martel's men smashed the windows in the front room of the house, lit the towels in their bottles, and threw them inside the front room. Then they stood back, took out their guns, and watched as the room caught fire.

It didn't take long before the front door swung open and Cameron's men came running out, coughing. They were easily picked off, one by one, as they ran out of the burning house.

Chapter Eight

"It's done," Martel said and ended the call.

Hareem looked at his Gucci Dive watch. Five minutes later, he watched Cameron come running out of Gianna's house, jump in his car, and speed off. Hareem waited a couple of minutes before he got out from behind the wheel, approached the front door, and rang the bell.

The door swung open. "You getting bold," Gianna said and held open the door for him to come in. She was wearing a light blue kimono, and as near as he could tell, she had nothing on under it.

"Bold niggas get what they want 'cause they take it. Weak muthafuckas don't get shit, 'cause they wait for somebody to give them shit."

"And you a bold nigga, huh?" Gianna asked as she walked past him. He grabbed her arm and pulled her to his chest.

"You fuckin' right I am. I took you, didn't I?" he replied while easing open her kimono. She stepped back just before his hand eased between her thighs, and she closed her kimono.

"You got that wrong," Gianna said and went to sit down on the couch. "I let you have some." She crossed her legs as Hareem sat down next to her. "But I ain't the one to be taken."

"So what's up with you, Gianna?" he asked as she picked up the television remote and started flipping through the channels.

"Nothing. Just watching TV."

Although Gianna was glad, even excited, that he was there, she was playing it as if his being there was no big deal. But it was a big deal. The question of whether he took her or she let him have some didn't matter.

He fucked me so good and so hard, I thought I was losing my mind. That shit was hot. Just the thought of it makes my pussy clench, Gianna thought.

"What's been up with you?" she asked as she looked at the dick print that was prominent on his thigh.

"Trying to make this money and survive in them streets, waiting patiently for another chance to be with you," Hareem said, moving closer and putting his hand on her thigh. "Wondering when you gonna let me take you out, show you how I treat a woman."

"You know I got a man. What if somebody sees us and tells him?"

Hareem shook his head. "Ain't nobody that nigga know gonna see us in Saint Augustine or Daytona Beach." Gianna smiled at the thought, because she rarely got out of Jacksonville. "Or better yet, why don't you let me take you to Miami?"

"I'd like that," Gianna said and turned toward him, releasing the grip she had on the kimono.

Hareem laughed. "I know that nigga don't take you nowhere."

She frowned. "We go to Red Lobster all the time."

"Because that's big time to him," Hareem said, taking advantage of his new access to her body. He eased her kimono open a little. "You ever hear of Safe Harbor Seafood Restaurant?"

"No. Where that at?"

"Jax Beach." He ran one finger between her breasts, then down to her navel. "It's the best seafood restaurant in Jacksonville."

"See, that's the kind of place I needs to be going," Gianna said and moved her hands from her lap.

"And I want to take you there," Hareem said as his hand reached between her thighs. "The restaurant is on the Jacksonville Beach boat ramp, so it's got a beautiful view of the water." He chuckled. "What kinda view you got from the Red Lobster?"

"The parking lot and I-Ninety-Five," Gianna said as Hareem patted her thigh. Her thighs parted for him, and his finger circled her clit.

"You deserved to be treated better than that." Hareem leaned forward, rubbing his thumb across and around her wet button. He eased two fingers inside her, and she gasped. "I want to give you everything," he said, fingering Gianna's pussy in and out slowly.

"I want you to give me everything you want me to have," she whispered.

Hareem eased another finger into Gianna and started to fuck her with his fingers, stretching her walls, and she tossed her hips back against them, making her pussy clench tightly around his fingers. But then Gianna wanted more, and she pushed him off.

"I need to take a shower," she said and stood up, gathering her kimono tightly around her.

"Let's go take a shower, then." Hareem stood up, and they kissed. He held Gianna's hand, and she led him into the bathroom to take a shower.

Gianna started to unzip his jeans, and he eased the kimono off her shoulders and let it drop to the floor. Her body was tingling all over in anticipation of him taking her again. She thought about their first night together, when he had blown on her nipples and bitten one gently. They'd been hard and wet, so he'd flicked each one. They had been sitting on the couch in a jacuzzi suite at the Hilton. Hareem had a big, thick dick. Gianna had got on her knees and leaned over to take him deep in her throat as he'd sat back to enjoy watching her work. Her skills were extraordinary.

After a quick shower now, Hareem finger fucked Gianna as she gave him a hand job. They got into bed, and she grabbed a rubber. He covered himself, and in one fluid motion, he was inside of Gianna, going deep, and she was tossing her hips to meet his thrusts.

"Damn, this pussy is tight," Hareem groaned.

"You're so fucking big," Gianna gasped.

Gianna's skin slapped against his, and Hareem grabbed her ass, then pulled her back toward him. She loved it, but she wanted him to taste her. Gianna pushed him off her, and when he saw her petting her mound, he got between her legs and pushed apart her fat lips. Soon, her thighs were slick and covered with her juices.

"Suck that pussy just like that," Gianna demanded.

She grabbed his head and held it there, because it was so damn good. When he inserted a finger and curled it against her G-spot, Gianna cried out. He told Gianna to kneel on the bed with her ass in the air. With a loud grunt, Hareem thrust his dick inside her.

"Fuck yeah!" he yelled.

Hareem began pumping in and out of Gianna quickly. It was so good that he had her screaming. Their rhythm was perfection, and both of them came hard.

Chapter Nine

After a night in which she tossed and turned repeatedly, Imani woke up tired. She never slept well when her father was out doing whatever it was that he did when he was out of the house. The fact that Brock was with him didn't make it any better. As she had tried in vain to find a spot in which to get comfortable, Imani had been consumed with thoughts of what Brock was doing and whom he was doing it to. She knew that she had absolutely no right to be concerned with what Brock was doing, much less be jealous about it, but there she was, both concerned about what Brock was doing and jealous of the person he was doing it to.

She finally was able to drift off the sleep once she accepted one simple fact. He had just got out of prison after ten years, and so he deserved to be elbow deep in some woman's pussy.

It just would be nice if it were mine, Imani thought as she got out of bed and went downstairs to work out in the home gym. *That's all right. If he's meant for you, you will have him.*

After her workout, during which she released all the pent-up aggression that she had built up the night before, Imani returned to her room to take a shower. Once the water had reached the perfect temperature for her, Imani stepped into the shower stall. She let the water caress her body before she picked up a loofah, applied some Olay ultra-moisture shea-butter body wash to it, and ran it over her skin. As the hot water washed over her, Imani thought about what she was going to wear that day, and then her mind drifted to thoughts of Brock and of making love to him. She closed her eyes and thought about Brock's rough hands traveling down to her stomach and settling between her thighs and about his hand petting her wanting mound and coaxing her lips open for him.

Imani put the loofah down, rinsed off, and let her hands caress her body. She ran her fingers across her nipples, down to her stomach, and then in between her thighs. She very slowly ran one finger up and down her slit. Her mouth opened unconsciously as Imani worked her sensitive button, plucked it and made circles around it, and then she dipped a finger inside. Once Imani felt her walls tighten around her finger, imagining that it was Brock moving in and out of her hard and fast, her body shuddered. Then she got out of the shower, dried off, wrapped a towel around herself, and left the bathroom to start getting dressed.

Once Imani had put on an Agent Provocateur "Tanya" cage bra and a strappy thong, she headed to the closet to pick out something to wear. Standing in her clothes closet, swaying to the beat in her mind, Imani chose an Escada "Python" jacquard three-quarter-length-sleeve dress. She complimented the outfit with David Yurman "Châtelaine" stud earrings with Hampton Blue topaz and Jimmy Choo "Romy" leather pumps. After taking one last look at herself in the full-length mirror, Imani grabbed her Tom Ford "Alix" tote bag and went downstairs to have some breakfast before heading to work.

Since Imani wanted to get into the office early that morning, and Kimberly was only just getting started on the breakfast feast that she usually prepared for the family, Imani planned to make herself a blueberry-almond-quinoa smoothie bowl and get out of there. When she got to the kitchen, the television was turned to the local news.

"The JSO and Jacksonville Fire and Rescue were called last night to a house in the Norwood area of Jacksonville. Witnesses say that three men threw Molotov cocktails inside the house and then shot the three men that were in the house as they tried to escape the burning structure. One of the deceased has been positively identified as Wilson Laurent, for whom the Jacksonville Sheriff's Office had an open warrant on drug charges. We'll have more information for you as it becomes available," said the TV reporter.

Imani shook her head, picked up the remote, and turned off the television just as Brock came into the kitchen. He had been up since six, so he had heard her when she went to work out and had wondered where she was going. When he'd heard her heels clicking against the hardwood floor in the hallway and on the stairs, he'd decided to come downstairs. She took all of him in—his broad shoulders, those muscular arms, and that sexy chest.

"Good morning, Imani."

And then there was that voice, which Imani could feel deep in her core.

"Morning, Brock," she said. She started making her smoothie and tried to act nonchalant about the Ermenegildo Zegna two-tone plaid jacket and slacks he was wearing, an outfit she'd bought for him.

He looks so good in that, Imani thought, and it occurred to her that she was enjoying shopping for Brock more than she had thought she would.

"How are you doing this morning?" He stood next to her as he poured a cup of coffee.

"Doing great." She could feel the heat radiating from him. "About to get outta here and head to the office."

"Mr. O said that we were gonna roll by there today, but I don't think he's gonna be up anytime soon," he said, enjoying the view of Imani's wide hips, round ass, and those long, sexy legs.

"Must have been quite a night," she said and turned around. Brock quickly looked away. "What kind of trouble did you boys get into?"

"No trouble. We went to Red's Steakhouse for dinner, and then we rolled out to the Westside, did a little barhopping, and then he showed me his place." Brock chuckled. "We had a few more drinks, talked a lot of shit, you know, about the old days. And then we came back here," he said, leaving out the part about how, after those few drinks, Stacy and her friend Deirdre came over to their table and Stacy put in work to satisfy his hunger. "It's the only place I know."

"So," Imani said, somewhat satisfied with his answer but knowing that there was more to it than that, "do you have any plans for the day?"

"None whatsoever." He took a step closer to her. "What did you have in mind?" Brock asked, and Imani's body trembled from the inside out.

"You can drive me to work," Imani said.

She was sitting down to enjoy her smoothie when she heard the doorbell ring. Shortly thereafter, De'Shane Jones and Lucius Cunningham came into the kitchen. While Brock had been in prison, both De'Shane and Lucius had risen to prominence, and now they were Mr. O's top arms and drug runners in the Southeast region.

"Hey, Imani," De'Shane said when he walked into the kitchen.

He and Imani had a good working relationship, one that he secretly wished with all his heart would turn into something deeper, but Imani wasn't the least bit interested in him. To her, he was just a moneymaker, and she couldn't imagine anything deeper than that. It wasn't that he was a bad-looking man; she just wasn't interested in him. The way that he saw it, it was just a matter of time before he wore her down.

"Guess we too early to eat," Lucius said.

"And my father isn't up yet," Imani told him, and then she introduced Brock. "He's gonna be driving for me and Daddy for a while, until he decides what he wants to do now that he's out."

While Lucius had never heard of Brock, De'Shane had. "Wait a minute. Your Brock Whitehall?"

Brock nodded. "I am."

De'Shane turned to Lucius. "Mr. O never told you about this nigga right here?"

"Nope," Lucius said, staring at Brock. He was mad because he used to drive Imani and Mr. O around sometimes. And as quiet as it was kept, he was into Imani and thought that he had a shot at her too.

De'Shane went on. "I don't know how true it is, but I heard he was in Chicago to do a deal with some bangers, and they tried to pay him with dope. When he tells them no deal, they throw down on him."

"What happened?" Imani asked, because she had never heard that story, and her father had told her plenty of Brock stories.

"They say this nigga took their guns and kicked both of their asses. Then he took their cash and left them their guns," De'Shane said.

Imani looked at Brock. "True story?" she asked, and Brock nodded.

"What are you? Some kinda super nigga or some shit?" Lucius asked.

Brock shrugged. "If that's what you think." He turned to Imani. "I'll be in the car when you're ready," he said and walked out of the kitchen.

Imani watched him as he went. She had always enjoyed the way he walked. That confident swagger always had an effect on her, and after that story, it had her juices flowing. She stood up.

"Excuse me, gentlemen," she said as she crossed the kitchen on her way to the front door. After taking a dozen steps, she stopped and turned back around. "Lucius. There's something I need you to do for me."

"What's that?" he asked, coming toward her.

"I have to run right now, so I need you to stop by the office sometime this afternoon, and I'll tell you what I need you to do for me," Imani said and continued walking to the front door.

Chapter Ten

When Imani got to the front door, she saw that the keys to her car, which she always left on a side table, were gone. She picked up her tote bag and walked out of the house. Brock had pulled her car around to the front of the house, and he was leaning against it now, with the front passenger door opened. He stood up straight when he saw her coming, hovered as she got in the passenger seat, and then closed the door for her.

"Where to, boss?" Brock asked when he got in the car.

"Don't call me that," Imani said, but she smiled, because that was what he called her father. "I have some business that I need to take care of at the port before I go to the office."

"How do I get there?"

"You remember how to get back to Butler Boulevard?"

"The highway?"

"Yes. That's where we're going. I'll let you know where to go when we get on."

Brock started the car and headed toward the highway, on the way to the Jacksonville Port Authority. For a while, the only sound in Imani's Volvo S90 hybrid was the sound of music. They didn't really know each other, so Imani and Brock had nothing to talk about. She had already asked him about his plans for the future and about his night. Imani was considering saying something about the difference between the weather in Atlanta as opposed to Jacksonville when he saved her the trouble.

"So what all do you do?"

"I do everything," Imani said proudly. "I handle both sides of the business." She went on to explain how she had taken the reins of the family business.

Things had been quiet for a while after Brock went to jail. At his trial, Arturo Vargas had testified that he had bought the M16 rifles for Vance to use in his turf war with Joaquin Herminio. He had been murdered at a popular Boca Raton restaurant a month before Herminio's trial started. For that reason, Warwick Vance, as well as Mr. O, had been laying low.

It was during those years that Mr. O had finally arranged and presided over the old-school sit-down with Roberto Petit-Frere and Warwick Vance that he'd been talking up for years. The peace that they made that day had held for years, but by that time, the landscape in Miami had changed and a new, more violent breed had come up behind them.

And then it happened. And after that, nothing was the same.

"I was in the office when the phone rang, and my mother answered it. Next thing I know, she is getting in her car, with her gun," Imani told Brock as he drove.

It was the Miami-Dade Police who had called. They had informed Imani's mother that they had a minor in custody, a Hareem Mosley. He had been arrested for simple assault after he got in a fight and for underage drinking. Hareem had told the police that his mother died a month ago and he was still living in their apartment. The police needed the boy's father, Orpheus Mosley, to come get him, or he would be turned over to child protective services.

Mr. O had never known that he had a son, but that didn't stop his wife, Julia, from chasing him around the house, firing shots, as he tried to tell her that he didn't know anything about a son. But Julia wasn't trying to hear that shit. She kept shooting until he finally left the house. He went to meet his son for the first time, and Julia filed for divorce that same afternoon. Mr. O never saw her again.

There was one thing that was certain about Orpheus Mosley: he loved that woman. She was his world. There were other women to be sure, but none of them meant anything to him. "Just someplace to bust a nut in," was what he was known to say.

Now his precious Julia was gone, and nothing meant anything to him. He was drinking too much, smoking way too much weed, and drowning himself in an endless sea of meaningless women to bust nuts in. He fell apart on the day he got the divorce papers. Mr. O didn't even bother to look at them: he told his lawyer to let her have whatever she wanted, and he signed the papers against his lawyer's advice. That was the day that he disappeared.

At the time, Imani was working toward her bachelor's degree in the Technical Management Program at DeVry, with a focus in business intelligence and analytics management. She was also doing a little work with the computer systems for Luxury Private Charters, separating and then transitioning years of information dating back to when her grandfather first started the business. However, with her mother out of the business and her father somewhere in the wind, not to mention the arrival of a new brother, whose mother had recently died, everything fell on Imani.

"So I had to step up," she told Brock.

That meant that there was no more room for the man-hungry party girl she had once been. Her plans to graduate from DeVry, land some high-paying job in LA, and leave Miami ended the day her father received the divorce papers. Her family may have been in disarray, but the charter business had to be run. There were deals in progress, and there was merchandise in the pipeline, and she had to step up and oversee everything.

As a young girl, Imani had heard the stories that her grandfather and then her father had told her of how the business was run, and as she got older, she had watched from a distance as they smuggled contraband, sold weapons, and dominated the dope game for more than a minute. Now, ready or not, Imani had to step up and handle it all. Her family needed her to do that.

"I had to learn everything there was to know about the weapon we were selling," she revealed.

"Which one was that?" Brock asked, glancing at her for a second, then returning his eyes to the road.

"The QBZ-95."

Brock smiled. "Tell me about it."

Imani turned slightly toward Brock as he drove. "The QBZ-95 is an assault rifle developed for the Chinese military. It fires the standard-version Chinese five-point-eight by forty-two millimeter round from a thirty-round magazine. The QBZ-95 is a select-fire rifle with a limited rate of fire of about six hundred fifty rpm. The effective range is four hundred meters, and it can be fitted to fire rifle grenades."

"Impressive."

"I know my guns."

"So did I."

"So I've been told," Imani said, because her father had told her that Brock was the best he'd ever seen and that she would do well to emulate him.

"Know what you're selling . . ."

"And the world will be yours," Imani said, completing the phrase that her father had repeated so many times to both of them.

Each looked at the other, and their eyes met. Imani felt a connection that went beyond their mutual interest in guns and the similarities between them that had arisen because they had had the same teacher. She felt an intimacy that went well beyond the physical attraction she'd been fantasizing about for years. She wondered if Brock felt it too.

From the moment he first saw her on the day he got out of prison, Brock had been physically attracted to Imani. His heart skipped a beat each time she spoke to him. He had seen the twinkle in her eye, felt the aura she was giving off, and had wondered if maybe . . . But Brock had quickly discounted the idea. After all, he had just got out of prison, they barely knew one another, and all they'd ever had were surface-level conversations.

But he felt it too. He felt what she felt. Whether either of them knew it or was ready to admit it, Brock and Imani were connecting on a deeper level—and this was just the start of it.

Chapter Eleven

"It's over there on your left," Imani said as they got closer to St Marys Seafood & More Express.

Brock parked the car in front of the restaurant. He looked over at Imani and saw that she was digging around for something in her purse. He got out and went to open her door. Imani held her hand out, and he smiled.

She's a lady, he thought.

Brock liked a woman who expected to be treated like a lady and who appreciated a man who knew how to treat her that way.

"Thank you," she said, accepting his hand.

"Anytime."

Brock watched her walk as he closed the car door. As he rushed to catch up with Imani, he wondered if she would stop at the door to the restaurant and wait for him to open it for her.

"What are we doing here?" Brock asked, and Imani stopped in her tracks. Then she stepped in front of the door and looked in her tote bag.

"We're here to meet two inspectors from the port," she said and discreetly nodded toward two men inside the restaurant who looked as if they had spent the night in their clothes. "That's them at the table in the far left corner."

Brock squinted as he looked in the restaurant's large front window. "I see them."

"One's name is Reed Allen. He'll be the one eating corned beef hash and eggs. The other is Miller Ford. He's having the shrimp and grits with bacon bits." She glanced at the door, and he opened it. "I'm going to introduce you, but they prefer to be referred to as Mr. Alpha and Mr. Beta. Don't ask. I'll explain why later," Imani said and approached the table. "Good morning, gentlemen."

"Morning, Ms. Mosley. Please, have a seat," Allen said.

"Thank you," Imani said. Brock pulled out her chair, and she sat down at the table. He waited until she nodded her head slightly before he went and sat across from her. "Gentlemen, this is Brock Whitehall. He's an old associate of my father's. Brock, this is Mr. Alpha and Mr. Beta," Imani said, and then she held out an envelope under the table.

"Good to meet you, Mr. Whitehall. Mr. O speaks very highly of you," Ford said and shook his hand. Then he put his hand under the table and felt for the envelope Imani was holding out. "I'm sure we'll be seeing more of each other as time passes."

"Y'all stay and have some breakfast with us," Allen said after Ford had eased the envelope into his pocket.

"I wish I could," Imani replied, and Brock stood up. "I have a million things to do today."

"Don't we all," Ford declared and shoved some shrimp and grits in his mouth. Imani rolled her eyes, because he was disgusting her, and she got up from the table.

"You gentlemen have a good day," Imani said and started for the door.

"Good meeting you, gentlemen," Brock said hastily and headed toward the door, where Imani was standing, waiting for him to open it.

She is so fuckin' fine, he thought on his way to the door.

Brock opened the door for Imani, and he felt her power as she passed by him. They walked to the car in silence, and he opened the passenger door for her to get in. Imani was excited about the possibilities as she waited for Brock to climb behind the wheel. She had enjoyed the nonverbal communication that she and Brock had shared inside the restaurant. It was a simple matter to know when to do this or not say that, but then again, it wasn't. Anytime Lucius or De'Shane accompanied her on these outings, they had to be told in advance when and under what circumstances to do certain things, and despite that, they often did something wrong.

Maybe it was the fact that she was a Brock Whitehall fangirl. But no matter the reason, as he got in the car, Imani was jumping up and down on the inside because seamless nonverbal communication would be an asset to them in their business dealings, and she was hopeful that it would carry over into the personal relationship she planned to build with Brock.

When Brock got in the car, he looked over at Imani. Everything about her turned him the fuck on. Her style, the way that she carried and wielded her power excited him. He had always had a thing for professional women, and powerful women were an aphrodisiac for him. *And Imani is so fuckin' fine.* Brock wanted Imani, and he decided in that second that he would have her.

"So what's up with Mr. Alpha and Mr. Beta?"

Imani giggled. "You remember Manny, don't you?"

"Manny Ramirez from the port?"

"Yes. When we were preparing to make the move, I reached out to Manny to see if he knew anybody here at Jaxport that we could do business with, and he handed us Allen and Ford. Naturally, he told us everything about them, and we checked them out, so we'd know what pressure points they'd respond to before we even made our approach. But when Daddy met with them, they said that they preferred to remain anonymous."

"I guess that made sense to them."

"Whatever, Brock. It makes no sense at all, but they do good work, so I ain't saying nothing."

"Where to?"

"Let's go get you a driver's license."

"I don't have the documents I need."

Imani tapped on her purse. "I have them."

"How did you get them?"

"Remember, I'm the one who put your stuff in storage." She paused to observe the look on his face. "I took your important papers, and I put them in a safe-deposit box. I knew we'd need them today, so I got what we'd need from the bank last week."

Brock took a second to think of all she had done for him. "Thank you for looking out for me while I was gone. I mean that." *Your father should have come to see me. Or better yet, your sexy ass could have come to see me.* "I appreciate it."

"I told you, this family owes you a debt that we can never pay. So it's me that appreciates you."

"We could go around this circle for the rest of the day."

"We could, but let's not." She smiled, and he breathed it in.

When they got to the tax collector's office for Brock to get his license, he took a number and they sat down to wait for it to be called. Whereas earlier that day they were searching for something to say, now they were chatting away about the legitimate business she ran and her expansion plans, as well as their mutual interest in guns. And, of course, there was running commentary about some of the people around them. Although she couldn't see it yet, their body language said that Imani and Brock were connecting as she hoped they would.

"Where to?" Brock asked once he was licensed to drive.

"You know how to use a navigation system?"

"I haven't been locked up that long," he said and looked at the dashboard. "But why don't you show me how to use yours?"

"Because you have no idea how to work it."

"Right," Brock said. They smiled at one another, and Imani showed him how to use the system as she set it for the Luxury Private Charters office on Heckscher Drive. The other company office was on the other side of the city, on Lakeside Drive, near the Ortega River.

"I imagine your father told them about his plans for me."

"Apparently. He was hoping that you would get out and say, 'Put me in coach.'"

"The plan was for me to pick up where I left off."

She didn't answer at first, because she wasn't sure what her father's plan for Brock was. Like her father, Imani wanted Brock to stick around, and even more so now that she was feeling him on more than just a physical level. "But I'll let you in on a little secret," she finally said.

"What's that?"

"He knew that when you got out, you would want to put it all behind you and say that you were done. But he thought that eventually, you would change your mind." Imani told him this in the hope that it would draw him in.

"He told you this?"

"My father tells me everything I need to know to do what I have to do for our family."

"I see," Brock said. *Because you run things in this camp.* "So what do you think?" he asked, because since Imani ran things, her opinion was the only one that mattered.

"About what you're gonna do?"

"Yes, what do you think I'm gonna do, boss?"

"I told you not to call me that," she said, smiling, because she liked the way he looked and sounded when he said it. "I don't think that you will change your mind."

"Why not?"

"You impress me as a man who once you make up your mind, you stick to it . . . unless you see a reason to change your decision, of course."

"Of course."

Imani adjusted her position in the seat so she was looking at Brock. "But I do think that as time goes on, you'll decide what you want to do and you'll work yourself into it." She turned away and looked out the window. "But I don't know you as well as my father does."

"That will change," Brock said confidently, because he planned to get to know everything about her. "I mean, since I'll be driving for you *and* your father for a while, we'll get to know each other better."

"I'm looking forward to getting to know you," Imani said as they arrived at Luxury Private Charters of Jacksonville. "I think that I can learn a lot from you," she added just to keep it professional.

Chapter Twelve

Luxury Private Charters was founded by Hughbert Mosley as Mosley Charter Service back in the days before Hughbert met Saulo Lorencio. When Mr. O took over the business in the eighties, he changed the company's name to Luxury Private Charters of Miami and the expansion began. Under the old man, the charter business was nothing more than a front for other activities, but Mr. O had a vision and transformed the business into a customer-focused private jet, boat charter, and limousine service. When he married Julia, she took over as operations manager, and she formed several strategic relationships with the finest operators throughout the world to provide an extensive network of quality operators and give customers access to every size and type of private jet, both domestic and international.

But that was before they got run out of Miami and had to sell the business. Now that they had relocated to Jacksonville, which wasn't as big a market as Miami, Imani's focus was on rebuilding the business. She still had access to the network of operators that her mother had built, so they had been able to transition their international business. With that established business still in place, Imani had taken some of the proceeds from the sale of their Miami business and bought two Cessna Citation M2 jets for use in both businesses. Then she had acquired a couple of yachts, got them in the water and earning, and then she had bought a fleet of limousines.

Her current focus was on the feasibility of buying another jet for local charters, though she toyed with the idea of sticking with the established network of operators to provide aircraft for that area of the business.

When they arrived at the office building, Brock got out and opened Imani's door. She held out her hand for him to help her out of the car. He took her hand and felt its warmth and didn't want to let go. Imani allowed her hand to linger in his as she took a step away from the car and walked alongside Brock, fighting the urge to keep holding his hand.

You're trippin', she thought as he opened the front door and held it open for her.

"Good morning, Imani," the receptionist said as she came in with Brock.

"Morning, Serena." Imani looked around the room, and seeing that they had everybody's attention, she decided to save some time. "Everybody, this is Brock Whitehall. He'll be driving for my father and me."

"Hello, everybody," Brock said and followed Imani to her office.

"Hello again, Mr. Whitehall," a woman said when she nearly bumped into him in the hallway.

"Good morning, Ginger," Brock said, surprised to see her in a striped linen shirtdress and not in her driver's uniform.

Again? "That's right. You picked him up from the airport," Imani said. "Anyway, this is Ginger Wright. She's our fleet manager."

"I thought you were a driver," Brock said.

"I started out as a driver, and I love to drive, so every once in a while, I'll take the VIP clients. And you, Mr. Whitehall, are the very definition of a VIP."

"Okay, enough of that," Imani said.

Knowing what a man-eater Ginger could be, Imani took Brock's hand in hers, and she pulled him into her office. Brock felt a chill come over him when she touched him.

"Good to see you again, Ginger," he called, and Imani closed the door behind them.

Imani had just sat down at her desk when Hareem burst into her office. He knew this got on her nerves, but that was why he did it. And she would always say, "Don't you know how to knock?" as her eyes narrowed.

"Don't you know how to knock, Hareem?"

"I do," he said and tapped on the door. "Happy now?"

"What do you want, Hareem?" Imani asked.

"I need to talk to you," Hareem said, and he glanced over at Brock, who sat in the chair in front of Imani's desk.

"Hareem Mosley, Brock Whitehall," Imani said. Hareem had been hearing larger-than-life stories about Brock ever since he'd come to live with his father.

"So you out, huh?" Hareem was not impressed.

"Free man and talking about it," Brock said, and they shook hands.

"Would you excuse us for a minute please, Brock?" Imani asked angrily.

Brock stood up. "No problem." He left her office and closed the door behind him.

"What's he gonna be doing?" Hareem asked, because he didn't need or want Brock in his business.

"What the fuck is wrong with you?"

"Me? What I do this time?"

"Me and Daddy both told you to make Diamond come to you."

"I am. I went by the house this morning to talk to Daddy about it, like he told me to, but he was asleep, so I didn't bother him!" he shouted, but Imani shook her head and kept her cool.

"Then tell me why I woke up to news about a house on fire and a triple murder?"

"I don't know what you're talking about," Hareem said, smiling slyly. "I was with a lady friend of mine last night."

"You really do think I'm stupid, don't you?"

Hareem said nothing.

"Would you like me to tell you which of your people were involved?" she said.

"Go ahead, Ms. Know-It-All."

"Pyromaniac Martel was calling the shots, and Jamarcus and Devonte were with him."

Since she was absolutely right—Martel was a pyromaniac, had been since they were kids, and Jamarcus and Devonte were there with him—Hareem said nothing.

"I told you once and I'm gonna tell you again, be careful not to start a war that you are not ready to fight."

Chapter Thirteen

"And I said I didn't have shit to do with it!" Hareem shouted and stormed out of her office and past Brock, who was talking to Ginger.

"Don't mind him." Ginger giggled alluringly as Hareem marched out of the building and slammed the front door. "That happens all the time."

After Hareem left the office, he got in his Dodge Charger Hellcat and sped away. Although he loved her and she loved him, there were days when he couldn't stand Imani, and this was one of those days. He hated that she treated him like he was stupid and didn't know what he was doing. As far as he was concerned, he knew exactly what he was doing. But there was no talking to Imani, and his father wasn't much better.

"If they knew what they were fuckin' doing, we wouldn't have got run the fuck outta Miami!" Hareem shouted at the top of his lungs as he sped up Heckscher Drive. "I'ma do this my way and show both of them that I'm smart! Smarter than her ass!"

His phone rang at that very moment, and he looked down at the display. It was Imani calling to smooth things over, like she always did.

"Fuck you, Imani! I got shit to do," he muttered and kept driving toward I-295.

A few minutes later, he dialed Martel's number. His right-hand man picked up right away.

"Where she at?" Hareem asked, wasting no time. He was looking for his ex-girlfriend, Lucinda Thompson, whom everybody called Loonie. She was the current girlfriend of Kevin Hedrick, another of Diamond's dealers.

"She's at Adventure Landing, by the beach," Martel reported.

"You got eyes on her?"

"Nope. But Devonte's on her."

"All right," Hareem said, and then he ended the call and called Devonte. When Devonte answered on the second ring, Hareem said, "Where she at?"

"Playing miniature golf."

"She alone?"

"Nah. She's with some other women. They all got kids with them," Devonte informed Hareem.

"Kids' playdate, huh? I'll be through there," he said and ended the call.

When he got to I-295, Hareem got on and headed for Beach Boulevard, on his way to Adventure Landing, a small amusement park that featured such attractions as Shipwreck Island Waterpark, miniature golf, laser tag, and the Wacky Worm Roller Coaster. There were batting cages, an arcade, and go-karts, and you could even feed alligators at Gator Alley.

After Hareem pulled in the parking lot at Adventure Landing and parked, he called Devonte once more. Devonte picked up.

"Where you at?" Hareem asked as he got out of the car.

"Still at miniature golf."

"I'll be there in a minute," Hareem said and headed that way. When he got there and found Devonte, he immediately asked, "Where she at?"

Devonte pointed.

There she was, at the fourteenth hole, with her mini club in hand, lining up a shot. He looked around for a woman with a baby carriage. There were a couple of carriages, but one woman in particular was holding on to the handle of her carriage like it was a matter of life and death, while the other was sitting on a bench, with the carriage next to her.

That's her baby, Hareem thought, staring at the first carriage.

"That's her," Hareem said aloud, his voice low, and then he casually worked his way over to a spot from where he could get a look at the baby.

Look at her. She is beautiful, Hareem thought when he caught a glimpse of the baby.

"Hareem? What are you doing here?" Loonie asked when she finally caught sight of him.

"I came looking for you."

Her fists hit her hips. "How did you know I was here?"

"I guess you forgot, I know everything."

"Right. You probably got Martel or somebody following me," Loonie said and got her carriage from the woman who was watching the baby for her.

"And what if I do have somebody following you? This is the only way I can get a chance to talk to you."

Loonie smiled. "What you want to talk to me about?"

Hareem pointed to the carriage. "I want to talk about her."

"What about her?"

"About her being my daughter."

Silence fell between the two of them. When Hareem smiled; so did Loonie.

Exasperated, Hareem broke the silence by saying, "What? Did you think I wouldn't find out, just because you ran home to your mom's in Palatka?"

Loonie smiled again. "What makes you think she's yours?"

"Look at her. She looks just like me," Hareem insisted.

"Just because she's light-skinned don't make her yours," Loonie said and started walking. But Loonie knew that the baby was his daughter.

Hareem caught up with her and pointed at the baby as they walked. "You're right. But what we can do is go to Any Lab Test Now on Atlantic, and we can settle this."

Loonie looked at him, Hareem looked at her, and each seemed happy to be with the other as they walked together.

"What happened to us, Loonie?"

Loonie stopped, the blissful look on her face disappeared, and she faced him. "You started fuckin' that skinny bitch, Cynthia, behind my back. Or you were fuckin' me behind her back? I don't know. Either way, you're a liar and a cheater."

Hareem hung his head. "You're right. I did that, and I'm sorry. Sorry because I let you get away."

"You didn't let me do shit, nigga. *I* left your lying ass." She went and sat down on a nearby bench.

At the time, Loonie had thought that she was falling in love with Hareem. She had thought that in him, she'd found somebody that understood her and accepted her for who she was, a somewhat high-strung, yet easygoing woman who was sometimes silly, but serious minded and determined. She'd liked that he was not trying to make her into the woman he wanted her to be. He had had her wide open for him when she found out about Cynthia, and that was why it had hurt so bad.

Hareem came and sat next to her, and she looked at him. Although Loonie still felt the hurt, seeing him again after all the time that had passed let her know that she still had feelings for him.

"I found out I was pregnant about a month after we broke up," Loonie said as Hareem looked between her and the baby.

"That why you ran to Palatka?" Hareem asked as he waved to the baby.

"I ran to Palatka to get away from your lying, cheating ass," Loonie said angrily, and then she paused, because her anger served no purpose at that point. She took a breath. "But by the time that I found out that I was pregnant, I had already gotten with Kevin. When I found out, I told him, and he got all excited and shit, thinking it was his baby, so I just went with it."

"But you know that's my baby, right?"

"We still getting a DNA test," Loonie said quickly. "But yeah, she's your daughter."

"What's her name?"

"Her name is Omeika Alondra Thompson," she said, leaning forward to reach into the carriage and pick up Omeika.

"That's a pretty name," Hareem said, thinking that he was glad that Loonie hadn't given his baby another man's name, as she handed him his daughter. He was instantly overwhelmed by emotions that he had never felt before. Hareem was holding his daughter, blood of his blood, flesh of his flesh, and he couldn't be happier.

"This is your real daddy, Omeika," Loonie said to the six-month-old baby girl.

"Hi, Omeika. I'm your daddy," Hareem said as his phone rang. Hareem held Omeika in one arm while he got out his phone and looked at the display. "I need to take this," he said, and Hareem handed Omeika back to her mother. "What's up?"

"You said to let you know if Marko came up short again this week," Chub said. "So I'm letting you know before I go kill this nigga."

"Hold up. Where you at?"

"At the crib."

"Sit tight. I'm coming." Hareem was about to end the call, but then he added, "And, Chub, that means you don't do shit until I get there. Understand?"

"I got you, Hareem. I'll be right here waiting for you," he said, and Hareem ended the call.

He looked at Loonie. "I gotta go handle some shit. But I still want to talk to you. Can you get away tonight?"

"Maybe." Loonie knew that she could get away, what she needed to decide was whether she wanted to.

"Meet me at my place after eight." He leaned in and kissed the baby. "Daddy has to go, but maybe Mommy will bring you with her when she comes."

"*If* I come," Loonie responded quickly.

He kissed Loonie on the cheek. "I hope you do. I love you, Loonie," Hareem said, and her anger came roaring back.

"And there it is." She shook her head. "You're still fuckin' that skinny bitch, but you say you love me."

"I do love you, Loonie," Hareem said, backing away from her. "And we'll talk about all the rest of that shit when I see you tonight."

"*If* I come to see you tonight!" Loonie shouted as he turned and walked away.

Chapter Fourteen

When Hareem pulled into Chub's apartment complex, he was surprised to see Martel getting out of his car and walking toward Chub's building. He honked his horn to get Martel's attention. Martel stopped and looked around, with his hand on his gun, and then he saw Hareem parking his Charger. Martel relaxed, walked over to the Charger, and waited for Hareem to get out.

"What's up, Hareem?" Martel asked.

"This nigga call you?"

"Chub said he had something going and that you were on your way." Martel saw the look on Hareem's face. "What's up?"

"He said that Marko was short again."

"That muthafucka," Martel muttered, shaking his head, because Marko had been warned more than once about being short.

"I told Chub to sit tight and don't do shit until I get there," Hareem said and stood fuming while he thought about what he was going to do. Then he walked around the front of his car, opened the front passenger door, reached under the seat, and pulled out his old .38 snub-nose. It was the first gun that he had ever fired. "Let's go."

As he walked with Martel to the building, Hareem thought about the day that his father had handed him that gun. "Let's see if you can shoot," Mr. O had said. When Hareem had fired the gun, he hadn't hit a damn thing. He smiled when he recalled that the very next day,

Imani had taught him how to handle a gun and how to shoot.

When Hareem and Martel went inside the building, they discovered that just about all their crew was in there. That made Hareem even madder than he already was. He'd told Chub to sit tight and do nothing, not invite the world, like they were coming to see a show. Knowing what he planned to do, Hareem kept his cool, because a lesson was about to be taught, so maybe everyone being there was a good thing. Hareem and Martel walked around the room, speaking, shaking hands, and high-fiving with the crew . . . until Hareem got to Chub.

"'Sup, Hareem?" Chub said, and he shook Hareem's hand. "Come on. Let me show you something." He led Hareem into the kitchen. Martel followed, and so did the rest of crew. There was Marko, gagged and bound to a kitchen chair with razor wire.

"What I tell you to do?" Hareem asked Chub and took the .38 snub-nose from his waist.

"You said to sit tight."

"Right. Is that what you did?"

"I thought—" Chub began, but Hareem cut him off.

"You thought? See, that was your first mistake." He glanced over at Martel. "Marty-mar, hold a gun to this nigga's head."

Chub's eyes opened wide as Martel took out his 9 mm and happily put the barrel to Chub's head. The room was quiet as everyone watched Hareem empty the bullets in his .38 on the kitchen table, and then he picked one up. Hareem put that one bullet back in the cylinder, spun it, and put the barrel to Chub's head.

"What I tell you to do?" Hareem asked Chub for the second time.

"I'm sorry, Hareem," Chub said, and Hareem pulled the trigger.

When the hammer clicked, Chub flinched, as did everybody in the room.

"What the fuck did I tell you to do?" Hareem shouted and pulled the trigger again when Chub didn't answer fast enough.

"You told me to sit tight!" Chub shouted.

"I say anything about going to get this nigga?" Hareem asked and pulled the trigger.

"No!"

"I say anything about calling . . . anybody?"

"You didn't, but—"

But Hareem pulled the trigger before Chub could finish his sentence.

"You do what the fuck I tell you to do." Hareem fired again at Chub, who, by that time, was fighting back tears and thinking that he was about to die over some bullshit.

A quiet buzz came over the room; there were two cylinders left, and everyone wondered if Hareem was really gonna kill Chub. Chub's hands shook a bit as he considered his chances of living through Hareem's next question.

"So what you gonna do next time I say to do some shit?" Hareem asked, but this time he didn't pull the trigger.

"I'ma do exactly what you say to do," Chub answered and said a silent prayer for his life.

"Right answer," Hareem said and pulled the trigger.

No shot was fired. Chub flinched, but he was glad to have survived this ordeal.

"That goes for the rest of you muthafuckas," Hareem growled. "When I say shit, when I tell y'all to do something, it's for a reason." He looked around the room and then back at Chub, put the gun in Chub's face, and pulled the trigger one last time.

Nobody was more surprised than Chub when no bullet left the gun and he was still alive, but Hareem had made his point. He looked around the room and could tell by the looks on his crew's faces that they had all gotten the point. When Hareem turned and walked toward Marko, he tossed Chub a bullet. Instead of loading it in the cylinder of his gun, he had actually palmed it.

"Now you . . . Marko . . . short again," Hareem snapped.

"I just need a couple of days, Hareem, and I swear I'll make it all right," Marko pleaded, thinking that Chub had just made a stupid mistake by not doing what he was told and yet Chub had nearly died today. Marko was late with the money. Again. He knew that he was going to die unless he could convince Hareem not to kill him.

"That's what you always say. You just need a couple of days." He turned to Martel and took out his nine. "Marty-mar, how much this nigga owe?"

"About twenty grand."

Hareem got in Marko's face. "It's more like seventeen thousand, six hundred, but we'll go with Marty-mar's number." Hareem stood up straight, then immediately got in Marko's face again. "What? You think it's cool that you always short, because we boys and shit? Huh . . . ? Is that what you think . . . ? You counting on me not killing your lying, thieving ass because we boys? 'Cause we came up together? Was that what you was thinking?" He backed up off Marko and looked around at his crew. "But that's the reason why we can't have this, none of it. Because we boys! And when one of us falls short, it hurts everybody. Now, because this nigga's short, everybody gotta hustle that much harder, because we got shit we trying to accomplish. We can't grow and we can't expand unless every one of you niggas is on his shit and making paper." He turned back to Marko. "Now I'm gonna kill you, unless somebody in this room gives me a reason not to kill your lying, thieving, 'just need a couple more days' ass."

When no one in the room said a word, Hareem raised his gun and shot Marko twice in the head.

Chapter Fifteen

It was just before four that afternoon when Brock got a call from Imani saying that she was ready to be picked up. Earlier that day, Imani had told him that she would be busy most of the day, so he had left the office and done what he used to do when he went to a new city. He'd got in Imani's car and driven around.

In his old life, whenever Brock went to a new city to do business, he'd arrive a few days early to get the lay of the land. He would start by checking out the meeting spot, if he knew where it was. Brock liked to be prepared for anything, so if shit went wrong, he would need to know how to get away. That was the first priority. He would drive around the immediate area to learn the streets; he'd check traffic patterns and police response times. Once he was satisfied with that, he'd expand to the surrounding areas and repeat the same process. During that time he would set up a safe house and position a couple of clean cars along his escape route, just in case he needed them.

Learning his way around Jacksonville wouldn't be all that difficult, but he planned to learn the territory by using his tried-and-true method, and then he would decide whether he was going to stay.

"Where are you?" Imani asked.

"I'm on Blanding Boulevard and . . . Park Street," he said as he drove through the intersection.

"You're not too far from our other location."

"I know. I was moving in that direction." Brock paused. "I thought it was a good idea since I'll probably drive you . . . *and* your father here sometime."

Imani picked up on that. "I do go there quite a bit." It was his first obvious bit of flirtation, and she hoped it wouldn't be his last. So she flirted back. "I like a man that's prepared for what he has to do."

"As you get to know me better, you'll find that I am an organized planner, so I'm usually very prepared for whatever in most situations."

"But I already know that about you," Imani flirted as a call came through on her other line. "Brock, I need to take this call. So we'll continue this conversation when you get here," she said and switched to her other line, pressing her thighs together, thinking, *That voice.*

"Just when things were getting interesting again," Brock said aloud. He made a U-turn and headed back across town to pick up Imani.

As he drove, Brock's mind was consumed with thoughts of Imani and where this budding flirtation—if it even was a flirtation—was going. And that made his next decision an easy one. Brock decided that he was going to stay in Jacksonville and see just where whatever this was, was going and how it was going to work out. He did have a concern, though.

Somebody that fine definitely has a man, Brock thought, but it didn't matter. If he was going to stay, Imani was going to be his, and nothing else was an option.

When he pulled into the parking lot at Luxury, Imani came right out and walked toward the car. Brock stopped the car, jumped out, and made it around the hood in time to open the passenger door for Imani.

"Thank you, Brock," she said, resisting the powerful urge to caress his handsome face as she got in.

He watched and enjoyed the sight of her legs as they swung into the car. "You're welcome, Imani."

"So, tell me all about your day," Imani said as soon as he was in the car. "What did you think of my little city?"

"I like it." He smiled. "What I've seen of it, anyway. It's nice."

Imani smiled, took a second to breathe, because she was glad he liked it here, and then decided against asking if he had decided to stay or not. "So what did you do?"

Other than miss looking at you? "I rode around, mostly. Anytime I come to a new city, that's how I learn my way around."

"See, I know that about you," Imani said excitedly. She smiled, kicked off her pumps, and put her feet up on the seat. The move made Brock lose all focus, and he had to stop short to avoid hitting the car in front of him. "You'd start by checking out the spot—"

"If I knew where it was," he interrupted. "Sometimes I wouldn't know where the meet was until the day of."

"But you had a work-around for that."

"Did I?"

Imani giggled. "Yes, you did."

"What was it?"

"Your general knowledge of the city. Since by that time you'd driven around most of the city, Mr. Organized Planner still felt pretty prepared." Imani paused. "See, I know more about you than you think."

"I'm flattered, but I'm curious to know why."

Because I've been your fangirl most of my life. "When I had to step up, my father taught me the business, just like he taught you." Imani crossed her legs, but this time Brock kept his eyes on the road. "But he said that you were . . . I don't want to give you the big head, but he said you were the best and I would do well to imitate you."

"I was good at what I did."

"No, Brock Whitehall, you were the best. So I used to do all the things that you used to do. Getaway, first priority.

Drive around the area to learn the streets, check traffic patterns, check police response times. I'd set up a safe house and drop off clean cars along the escape route, just like you did." Imani smiled. "According to Daddy, anyway."

"All true. That's exactly how I used to do it."

"But I added a little idiosyncrasy of my own."

"What was that?"

"I would always make a big deal of my arrival time." Imani put one finger coyly on her bottom lip. "You know us pretty girls like to make an entrance." They shared a laugh, and it felt good to both of them. "So once I had everything set up, I'd drive to the closest airport, fly out, and fly back into the city the next day."

"I'm sure that worked well for you."

"It did."

"Being the most beautiful woman in the room must have its advantages."

"I wouldn't go that far and call myself the most beautiful woman, but I truly thank you for the compliment," she said, feeling warm and kinda gooey inside.

"So where would you like to go, boss?" Brock said, and Imani didn't tell him not to call her that.

"Have you eaten today?" she quizzed.

"I grabbed a burger around one."

"What do you like to eat?"

"Food. The better question is, What do *you* like to eat? I mean, I don't even know what that stuff you were eating was, but it looked pretty healthy. So what are you? Some type of vegetarian?"

"Oh my God, no. As much as I love a big, thick, juicy well-done steak and some blackened mahi-mahi," Imani said suggestively, and then she nodded her head in acknowledgment of his point. "Okay, yes, I do eat pretty healthy, but that is how I stay in shape."

"And you are that," he said, looking over at her.

"So, what do you want to eat?"

"I think you already said what we're having to eat, and since this is your town, I'm just waiting on you to tell me where to go, because I'm starving."

"I know just the place. The mahi-mahi is excellent. You are going to love it," she told him.

"I ask again, where to, boss?" Brock asked, and Imani told him how to get to the Julington Creek Fish Camp on San Jose Boulevard, where they dined on broiled oysters with horseradish-bacon cream, blackened mahi-mahi with tasso ham gravy, and the daily chef's steak.

"What wine do you recommend?" Imani asked their server.

"The Elk Cove pinot grigio. It has a lush and vivid mix of grapefruit, lemon curd, and candied orange peel undertones, to both surprise and delight your taste buds."

"We'll try a bottle of that," Imani said and handed their server back the menus.

The meal and the conversation that surrounded it were excellent. By the time their server came to ask about dessert, both of them were feeling good about the night they'd had and especially about the possibilities for the future. But there was one question that Imani wanted to know the answer to. It was a question she'd asked her father ten years ago.

"Mind if I ask you a question?" she said, and Brock laughed.

"You've been asking me questions all night, and you haven't bothered to ask if I mind until now."

"This question is personal."

"So was every other question you asked," he said, still laughing. And then he wiped his mouth and sat up straight. "Go ahead and ask me what you want to ask me."

"Why'd you do it?"

"Do what?"

"Kept your mouth shut and do ten years for Daddy?"

"What was I supposed to do?"

"I get that. You did what you had to do to get Daddy out of there that night. But why didn't you jump in the car with him and get both of you outta there?"

"Because it was a setup. The ATF and the FBI were involved. Somebody had to take the fall. Better it be me than your father."

"That's loyalty." Imani picked up her glass. "A man of honor."

And that makes you that much sexier, Mr. Brock Whitehall.

Chapter Sixteen

It was after eight when Hareem arrived at his river-front condo. He got out of the car and looked around for Loonie's big-body Benz. He didn't expect her to be on time; that simply wasn't her style at all. Loonie would get there in time to make a dramatic entrance. When Hareem didn't see her car, he went inside.

Hareem wasn't actually sure if she would come, but he hoped that she would and that she would bring his baby. He didn't need any damn test to tell him that was his baby. He could feel it when he held her in his arms. If it wasn't for Marko and Chub's bullshit, he'd have spent more time with Loonie and the baby.

After Hareem had killed Marko, he had had to hurry to pick up Cynthia from her office, because she had planned for them to attend the Florida Commercial Real Estate Symposium. She was excited about hearing the keynote speaker, Levy Spencer, the chairman of the Americas Research Corporation.

The pair might have seemed like an odd couple to some, but there was a method to what they were doing. Money. Cynthia loved Hareem, but she had no delusions about who Hareem was, and she didn't harbor any thoughts of trying to change him. He was a drug dealer and a killer, but that didn't bother her, because drug dealers who murdered had money, and with that money, she would be free to invest, once the money was properly laundered, of course. That was the program she had sold Hareem, and that was why he had started fucking Cynthia behind Loonie's back. But secrets never stay secrets for long.

It had hurt Hareem when Loonie found out about Cynthia and left him. He really did love Loonie. Naturally, he didn't realize how much that he loved her until she was gone. But, unfortunately, by the time he realized it, Loonie had disappeared and was nowhere to be found. He had had to hire the private investigator that Alexis Fox had turned him on to so he could find her. It was the investigator who had told him that Loonie was pregnant.

They were good together, and now Loonie had his daughter. Hareem knew that he had to find a way to work it out so he could have his love, his daughter, and his moneymaker.

It had been a few days since he'd been at his riverfront condo, so he straightened up the place a little before Loonie got there. He laughed when he thought about how they had that big-ass house that Imani wanted, but none of them really *lived* there, though she did sleep there more often than he or his father did. Most days he went there only to have breakfast, and that was more because Kimberly was a great cook, and not because he had a desire to eat with his family, which was something that his father believed in. Mr. O thought that they should try to have one meal together as a family at least once a day.

Now that the place looked and smelled better, Hareem sat down on the couch in the living room and relaxed and hoped Loonie would show. As it got closer to nine o'clock, Hareem started to think that she wasn't coming over. Maybe she couldn't get away from Hedrick, he thought, and then he decided to give her five more minutes. If Loonie didn't show up, then he would call Gianna and see what was up with her, even though he was done with her.

"Or maybe I'll hit the bars and find something new," he said and stood up.

Hareem was about to grab his keys from the kitchen counter when he heard a light tapping on the front door. He got his gun from under one of the throw pillows on the couch and went to the door. He got excited when he looked out through the peephole and saw Loonie standing there with what looked like a car seat in her hands. He unlocked the door and quickly jerked it open.

"Shhh," Loonie whispered, with her index finger over her lips. "She's asleep."

"Okay," Hareem whispered and took the car seat from her. "Come in."

When he brought the baby inside, Loonie took her from the seat and carried her into the bedroom.

"Did she wake up?" Hareem whispered when he joined her.

"No. She's like you. She'll sleep through anything. It's just hard getting her to go to sleep, 'cause she's nosy and she be fighting it," Loonie said. Omeika's parents tiptoed out of the bedroom and left their baby girl to sleep.

"Okay, I'm here," Loonie said with her hands on her hips.

"And I am so happy you came."

"What you wanna talk to me about?"

"Why don't you have a seat? Make yourself comfortable," he said, and Loonie moved toward the couch. "Can I get you something to drink?"

"What you got?"

Hareem stopped and smiled. "I got whatever you want."

"I'll bet. I'll have some of that Cîroc citrus vodka I know you got chilling in the refrigerator."

"See how well you know me," he said and went into the kitchen to make them drinks. "You know what I was thinking about while I was waiting for you to get here?"

"You were praying that I would come?"

"No." Hareem laughed. "You remember that day we were fucked up—"

"We were always fucked up in those days," she said and laughed and thought about all the time they'd spent together. "Before noon most days. You gonna have to be more specific if you want me to remember."

Hareem walked over to the couch, handed her a glass, and sat down next to her. "We were riding, drinking, burnin' that good-good, and you said you wanted to go to the movies, but you wouldn't go in unless you could bring the bottle."

She laughed. "What were we drinking that day?"

"Henny."

"That's right, straight to the head," she said and took a sip of citrus vodka. "I remember we went to Walmart, and I bought a purse big enough to put the bottle in."

"And then we smoked another one before we went in."

"And we fell asleep halfway through the movie."

"We did wake up at the end."

By that time, they were both laughing hysterically, and Hareem was enjoying the sound and the feel of it. Loonie remembered that they had laughed a lot those days and that she had enjoyed being with him, because they had had so much fun.

"I needed that," she said once the laughter had subsided. "But you still haven't said what you want to talk about." She paused and looked at him. "Or did you think I would come through the door, my clothes would magically fall off, and you'd fuck the shit outta me? Was that what you were thinking was gonna happen here?"

"No, but now that you mention it, it would have been nice."

"Not happening."

"Then I'll just tell you. I love you, Loonie, and I want to know if there is any way that we can find our way back."

"Back to what? Back to being together?"

"Yes. We were awesome together."

"One problem. You got a woman."

Hareem swallowed hard. "She's business," he said, and Hareem took his time and explained their relationship. "Like I said, just business. But you got a man too."

"Honestly?"

"Honestly. You can tell me anything."

"I hate that muthafucka. I mean Kevin was really nice and sweet and shit when he used to come down to Palatka to see me, but ever since I had the baby and moved back up here . . ." Loonie shook her head. "It's like he does shit just to get on my nerves."

"Get rid of him," Hareem said with a wave of his hand.

"He won't go," she said passionately.

Hareem smiled, because this had just become about business. "Maybe I could help you with that."

"How?"

"Put the nigga out of business." And take his family back.

"How you gonna do that?"

"How much do you know about his business?"

"Everything." Loonie smiled. "He used to take me everywhere with him."

"You know where his stash house is?"

"I sure do. I know where all his stash houses are," Loonie said and rattled off the address of one. Then she told him how the place was set up.

"Thank you, bae," he said and took out his phone. He called Martel, and his right-hand-man picked up on the first ring. "'Sup, Marty-mar? I got something I need you to do. Something you're gonna enjoy," Hareem said, and then he told Martel about the stash houses and what he wanted him to do.

"You're right. I am gonna enjoy the shit outta that for sure," Martel said.

"Text me with it when it's done."

It was a couple of hours later when Hareem received the text he'd been waiting for. He and Loonie had been having a good time, burnin' that good-good, watching movies, and doing shots of Cîroc citrus vodka. All the text said was, Done, but there was a video attached. Hareem pressed the arrow on the phone's screen, and a burning house appeared. He handed the phone to Loonie.

"Recognize the house?" he asked her.

"That's Kevin's stash house," she said excitedly, then hugged and kissed Hareem on the cheek.

That one kiss led to another and another, and Loonie's resistance and her determination not to have sex with Hareem got weak. Soon she was in his arms and he was carrying her to the bedroom.

Chapter Seventeen

It used to be the same routine every morning for Imani. Her internal clock always, without fail, woke her up before her iPhone alarm went off at eight thirty. Since the phone was in her hand, she'd check emails before she headed downstairs to the gym for a workout. While Imani put in work, she'd mentally walk through her priorities for the day. Then she'd shower and get dressed, head to the kitchen to eat a healthy breakfast, follow up with or make new connections, and then it was off to the office sometime around ten or ten thirty.

But not anymore.

Since Brock had got out of prison and moved into the house, everything about her routine had changed, and it went beyond just her morning rituals. Now her day revolved around Brock, and she'd even work around him. It had all begun the morning she strolled into the gym and found Brock dressed in the 2UNDR boxer briefs she'd bought for him and no shirt. Sweat was dripping off his deep chocolate skin. After she'd got her eyes full, and he'd apologized for the way he was dressed, Imani had promised to take him somewhere to get something more appropriate to work out in. They'd worked out together that morning and planned to hit it again the next morning.

"See you at seven tomorrow morning?" he'd said.

"I was thinking more like eight thirty," Imani said, thinking that she could set her alarm for eight fifteen.

"Seven thirty?"

"Eight o'clock and you have a date."

"It's a date." Brock grabbed his towel and headed toward the door. "A date. I think I like the sound of that."

Imani watched him walk away. His confident swagger was looking good in those briefs.

Now that Imani was working out with Brock every morning, there was no more mentally walking through her priorities for the day as she exercised her muscles. Other than her business, he was her priority. And once they showered and dressed each morning, there was no more following up with connections. Now it was all about the conversation with the family over breakfast. And instead of rushing off to the office as soon as breakfast was over, Imani busied herself around the house until her father was ready to go, because, after all, Brock was his driver.

In spite of the fact that Mr. O tried to monopolize Brock's time, Imani would always find some way to spend some part of the day with him. And even on days when she couldn't, Imani wasn't worried, because most nights belonged to her. Since they both loved to eat, they routinely hit a restaurant after work, and then they'd find something else to do. In Imani's eyes, she had the perfect tall, dark, and handsome man, and he thought that she was the most beautiful woman that he had ever seen.

Although they wanted to strip each other down and fuck until they passed out, they refrained. They were forming a friendship, a bond between them that could develop into so much more. It was a fact that everyone around them could see.

"Them two just need to go on and fuck and get it over with," Kimberly said, shaking her head, one morning, after Imani had chased Brock out of the kitchen as they laughed like children.

That same evening, Imani decided that she would surprise Brock with tickets to go to the St. Johns Town Center and experience The Escape Game, an escape room adventure. Players entered an immersive environment and had sixty minutes to follow the clues, solve the puzzles, complete the mission, and escape.

However, all of Imani's plans went out the window when they left Luxury Private Charters and Mr. O said, "Brock, I need you to drop Imani at the house. I need you to drive me somewhere."

"Yes, sir," Brock said and started for the house.

"Where are you going?" a pouty Imani asked.

"I have some business to take care of."

"If it's business, that is all the more reason that I should know where you're going."

Mr. O nodded. "That makes sense."

"So where are you going?"

"I have some business to take care of," Mr. O repeated. Imani folded her arms across her chest. "She gets pissy when she doesn't get her way."

"Whatever, Daddy," Imani said and sank deeper into her seat. First, he had ruined her plans for the night, and now she was getting excluded from business.

"But she is so adorable when she gets all pouty like that, isn't she?" Mr. O went on.

"Yes, she is *so* adorable," Brock said, and that made Imani smile, and she came back to life.

Therefore, the entire way to the house, Imani pressed her case for why she needed to be there with her father if it involved business. Her father basically agreed with almost everything she said, but he still told her that she wasn't going. Each time one or the other would try to involve Brock in the discussion, which at times seemed more like an argument, he would repeat, "Staying out of it."

But the discussion continued until Brock parked in front of the house.

"You're still not going, Imani," Mr. O declared.

"Okay, fine. If it's business, that means you'll tell me about it in the morning, right?" Imani asked as Brock got out of the car.

He knew that no matter what she said, her father wouldn't relent. Brock rounded the hood, opened Imani's car door, and helped her out. They headed to the front door and looked at one another when they reached the house.

"I guess this is good night," Imani said, closing her eyes and dropping her head sadly.

"I guess so, since I don't know where we're going."

"Yeah." Imani looked up into his eyes. "Good night."

"Good night, Imani."

And then they stood looking at each other until Imani reached for the doorknob and Brock turned to walk away.

When Brock got back in the car, it occurred to him that part of Imani's disappointment with not being allowed to go tonight stemmed from the fact that she had made plans for them. He remembered a couple of nights ago, over dinner, they'd talked about how they were both planners when it came to business, but they loved being totally spontaneous when it came to everything else.

One day I'll surprise you and plan something for us to do, Imani had said, and Brock wondered now if she'd made good on her threat.

"Where we going, boss?"

"Hyatt Regency Riverfront."

"Any particular way you want to go?"

"Doesn't matter." Mr. O looked at his watch. "But take your time." *Make the muthafucka wait.*

"The scenic route it is."

"Tell me something," Mr. O said after they had driven awhile. "What do you think of Hareem?"

Imani thinks he's out of control. "I don't know enough about him to really give you anything more than a gut answer."

"And your gut says?"

"That he's young and needs guidance," Brock said. It was a kinder way of saying that he was out of control.

"And I've tried with him. Tried to share my knowledge and experience in the game, but the boy is headstrong, arrogant, stubborn, and thinks he has something to prove, and that's what scares me most about him."

"Why?" Brock asked, but he had a feeling that he already knew the answer.

"Because he reminds me of me," Mr. O answered, just as Brock expected. He used to tell Brock of the days when he was a arrogant young man who wanted to prove to his father that he knew a better way.

"It worked for you."

"It did, and he came up here and damn near controls this market, so I try not to give him too much shit about how he runs his program." Mr. O chuckled. "I leave that to Imani."

"He'll be all right."

"From the first day he came to live with us, he has felt that he has to prove he belongs. He had a rough life before he came to live with us. His mother was an addict. You know the story."

Mr. O paused to reflect on those early days when Hareem first came to live with them. Julia leaving had broken him. He had been too consumed with his own problems to give Hareem the attention that he needed. That had fallen on Imani.

"Maybe I gave him too much, too much stuff to make him feel better. Let him have too much freedom, when I should have kept him close to me and done more talking," he mused.

"Do I know his mother?"

"I don't even remember his mother." Mr. O dropped his head. "It was the one thing that Julia couldn't forgive me for, and she left me. If it wasn't for Imani stepping into the role, we wouldn't be in the position we're in today." *A role I was grooming you for*, Mr. O thought but didn't say this.

Chapter Eighteen

When Brock and Mr. O arrived at the Hyatt Regency Jacksonville Riverfront, Brock parked in the garage, and they went into the hotel for Mr. O's meeting. He escorted Mr. O to the elevator and waited until it came. When the doors opened, Brock took a step forward, but Mr. O held out his hand and stopped him from getting on the elevator.

"Why don't you wait for me in the bar?" he said and stepped onto the elevator.

"Yes, boss," Brock said as the doors closed, and the situation immediately made him anxious.

Brock would have felt better about Mr. O's decision to go up alone if he had told him whom his meeting was with. He stood there and watched to see which floor Mr. O got off on. When the elevator stopped on the twelfth floor, Brock went to Tavern, the hotel bar.

Mr. O got off the elevator and knocked on the door of suite twelve-twenty. It took a while, but when the door opened, the first thing Mr. O saw was the smiling face of Moreno Fernandez. Without a word, Fernandez stepped aside, and Mr. O walked into the suite. Fernandez closed the door and followed Mr. O to the table in the suite. Both men unbuttoned their jackets and reached for their guns with their left hand. Then each man unloaded his weapon before laying it on the table.

"Ferdie," Mr. O said and held out his hand.

"O," Fernandez said, and the friendly rivals shook hands.

They had known about the other for years and had a mutual respect for one another. It was only by chance that they'd met when they were both pursuing the same client, who was looking to buy Bushmaster M4-type carbines. The meeting had been set at a bar, and the client had stood them both up. Since they were in the same business, this had given them a chance to talk to somebody who understood their world, and a friendship had developed. Until it came to business. Each of them believed that you didn't have friends in business, just competitors and enemies.

"How's your daughter? Imani, isn't it?" Fernandez asked as both men took a seat at the table.

"You remembered." Mr. O chuckled because he couldn't remember any of Fernandez's daughters' names. There were so many. "Imani is fine. I have a son now too," Mr. O said proudly.

"Really? A surprise, I take it."

"A big one."

"I have several of those myself," Fernandez said and laughed. "How old is he?"

"He'll be twenty-one soon." Mr. O chuckled, but then his game face returned. "So, why am I here?"

"I'm getting pushed out."

Mr. O chuckled because he knew all too well what that felt like. "By who?"

"I am being pushed out of my own organization by some people that work for me," Fernandez answered. Then he paused. "And others," he added. "I believe that they're responsible for the recent attempt on my life."

"I understand. What can I do to help?" Mr. O asked graciously, but at the same time, he was wondering, *Why come to me?*

"I need money."

"How much money?"

"Three hundred grand. And I need it in cash."

Mr. O leaned back and thought about it. It wasn't about the money; a few hundred Gs was nothing. The question was, Did he want to get involved in Ferdie's problems? "Sure, Ferdie." He stood up and held out his hand. "Give me a day or two to put the cash together."

Fernandez stood up, and with both hands, he shook Mr. O's. "Thank you, O. I really appreciate this."

"No worries," Mr. O said and reached for his gun.

"You in a hurry?"

"Not especially."

"Have a drink with me before you go," Fernandez said.

"All you had to do was offer," Mr. O said and reclaimed his seat. "But just one."

It was just about the time when Brock looked at his watch as he sat at the bar. Although it had been only thirty minutes since he and Mr. O had parted ways, it felt like an eternity. Maybe there was nothing to worry about. After all, they were at a hotel, and maybe Mr. O was there to meet a woman. If that was the case, Brock understood keeping Imani out of it. But if that was the case, why not just tell him? *Why all the mystery?*

"Is this seat taken?" a female voice asked, snapping him out of his thoughts.

Brock turned toward the voice. "No." The woman was beautiful, and that made him smile. "Please have a seat."

"Thank you," she said and signaled for the bartender without success.

Brock picked up his drink, took a sip, and then turned to take all of her in. Her jet-black hair was parted down the middle, and thick braids framed her honey-kissed skin, her chiseled features, and her dark eyes. He turned away.

As she continued to try to get the bartender's attention, Brock looked at his watch and couldn't help but notice the way her purple Stella McCartney mock-neck mini-dress hugged each of her curves, as if the dress had been designed for her. He finished his drink, put the glass down, and signaled for the bartender. He came right away.

"Another Jack?"

"Yes. But the lady was trying to get your attention," Brock said, and she smiled.

"I'm sorry." The bartender put a napkin down in front of her. "What can I get for you?"

"Cuba libre please," she said in a soft and sultry voice.

"I'll be back with those in a minute," the bartender said and went off to complete his tasks.

"Thank you," she said, and then she looked at him. "Have we met?"

"I don't think so. I think I'd remember you."

"You look very familiar to me. If you don't mind me asking, where are you from?"

"Miami."

"I'm from Madrid, but I spend a lot of time in Miami."

"I don't live there anymore." He chuckled. "I've been living in Atlanta for the past ten years. I just recently moved here."

She looked disappointed. "Well, maybe not, but you look so familiar to me."

"I just have that kind of face," Brock said as the bartender returned with their drinks and set them on the bar top.

She picked up her glass. "Renata Cano."

"Brock Whitehall." He raised his glass. "Nice to meet you."

"And you. So what brought you to Jacksonville?"

"I have some friends here, family really. They invited me down. I like it here," he said and thought about Imani. "I'm thinking about staying. What about you?"

"Just visiting. I'm here to meet somebody who's staying here at the hotel," Renata said.

From there they got into a lively conversation about Miami, and it went on until Brock saw Mr. O coming toward the bar.

He finished his drink and signaled for the bartender. "As much as I'd love to stay and talk some more, I have to go," Brock said as the bartender arrived. "Check, please."

"Well, it was nice meeting you." Renata smiled and held out her hand. "And it was very nice talking to you."

"Believe me, it was my pleasure. It reminded me of home," he said as Mr. O made it to the bar. He waved and kept walking toward the exit. Brock stood up and tossed a couple of twenties on the bar top.

"Maybe we'll bump into each other again when you have more time to talk," Renata said. "Or maybe I'll see you next time you're in Miami."

"I'd like that," Brock said, and they exchanged numbers. "Good night, Renata. It was very nice meeting you." He then left the bar to catch up with Mr. O.

Chapter Nineteen

On the way home from the Hyatt, Mr. O called Kimberly and told her they were on their way, so she had dinner prepared and ready to serve when they got home. Brock hoped that there was still time to do whatever it was that Imani had planned for them to do that evening.

If she had something planned.

He was disappointed that Imani wasn't home when they got there. He sat down to a meal of zucchini boats and rigatoni with sausage, thinking that maybe he was wrong. Maybe he was getting ahead of himself when it came to Imani. Maybe she was just being friendly by showing the new guy around the city. After all, Imani was her father's loyal soldier. It would only make sense that she would do everything she could to accomplish Mr. O's objective, and his objective was to get Brock back in the game.

So you need to slow down and keep things in perspective.

For dessert, Kimberly served them homemade cheesecake brownies. It was then that Mr. O announced his intentions for the evening.

"I'm gonna head out tonight," he said and took a bite of his brownie.

"I'll bring the car around," Brock said before shoving his last bite of cheesecake brownie in his mouth.

"No need. I got this tonight."

"You sure?"

"Yeah, I'm sure." Mr. O chuckled. "I think I can get some pussy by myself."

"I know that, boss. But what about your security?"

"This ain't Miami, son. Up here, I'm a legitimate businessman. Cops ain't hunting me, and I have no enemies," he said, getting up from the table. He headed upstairs to change. His response made it obvious to Brock that Mr. O didn't need him to drive him; he had asked Brock to drive only to keep him around.

With nothing to do and nobody to do it with, Brock got up from the table and went into the game room. He made himself a drink, picked up a pool stick, and racked up the balls. This was the first time he'd picked up a cue in ten years. His plan was to hang around and see if Imani came home, and then maybe they could do something together.

Didn't you just say you were going to slow down and keep things in perspective? he thought as he broke the balls. The six ball went in a corner pocket. *You still got it.*

After a few games and a few drinks, Brock assumed that Imani wasn't coming home any time soon, and went upstairs to his room. Seeing that he wasn't tired or ready to sleep, Brock propped up some pillows, turned on the TV, relaxed, and thought about his future. He pondered getting his own place and a car of his own.

It was fifteen minutes later when Imani finally got home and parked in the garage. She was disappointed that she didn't see her father's car. To her, that meant Brock wasn't home. After Brock had dropped her off at the house earlier, Imani had decided to go to the St. Johns Town Center to see if she could use her tickets to The Escape Game the following evening. And since her dinner plans had been ruined as well, Imani had gone to Maggiano's and dined alone on their salmon with crispy Calabrian shrimp.

Imani climbed out of the car and entered the house. When she went upstairs to her room, she was surprised to see light coming out from under Brock's bedroom door. Her first thought was to go knock on the door and see if he wanted to do something with her. She started down the hall, but she quickly changed her mind. Imani went to her room and shut the door, thinking that she needed to slow her roll.

She changed out of her clothes and crawled under the covers. As she lay in bed, Imani thought about her decision not to knock on Brock's door. Although she was pretty sure that Brock was feeling her the same way she was feeling him, she didn't want to seem like she was chasing him or trying to force herself on him.

At seven forty-five the next morning, Imani's internal clock woke her up before her iPhone alarm went off. She rolled out of bed and started getting dressed to go work out. As she was leaving her bedroom, she turned off her alarm, and then she headed downstairs to the gym. As she expected, Brock was already in there, jogging on the treadmill. She stood there quietly watching him for a while, admiring how good he looked in the Gymshark sport shorts and the Critical Drop Arm Tank that she had gotten for him to wear while he worked out.

Imani dropped her towel on a bench. "Good morning, Brock."

He turned off the treadmill. "How are you, Imani?"

"I am doing great this morning," she said, enjoying the sight of sweat dripping off his muscular frame. "What about you?"

I missed you last night, he thought. "Great. I slept like a baby last night."

Imani assumed her opening yoga pose. It was called Balasana, or the Child's Pose, and was a hip-opening exercise that increased mobility and flexibility and allowed for a greater range of motion. Brock stopped to watch her before moving on to the cage workout machine, because he was into the way her round ass rested on her heels when she stretched to engage her core muscles.

"Where did you and Daddy go last night?" Imani asked as stretched.

"Did you ask your father?"

"No." She giggled. "And he'll just say that he went out."

"If that's what he'll say, then that's where he was."

"You're just as bad as he is." Imani stretched some more, and Brock held his breath. "I'll ask him when he gets up."

"Is he back?"

Imani tensed. "What do you mean, is he back?"

Brock started walking toward her, and Imani held her breath. "I mean, is he back from wherever he went last night?" he said.

Imani rocked back on her heels. "I thought you two were together."

"We were. Then, when we got home, he said he was going out and he didn't need me to drive for him." He started to tell her what her father had said about getting pussy by himself, but it wasn't necessary. The point had been made.

"And you let him drive himself?"

"Yeah, he said—" Brock began, and Imani held up her hand.

"Daddy may think that he is all right to drive himself, but he's not. He has early-stage cataracts, and he can't see very well at night anymore."

"I did not know that."

"Why did you think I wanted him to get a driver?"

"I thought that was just a reason to get me to stay."

Imani remained silent, as if she'd been caught in a secret. "It was, but that doesn't mean that he doesn't need a driver, because he does," she finally confessed.

"Understood. Next time he tries that, I'll insist that I drive him where he wants to go and pick him up when he's done."

"Thank you, Brock."

"No problem."

Imani laughed lightly. "He probably went to see Anissa."

"Who is that?"

"A woman half his age. He hasn't told her how old he is, and you driving his blind ass over there would have made him feel old." She laughed again. "Older than he is."

After they completed their workout, showered, changed clothes, and had breakfast, Brock took Imani to work. Since her father hadn't made it home by the time they left the house, Imani called him, but Mr. O did not answer. A few minutes later, he sent her a text that said, I'm fine.

Once he walked Imani to the building and held the door open for her, Brock told her that he'd be back when she called, and then he went back to her car and drove away. Imani stood there for a second or two, wondering what had just happened. The morning had been going great between them. They had had a good workout together, the conversation over breakfast had been engaging and at times hilarious, and that good feeling had continued in the car on their way to the office. Imani went to her office, wondering if she had done something or said something to make him mad. She shook it off.

And they say we're the sensitive ones, she thought and got to work.

But there was nothing wrong, nor had she done something or said something to make him mad. Now that Brock had decided to get a car and a place to stay, he wanted to get right on it. And so, when Imani called to say that she was ready to leave the office, Brock picked her up and took her to see the Infiniti Q60 he had picked out and then drove by the apartment he had selected for himself.

Imani was a little disappointed that he wanted to move out of her family home, but then she thought that it may be a good thing.

They lived in her father's house, and Imani would feel uncomfortable having hot sex when her father was in the bedroom down the hall. That was why she had got her own place. *Maybe he feels the same way*, she surmised. And that single thought made her feel better about the situation.

"I'll work out the financing in the morning for you," Imani promised as they drove off.

"Thank you, Imani," he said with a smile that showed how much he appreciated it. "And I appreciate you," he added, and Imani's smile broadened.

"Anything you want or need, you just have to let me know, and I will make it happen for you."

"That's because you're all things to all people, right?" Brock asked, and Imani took a moment to think before she answered.

"No. Not all things to all people. I just want to be all things to you," Imani said, and Brock took his eyes off the road to glance over at her. They stared into each other's eyes for a split second before he focused back on the road.

Brock was caught off guard by her words. "I want to be that for you too," he said and had to slam on his brakes to avoid hitting the car in front of them.

"You want me to drive?" she giggled. "You seem a little distracted."

"I think you're enough to distract any man. But that's not the point."

"What is the point, then?"

"I'm hungry, so where do you want to eat?"

Imani thought for a second or two. She had planned for them to go and experience The Escape Game at Town

Center, so she picked a restaurant that was close by and chose Seasons 52. Fifteen minutes later they parked and headed inside the restaurant.

"What are you having?" he asked once they were seated.

"I was thinking about the cedar plank roasted salmon, but I had salmon last night," she replied as she looked over the menu.

"Where did you eat last night?"

Imani put down her menu and folded her hands in front of her. "Tell me where you and Daddy went last night, and I'll tell you where I ate."

Brock raised his menu so that it covered his face. "I think I'll have the filet mignon and Maine lobster tail."

Imani giggled at his evasiveness, and she chose the wood-grilled filet mignon.

After dinner they headed to Town Center to play The Escape Game. They decided to try the Space Station. According to the game, their spaceship crash-landed on the surface of Mars. Radiation levels were rising fast, and they had to get the spaceship's systems back online and relaunch the vehicle into orbit in order to make it out alive, along with the four other crew members they met when they got there. They were able to escape from Mars and had a great time doing it, and they even made some new friends in the process.

When they got back to the house, Brock and Imani had a drink in the great room and talked about how much fun they had had together. Once Imani announced that she was tired and going up to bed, Brock walked her to her bedroom door.

"Good night, Imani. I had fun with you tonight."

"I did too," Imani said, and they stared at each other before they stepped closer to one another and shared their first kiss.

"Good night, Brock," she said when the kiss was over. And then she turned and went into her bedroom.

As Brock walked down the hall, he saw light coming out from under Mr. O's door.

"Definitely need my own place," he mumbled to himself.

Chapter Twenty

The next morning, after their workout, which was laced with flirtatious comments and longing glances, which spoke volumes about the way they were feeling about each other, Imani headed upstairs and got dressed. She grabbed a couple of coconut-quinoa breakfast bars and left the house without waiting for Brock and her father. There were a couple of deals in motion that Imani had to handle, and there were some financial arrangements that needed to be made, and she wanted both done by the end of the day.

When Brock came downstairs for breakfast, Mr. O told him Imani had already left the house. As he fixed his plate, Brock wondered if she had left early because of their kiss the night before.

It was just a kiss, he told himself. They didn't tongue each other down, nor did their hands roam each other's body to check out what the other was working with. It was just a kiss.

I was looking at her, she was looking at me, and it just happened, he thought as he sat down at the table. But then he thought that if anything was wrong, she would have said something while they were working out this morning.

It was just a kiss, but it was *that* kiss and the words *I just want to be all things to you* that had kept him up thinking most of the night. Then he had got up in time to work out with her, so now he was tired.

And for that reason, after Brock dropped Mr. O at the office, he went back to the house and got in bed. On the way back to the house, he had thought maybe he should have gone inside the office and said something to Imani. To make sure that everything was all right between them. He yawned as he lay in bed now and quickly reminded himself that he had seen her two hours ago and she'd been fine.

It seemed like his head had just hit the pillow when his phone rang. He picked it up and answered the call.

"Hello."

"Did I wake you up?"

"Yeah, but it's cool."

"I'm sorry."

He looked at the time; it was just after two o'clock. "You ready to go already?"

"No, but I would like you to come up here," she said, and he could hear the excitement in her voice. "There are some things that I want to talk to you about. But it's no rush."

"I'm on my way," Brock said and ended the call. "Told you it was nothing," he said aloud and got out of bed and jumped in the shower. And then he was off to see what Imani wanted.

When Imani saw the car pull into the parking lot as she stood in front of her office window, she got excited, because she'd been thinking about him all day. She had devoted a large part of her day to Brock, and she wanted to share what she had done for him. Imani meant what she said when she told him that she just wanted to be all things to him, and she was ready to back her words with action.

Imani's office door was open and she was standing on the threshold, so Brock caught a glimpse of her as soon as he came into the building. She smiled brightly and waved as he made his way to her office door.

"What's up, Imani?" he said and leaned on the doorjamb.

"Hey, Brock." She put her hands together apologetically. "I am so sorry that I woke you up."

"It's no problem. They tell me sleep is overrated."

"They lied. Sleep is wonderful," she said, and they laughed.

He pushed off the doorjamb. "What did you want to talk to me about?"

Just then Mr. O rounded the corner. He was carrying a briefcase. "Brock!" Mr. O called. "I'm glad you're here. I was just about to call you." He came to a stop in front of Imani's office door.

"What up, boss?" Brock said and winked at Imani.

"I need to make a run," he said. "Come on."

"Now?"

"Yes, now. Come on."

"But I was—" Brock began, and Mr. O saw the look on his and Imani's faces.

"You two need to fuck and get it over with," Mr. O announced.

"Daddy?" Imani exclaimed, with a frown on her face. But she agreed. She did need Brock to fuck her.

"You do. Just not now." Mr. O tapped Brock on the arm. "Come on. Let's go."

"Right behind you, boss."

"Call me when you're done, please," Imani told Brock and then watched him as he made his way down the hallway.

"I will," Brock called over his shoulder, and once again, he left Imani disappointed because her plans had been put on hold.

"Where to, boss?" Brock asked when they got in the car.

"The Hyatt."

When Brock and Mr. O arrived at the Hyatt Regency Riverfront, Brock parked in the garage before going into the hotel. However, this time when the elevator came and the doors opened, Brock took a step to get on.

Mr. O knit his brow. "Why don't you wait for me in the bar?"

"No," Brock insisted and got on the elevator. "You coming?"

Mr. O shook his head. "Niggas," he said and got on the elevator.

The minute the elevator doors opened, Mr. O marched off the elevator, and Brock had to hustle to keep up. When he got to suite twelve-twenty, Mr. O knocked on the door and waited for Moreno Fernandez to answer. When no one opened the door, he knocked harder, but still, nobody came to open it. Mr. O looked at his watch and thought about waiting in the lobby or the bar for Fernandez to get there.

"Let's go home," he said finally and turned to make his way back to the elevator, thinking that if Fernandez still needed the money, he knew how to call.

"What was that about?" Brock asked when they were on their way to the house.

"I was supposed to be meeting Moreno Fernandez at the hotel, but you saw, he was a no-show."

"What were you meeting Ferdie for?"

Mr. O explained to Brock that he had planned to meet Fernandez because the man was being pushed out of his organization and needed to borrow three hundred thousand dollars in cash.

"That what's in the briefcase?" Brock asked.

"Yes."

For the rest of the trip to the house, neither Mr. O nor Brock said anything. Even though they weren't talking to each other about it, they were thinking about the same thing. Fernandez was getting pushed out of his own business by his own people, and they may have made an attempt on his life. As Brock drove, both he and Mr. O considered the possibility that another attempt had been made, and this time Fernandez's henchmen had been successful. Therefore, the question they both were thinking about was how Mr. O's meeting with Fernandez was going to affect them.

When they arrived at the house, Mr. O ignored Kimberly's question about dinner, went straight to his office, and shut the door.

Chapter Twenty-one

It was after five that same evening when Imani shut down her laptop, left the office, and went home for the evening. She was surprised when she pulled into the garage and saw that her father's car was there. She got out of her own car and touched the hood of his as she passed by.

"Still warm," Imani said, then walked into the house.

"Hello," she called from the foyer, but she got no answer, so she continued farther into the house. "Anybody here?"

"Back here!" Brock shouted from the game room. When Imani came into the room, Brock was standing at the bar, fixing a drink.

"I thought you were going to call me?" she said the second she saw him.

"Hey, Imani. It's good to see you."

She walked to the bar and stood next to him. "Hey, Brock. It's great to see you too."

"You want a drink?"

"Thank you," Imani said, resisting the overwhelming urge to kiss him on the cheek. "Now, I thought you were going to call me."

"I was just about to call you."

"But you needed a drink first." Imani nodded playfully. "Well, now you've had your drink," she said, quoting a line from *The Godfather*.

"Okay, Don Vito," Brock laughed.

"So I'm guessing that you're not planning on telling me where you two went or what was in the briefcase, are you?"

Although Brock was concerned about Mr. O's involvement with Moreno Fernandez, he decided not to share his concerns with Imani. "No. I would never betray his confidence, or yours, for that matter."

She smiled. "Good answer, so I'll let it go." But it was more like she was putting her question on hold for the moment, because Imani needed to know.

"Good," he said, because if she asked him again with those soulful eyes, he might tell her everything. Brock wanted to be everything for her, give her whatever she needed, but there were lines of trust and integrity that he wouldn't cross. At least not without a good reason, and her soulful eyes weren't enough.

"Where's Daddy?"

"He went into his office as soon as we got back."

"Hmm," Imani said, like she had read something into him going straight to his office, but she actually hadn't. She just hated to be in the dark when it came to business. So she was concerned. What was in the briefcase, and whom did he go to meet? she wondered. Imani respected the position that Brock was taking, and would probably appreciate his moral compass more when it was her confidence he wouldn't betray, but right now, Imani needed to know what was going on.

Because I'm sure that there was money in that briefcase.

"So what did you want to talk to me about?" Brock asked to change the subject before she asked another question about the briefcase. He could see the excitement return to her face.

"Come on. I'll show you," Imani said. She grabbed his hand, and they headed toward the garage. She pulled her car keys from her pocket, and Brock tried unsuccessfully to grab them out of her hand. "I'll drive," she told him.

Although she had said that she would let it go, Imani couldn't let it go. She was concerned about her father, and for a change, it wasn't about his health. Over the years, Imani had gone from being his student to being his trusted confidante to being his business partner. He rarely did anything without talking to her about it first and would often acquiesce to her suggestions. That was why this issue with Fernandez bothered her so much.

Brock had been in prison for the past ten years; therefore he had no idea about how the relationship between her and her father had evolved. So as she drove up A1A, Imani told Brock about the business and her role in it. She stressed the need for information and how that information was the key to making it all happen.

"I hear you. I do. I don't know exactly what's going on, but trust me, I'm on top of it," he assured her. He paused and then looked at Imani as she drove. "I would never let anything happen to your father."

"I know that."

And she did. Imani knew how much affection Brock had for her father.

"So I'll make you a deal," he said, because he knew that she was right. If something was going on with Fernandez, she did need to know.

"What's that?"

"If whatever this is becomes an issue, I will tell you everything that I know. Fair enough?"

"Fair enough," Imani said as she put on her turn signal. "We're here."

"Where is here?"

"You'll see," Imani said and turned into a place called The Park at Atlantic Beach.

"Who lives here?"

Imani didn't answer; she parked in front of the leasing office.

"I take it you know her?" Brock asked when a woman came out of the office, smiling and waving.

"Yes, I do. Come on. I'll introduce you," Imani said, and they got out of the car.

"Hey, girl," the woman called.

"How you doing?" Imani asked her, and the two women embraced. "Brock Whitehall, I'd like to introduce you to my friend and business associate, Alexis Fox."

"Nice to meet you, Mr. Whitehall."

"It's Brock, and it's nice to meet you too." *With your sexy fuckin' ass.* "Mr. O speaks very highly of you." And he wasn't lying.

Dressed conservatively in a silk dupioni belted dress from the St. John Collection that featured a necktie on a widespread collar, a V-shaped neckline, long sleeves, and button cuffs, Alexis Fox was a beautiful woman, and even in that conservative dress, she was extremely sexy.

Imani looped her arm in his, and they started walking. The move caught him off guard, and that made his body tremble a bit. There had never been a woman who had had an effect on him the way Imani did. He tried to rationalize it by thinking that he'd been in prison for ten years, and so any fine woman would have an effect on him. It was easier to think that than to admit that he was falling in love with Imani.

"This morning, while I was getting ready to start working on getting you the place you said that you wanted, I thought about this place," Imani told him.

"Since you own this place," Alexis said as she walked alongside them.

"You own this place?" Brock asked as they walked toward one of the buildings.

"*We* do," Alexis said quickly, correcting him. Her ambition was to build an empire for herself, and owning this property with Imani was just one link in the chain.

"And we're converting the apartments to condos," Imani said when they reached the building. They went inside, and Alexis unlocked the door to one of the units.

"Have a look around and tell me what you think," Imani said as the three of them filed into the unit.

As Brock walked through the three-bedroom, two-bath unit, Imani and Alexis talked among themselves about the state of the property, how the conversions were going, and how the renovated units were selling.

"So what do you think?" Imani asked once Brock had finished his walk-through.

"It's nice," he said, but Brock wanted something with more space.

"But?" Imani questioned.

"The master is fine, but the other two bedrooms are a little small," he said, and the ladies looked disappointed.

"This is actually our model," Alexis said quickly as Brock and Imani moved toward the door. If he wasn't interested, that was the end of it, but Alexis wasn't going to let him go that easily. "You need to see a unit without any furniture."

"No need for that," Brock said once they got outside. "I'll take this one. On one condition."

"What's that?" Imani asked anxiously, knowing that she would do whatever he wanted.

"I want two units, one on top of the other." He paused. "Renovate the first level to my specifications, build me some stairs to the top unit, and we have a deal."

"Sold," Alexis said quickly.

"Oh, and I'd like it to be in a building in the back."

"Let's go pick you out a building," Alexis said excitedly, and she rushed off to get the golf cart.

"You sure?" Imani asked.

Brock nodded. "Yeah, I'm sure."

He stepped closer to her and put his arms around her waist. Imani raised her arms and put her hands on his shoulders. She looked up at him.

"I meant it when I said that I want to be everything to you," he said and kissed her.

This kiss was nothing like their first kiss. This time, each of them put their body into the kiss, and Imani felt it deep in her core. Brock's kiss was demanding, as if he was saying, "You're mine. These lips, that tongue, and this body were made just for me."

This kiss was passionate, and Imani felt her body begin to quiver as their tongues danced. His kiss was dizzying too, and the heat from his body seemed to cover her. She felt loved, safe, and protected in his arms.

"If y'all need a minute, I could ride around for a while and come back," Alexis said when she drove up in the golf cart.

"No need," Imani sighed as their lips slowly parted. She took a deep breath. "We're ready," she said, and they joined Alexis on the golf cart to pick out a building for Brock.

After picking out the building and the units he wanted, Brock and Imani got ready to leave The Park at Atlantic Beach.

"So, do you have any more surprises in store for me?" he asked once they were back in Imani's car.

"As a matter of fact, I do," Imani said as they drove away. She had spent the day making arrangements for Brock, so now she was driving him to sign for the Infiniti Q60 he wanted.

Twenty minutes later they reached the Infiniti dealership.

"Paperwork is already done, Ms. Mosley. All I need is for Mr. Whitehall to sign on the dotted line," the sales manager announced when Imani and Brock walked through the front door.

And once the paperwork was done, the manager handed Brock the keys, and he and Imani went out to look at the car. He kissed her forehead and put his arms around her and lifted her head. Brock kissed her lips tenderly, and when their lips parted, that was when Imani told Brock that she was hungry.

"But I don't want to eat anything too heavy," Imani said and slipped her hand in his as they walked back to her car.

"What did you have in mind?"

She let go of his hand once they got to her car. "Follow me," she said, smiling, like she had a plan worked out. She watched him walk back to his car. Brock got in, started up the car, and waited for Imani to lead the way. She climbed behind the wheel and pulled up alongside him, and Brock rolled down his window.

"Try to keep up," Imani said and floored it.

"Oh, no, you didn't," Brock said, slamming the car into gear and tearing out after her. The pair sped up A1A, weaving between cars, each trying to gain the advantage.

After following her for a while, he had to admit, "She's good."

Although he did his best to overtake Imani, Brock never did get the better of her before she turned into the parking lot at Pusser's Bar and Grille in Ponte Vedra Beach. They sat outside, watching the sunset over the western sky and talking about this and that while they shared Calypso Fish Tacos and lobster rolls.

"What do you want to do now?" Brock asked as they walked hand in hand out of Pusser's.

"Follow me," Imani giggled. "And this time, I'll drive slow so you can keep up."

"If you tell me where we're going, I'll beat you there," Brock said confidently.

"That sounds like a challenge."

"It is."

"Challenge accepted."

She gave Brock an address on First Street in Jacksonville Beach. But it didn't matter. Imani still arrived five minutes before him, because she ran a light at Solana Road to gain the advantage.

Chapter Twenty-two

Imani got out of her car and leaned against the trunk while she waited for Brock to arrive. As he pulled into the lot, he could see her. To him, Imani was a vision in red. There was a light breeze blowing through her hair, and the light of the moon caressed her face. She looked so good to him in the Alexandre Vauthier asymmetric draped dress, and the red Christian Louboutin red-sole pumps made her dress pop. It made him want her, but that had been the case since the first time Imani came in the room and walked toward him. She waved when she saw him, and he parked his new ride as close to hers as possible. Imani pushed off her car and walked over to his driver's door.

"Finally made it," she said when he opened the door.

"Finally." He hated to lose, especially to Imani. He would have run the light too, but the eighteen-wheeler coming through the intersection had made that a bad idea, and he'd slammed on his brakes.

"I believe you lost the challenge. When do I get my prize?"

"We never settled on a prize."

"No, I guess we didn't, but I'm sure I'll think of something."

"So, who lives here?"

"I do." Imani paused, and they each took a step toward the other. She looked up into his eyes. "I stay here sometimes, when I want some privacy or just need some time to myself," she explained as they started toward her building.

"Everybody needs some time to themselves, and you, being all things to all people—"

"And I said that I was only all things to you," she interrupted.

"So I can understand that," he said and excitedly walked alongside her. Excited because he was hoping that being at her place would lead to him being inside her.

"I thought that you would understand. You seem like a very private person."

"What makes you say that?" he asked and held the door open for her.

"Something about the look on your face every time I say that I packed up your stuff," she said and pressed the button for the elevator. "And that I have all your important papers."

"At first, it did feel kinda creepy, because, yes, I am a very private person, and the idea of you going through my stuff . . . I don't know. I felt . . ." Brock paused as he searched for the right word.

"Violated?"

"Yeah." The two got on the elevator when it came, and took it up to the fourteenth floor. "It's like you know more about me than anybody."

"They say you can tell a lot about a person by their stuff."

"Exactly," he said and followed Imani to her condo. "But then, after a while, I don't know . . . You knowing everything about me felt comfortable. Like you're supposed to know everything about me."

"I don't know *everything* about you, but I want to." She unlocked the door, and they went inside. "Let me give you a quick tour," she said as she stood in the foyer.

She guided him down the hallway and opened the door to the first room. "This is my office. That's a bedroom across the hall." They walked farther down the hallway. "That's the laundry room," she said, pointing. She made her way to the kitchen and then showed him the dining area and the living room.

"This is nice, Imani," Brock said as he followed her into the living room. The living-room walls and the furniture were white and trimmed with rich East Indian rosewood.

"Thank you."

Since she knew what they had come there to do, Imani thought about telling Brock that she was going to her bedroom to change into something more comfortable and coming out naked.

"That's my bedroom," Imani said matter-of-factly as she pointed to a room just off the living room on her way to the French doors that led to the balcony. "But this is my favorite spot in the house," she said as she opened the French doors wide, as if she was presenting the Atlantic Ocean to him. The view of the ocean from her balcony was breathtaking. "Isn't it beautiful?"

"It is," Brock said, but he wasn't looking at the ocean. "But not as beautiful as you."

"Thank you," Imani said and led him back inside, bouncing between exhilaration, euphoria, anxiety, and panic, because she had anticipated this moment for years. "Can I get you something to drink?"

"Thank you. Whatever you have is fine."

"Have a seat and make yourself at home," Imani said as she went behind the bar, hoping that he'd be spending a lot of time there.

"I want to thank you for all you did for me today," Brock said and sat down on the couch.

"You're welcome. It was my pleasure."

"And you got it all done so fast."

"You told me what you wanted, so I got right on it for you."

"That's why you ran out of the house this morning."

"I knew that you would figure that out all by yourself," Imani said as she brought their drinks over.

"Thank you," he said when she handed him his glass.

Imani sat down next to him and felt a rush of excitement in anticipation of what was to come.

Brock leaned close to ask, "What are we drinking?"

"We're drinking Jack Daniel's Single Barrel." Imani leaned toward him and put the glass to her lips. "The Eric Church edition."

"Smooth," he said after he took a sip. "I didn't know you drank Jack."

"I've developed a taste for it lately," Imani said before taking a sip and then resting her glass on the coffee table.

Brock shot back the rest of his drink and put his glass down on the table next to hers. "I guess this is the part where I kiss you," he said softly as his hand glided across her cheek and gently pulled her close.

Brock's kiss was slow and passionate, yet hard and hungry all at once, as if he were exploring the inside of her mouth. Their tongues danced and his hands cradled her face as he kissed her with fervor. Imani could feel his hunger for her, and her desire to have him inside her made her body ache. Their lips parted, and their bodies shuddered from how intense this moment between them was . . . and from what was still to come.

Brock ran one hand through her hair and pulled her closer to him with the other. Imani wrapped her arms around his neck as she leaned in and gave him a ravenous kiss. Then he pulled down her zipper and eased the dress off her shoulders.

Her head fell back and her eyes drifted closed as he kissed her neck, caressed her skin, making Imani wetter for him. He unhooked her bra and pulled the straps off her shoulders. Then Brock's hot lips and tongue blazed a torrid trail from her neck down to her chest, stopping only to linger at Imani's beautiful breasts.

"Magnificent," he managed to breathe out before he lowered his head and ran his tongue over her nipples. Then Brock pressed them together and devoured both nipples in his mouth.

"That feels so good," she sighed, holding on to his head.

Brock quickly pulled Imani on top of him and cupped her face. "You are so beautiful."

Imani's clit began to swell as she ground her body against his dick while he feasted on her erect nipples. She cried out over the sensation of his tongue, his lips, and his teeth teasing and sucking her nipples.

"That feels so good." Imani reached out, caressed his face, and forced herself to push off Brock and stand up. She quickly kicked out of those red sole pumps and let her dress fall to the floor. "And I want more," she said in a whisper.

Brock stood up. Imani unbuttoned his shirt and then helped him take it off as he fumbled with his belt buckle, trying to get out of his pants as quickly as possible. When he stepped out of his shoes, Imani slowly dropped to her knees and pulled down his pants and underwear.

"Magnificent," she said softly, holding his dick in her hand, before she moaned. She was about to take him into her hot, wet mouth.

I don't care how big a fangirl you are. First sex rules still apply, Imani thought and stood up.

She held out her hand. "Come with me."

Brock took her hand, and she led him into her bedroom. Once she got to her bed, Imani pushed Brock lightly. He fell on the bed, and she got a condom from her nightstand, and then he watched as Imani put it on him. Brock reached out and pulled her onto his lap. Imani was so wet and throbbing with the need to feel him buried deep inside her, she straddled his thighs and slid down on his thick dick. She sighed, because she had wanted this moment to happen since she was fifteen, and now she begged silently for this moment to never end. Imani cried out in ecstasy as she bounced up and down hard on his dick, his kisses muffling the sounds of her screams.

Brock's thrusts were deep, hard, and intense, and Imani was rolling her hips so he could hit her spot with each powerful thrust. His hands gripped her round cheeks, as if he was encouraging her to ride harder. Her eyes widened, her breath caught in her throat, her mouth opened, and her muscles tightened their firm grip on him.

"I'm coming, I'm coming, I'm coming!" Imani screamed, gyrated on his dick. She felt the sensation radiating throughout her body, and Imani exploded.

Chapter Twenty-three

When Imani woke up the next morning, she sat up, yawned, and got in a good stretch. Although her body was a little sore in places, she felt amazing. Imani had needed that; she had needed to feel Brock inside of her. The way that he had worked her body was slow and very thorough. He hadn't missed any of her hot spots, as if she had directed him to each one and told him just how she wanted it. There'd been no need for that, though. Brock had given it to Imani in ways that had her shaking and screaming until early in the morning.

"Good morning, beautiful," Brock said, and it startled her a bit.

"Morning." She lay down closer to him. "How long have you been up?"

"Since six," he said and leaned over to kiss Imani. "You know how your internal clock wakes you up? Mine does the same thing. I've been getting up at six for the count for ten years."

"I understand." Imani rested her head against his chest, and Brock put his arm around her. "What time is it, anyway?"

He picked up his phone. "Eight twenty-seven."

"I guess we're not working out this morning."

"I wouldn't say that," Brock said, gently lifting Imani's face and pulling it toward his. He kissed Imani deeply, slowly teasing her tongue with his.

When their lips parted, Imani sat up and knelt on the bed, with her ass in the air. "Come get it."

Brock got up, adjusted her ass so it was in a perfect position, and penetrated her. His strokes were slow and sensual; her walls rippled around his length, making Imani moan with pleasure. Brock pumped in and out of her slowly and very deliberately, because he wanted to make it last forever. Imani's sex was incredible. It was so good that it had him hollering, "Get it!" each time she brought it down on him.

When Brock picked up his pace and began slamming into her hard and fast, her walls clenched around him. The sensation blew his mind, and he began pumping in and out of her furiously, until they shouted as they came together.

Afterward, they lay there, hearts still pumping, their chests rising and falling as their breathing slowed, staring into each other's eyes until the moment passed. Imani snuggled close to him.

"You made me hungry," she said after a while.

"Yeah, me too."

"Then we need to go," Imani said. "Because there is no food here."

Brock rolled on his side and kissed her. "No food at all?"

Imani shook her head slowly. "The only thing in my refrigerator is bottled water."

"You don't cook?"

"I can. I used to cook, and I was a pretty good cook. I used to cook all the time after Mommy left." Imani rolled into Brock's arms. "But when we moved here and Daddy hired Kimberly and she served us that first meal, that was the day I stopped cooking. The woman is incredible."

"She really is." Brock kissed her.

Imani looked into his eyes. "So, sexy man, as much as I'd like to lie here all day long and do this with you, I have to work today." Imani sighed, and it made his dick hard.

Her work schedule was indeed full. De'Shane was in Rio Rico, Arizona, making the delivery on a shipment of Bushmaster Carbon 15s; she had her monthly meeting with Ginger to review the client reports; and she had to finalize a proposal for a potential new client. So she couldn't slack off today.

When they got to the house and walked into the dining room, her father, Lucius, and her brother were just finishing up breakfast. Imani was surprised to see that Cynthia was there with Hareem. There was only a cup of coffee in front of her, so it was obvious that she hadn't come there to eat. Cynthia was the managing director of her parents' real estate brokerage, and she was always at her office at that hour of the morning. However, this morning she had gotten a text with an image of Hareem asleep in the bed of some woman who was wearing a light blue kimono. Not feeling it necessary to rock the boat over it, Cynthia had decided that the thing to do for the time being was to keep Hareem close for a while. She would deal with this woman if it became necessary.

Imani leaned close to Brock.

"Don't say a thing about me being in business with Alexis," she whispered, and he nodded.

Her father was the first to see them when they came into the dining room, and he chuckled. "Y'all finally did it." He chuckled some more. "Took you long enough."

"Finally did what?" Hareem asked. "Took them long enough to do what?"

"Mind your business, boy," Mr. O said and sipped his coffee.

Hareem looked at Imani and smiled. "Wait a second. Wasn't you wearing that yesterday?" He started laughing. "Maybe now you won't be so uptight all the time."

"What y'all talking about?" Lucius asked.

"Mind your business, Lucius," Mr. O said.

"He fucked her," Hareem said, and Cynthia punched him in the arm.

"What!" Lucius said, with a wicked scowl on his face. He had wanted to get with Imani for years. *Then this nigga shows up.*

Brock pulled her chair out, and Imani sat down. "Thanks for putting my business on the street, little brother. Know it when it comes back to you," she said.

Hareem was about to say something, because he knew that was a real threat, especially with Cynthia sitting right across from her, but he was too slow.

"How are you, Cynthia?" Imani asked.

"I'm doing great, Imani. How are you?"

"I'm wonderful. You haven't met Brock, have you?"

"No, I haven't."

"Cynthia Miles, this is Brock Whitehall."

"It's good to meet you, Cynthia," Brock said.

"As you can tell, and I have no idea why, she is Hareem's girlfriend," Imani explained.

Cynthia nodded. "Nice to meet you too, Brock."

"Cynthia's family owns a real estate firm," Hareem said proudly.

Cynthia didn't waste any time. "Yes, they do, so I'm hoping that if you decide to stay in Jacksonville, you'll allow one of my agents to show you some properties."

"If I decide to stay, I certainly will," he said, glancing at Imani.

"Oh, yeah, he's staying," Hareem said, looking at the way Imani and Brock were gazing at each other. He pushed back from the table and stood up. "It's about time for us to get out of here."

When Cynthia took her cue from Hareem and rose from her chair, Mr. O and Brock stood up, as gentlemen did when a lady was leaving the room.

"Always good to see you, Cynthia," Mr. O said, glancing at Lucius, who hadn't moved a muscle. Although he had never had a chance, Lucius was still brooding over Imani fucking Brock.

"I promise it won't be as long between visits," Cynthia replied. "Imani, it was good to see you. And, Brock, I hope that I'll see you again."

Hareem and Cynthia left the house, got in his Charger, and drove away. He needed to get Cynthia out of there before Imani had a chance for payback. That would be the last thing that he needed for Imani to do, especially when he was trying to rebuild his relationship with Loonie and have a relationship with Omeika. Imani's interference would ruin everything.

"You shouldn't have done that to Imani," Cynthia said.

"I know. And I'm gonna apologize to her. But Lucius has been sucking up to Imani for years, going out of his way to do shit for her, and she treats him like he doesn't exist until she wants him to do something for her."

"What you're saying is that she treats him like an employee," Cynthia said.

Hareem laughed. "You right," he agreed and looked over at Cynthia as he drove.

He was trying to figure out how he was going to tell Cynthia about Loonie and Omeika and, more importantly, how was he going to convince her to accept the relationship that he wanted to build with them. After spending most of his life without a father, Hareem wanted Omeika to have the relationship that he had never had with his father. He was determined to have his love, his daughter, and his moneymaker. As he drove, he thought about how unfair that it was to consider, much less call, Cynthia nothing more than his moneymaker. But he didn't feel about her the way he felt about Loonie. Hareem loved Loonie, and despite what people would tell you, you couldn't truly love two women at the same time.

That shit is impossible.

But he did have strong feelings for Cynthia; he just wasn't in love with her. But she was good for him, and he had to admit that they were good together. Hareem appreciated that Cynthia had taken the time to understand him, who he was, what he had gone through as a child, and the things he wanted out of life.

"Where are you going?" she asked when she noticed that he wasn't driving toward her office.

"I was thinking about you and me having a little after-breakfast breakfast."

She smiled. "I want to, but I can't."

"Come on, Cyn," he said, calling her by the pet name he had given her, because under that business suit beat the heart of a sexual demon. "Spend the day with me." Hareem reached under her skirt.

"No." She swatted his hand away.

"Come on, Cyn. We can lie in bed and fuck all day, like we used to."

"That's sure sounds good," Cynthia said and thought about those days.

Before her mother had made her managing director of the brokerage, Cynthia has been a real estate agent who spent most of her days fucking. Now, as a member of top-level management, Cynthia was much more responsible, and that had been her mother's point in promoting her. But she did miss the old days.

"Okay, but just a quickie, and then I gotta go," she said, and Hareem drove a little faster.

Chapter Twenty-four

Since neither Hareem nor Cynthia knew the meaning of the word *quickie*, it was almost noon when they left the house so he could take her to work. Knowing his proclivity for sleeping with other women, having Hareem take her to work and pick her up every day was one of her means of controlling him. She had always known about his other women, even in the beginning. In fact, he had been sleeping with three women when she met him. Two she had run off personally, and the other had moved to Palatka.

Although it bothered her, Cynthia had resigned herself to Hareem's dalliances. It really wasn't so hard, since she saw other people too, although Hareem didn't know it. She wasn't ready to give up that part of herself or share it with Hareem. But somebody sending her images, that was another matter entirely. She couldn't see the woman's face in the image; it was taken from an angle that allowed her to see only the kimono and a bare shoulder, with Hareem asleep in the background. Cynthia would find out who had sent it and would shut her down if the issue persisted.

After Hareem dropped her at the office and drove away, he picked up his phone to call Loonie. Omeika had a doctor's appointment that afternoon at one, and he had promised to take them. He unlocked his phone and saw that she had called twice in the past hour and had sent a text. Hareem dialed her number.

"About time you called me back," Loonie said when she answered the call.

"I'm sorry. I was in the middle of something when you called."

"I'm sure you were right in the middle of that skinny bitch's thighs."

"I was—" He started to make up an excuse, but Loonie cut him off before he could get it out.

"Don't bother explaining. I just need to know if you're coming or not. It doesn't matter to me. I got a car, and I am more than happy to drive myself. You the one that said you wanted to be there."

"I do wanna be there, and I am on my way right now."

Loonie looked at her watch. "All right, Hareem, you need to be here at exactly twelve thirty, because at twelve thirty-one I'm in the car and I'm gone."

"I'll be there. I love you," Hareem said and ended the call before Loonie could say anything.

She put the phone down and picked up Omeika. "We gonna see how this thing with your daddy goes." She kissed her on the cheek. "But Mommy's not gonna take but so much of his shit."

All Loonie wanted was what was best for her and Omeika. She wouldn't call what she felt for Hareem love, but she did have feelings for him, and he was her baby's father. Loonie had gotten the results of the DNA test, and Hareem was indeed Omeika's father. He at least deserved a chance to step up to the role. She was willing to try to go along with Hareem's plan and see how it went. But Loonie had set definite limits on what she was willing to do. And him continuing to fuck Cynthia and thinking he was gonna fuck her too was where she had drawn her line.

When Hareem zoomed into the parking lot, Loonie had already put Omeika in her car seat and was about to get behind the wheel. Therefore, instead of moving Omeika from one car to another, Hareem got into Loonie's car, and she drove them to the doctor. Having him there, being able to share the experience of her six-month checkup with him felt good to her.

Although she hadn't been alone during her pregnancy—she'd been with her family, and Hedrick had come to see her and take her out every once in a while—Loonie had nonetheless felt lonely. Loonie had understood, though, that since her girlfriends weren't pregnant, they wanted to hang out, and since Loonie wasn't in hang-out mode, they gradually drifted apart. Today with Hareem was the first time in a long time when she didn't feel as if it was just her and Omeika.

When they got back to her place and took Omeika inside and put her down for a nap, mother and father talked about the doctor's appointment. In the middle of this conversation, Imani called Hareem. To give them some privacy, Loonie got up and went into the kitchen to get her quart-sized cup of water. She checked on Omeika before coming back into the living room.

"No, there's nobody else I want there," Hareem said into his phone.

"You sure? Kimberly hired a caterer, so they'll be plenty of food," Imani told him.

"Yeah, I'm sure." He looked at Loonie as she sat down next to him. "Imani."

"What?"

"I'm sorry about that shit this morning."

"No, you're not. You're just afraid of what I might say to Cynthia." Imani laughed a little. "Only reason you did it was to fuck with Lucius."

He chuckled. "You know me too well."

"You're my little brother, and I know you better than you know yourself." Imani giggled. "Besides, Lucius needed to know, so he knows he ain't ever getting any of this, so he can stop trying."

"You're welcome."

"Bye, Hareem."

"Even though you get on my nerves sometimes, I love you."

"And you know the feeling is mutual, right?"

"Bye." Hareem put down the phone and looked at Loonie. She had a big smile on her face.

"What?"

"Nothing. I'm just glad that you and your sister are getting along. I remember that wasn't always the case with you two."

"We have always got along. We just get on each other's nerves sometimes. But since the day I came to live with them, Imani has always had my back, and she would do anything for me. And I would do the same for her," he said. He picked up the remote and turned on the TV. They watched *Jerry* for a while, before Loonie had a question.

"You tell her about Omeika?"

"Not yet."

"When you gonna tell her?"

"I'm gonna tell her and my father after the party," Hareem said, and right away he knew he had messed up.

"What party?"

Hareem took a deep breath and turned to her slowly while he thought about how he was going to answer. "Imani is planning a party for my twenty-first birthday," he said, deciding to go with the truth.

"That's nice of her to do that for your birthday," Loonie said and went back to watching *Jerry*.

It wasn't the response that Hareem was expecting, but he would take it. So Hareem went back to watching *Jerry* too. It was a story about two cops who had ignored calls in order to have sex in their police car. Then a commercial came on, and Loonie dropped it.

"I wanna go."

"Go where?"

"To the party."

"No."

"Why not?"

"Because I don't want any kind of problems that day."

"What? You think I don't know how to act?"

"No, it's not that."

"Well, what is it, then?"

"You know Cynthia will be there—"

"Don't tell anybody who I am. I know how to behave myself," Loonie said, interrupting him.

"No, um, no," he said, shaking his head.

"Why not?"

"Ain't no way you and Omeika gonna be in that house and my family not know who y'all are. That ain't happening."

"Okay." Loonie nodded. "I can understand that. And that is not how I want to meet them, anyway. But know this, Hareem. I ain't the other woman, and I damn sure ain't no side chick. That is not what's happening here. You wanna fuck, go fuck that skinny bitch you left me for. I am your daughter's mother, and I expect . . . No! Fuck am I saying? I *demand* to be treated with respect."

"I know, and I'm good with all that," Hareem said, because this wasn't about sex for him. "And trust me, as soon as all this is behind me, I promise that I'm going to take you to the house and introduce you to my father and my sister."

"And Cynthia? When you gonna tell her?"

"After I tell my family. But I *will* tell her. You and my baby ain't no secret," he said just as his phone rang.

He looked at the display; it was Gianna calling. Since she couldn't tell him anything about who Diamond was, and he had gotten all he needed or wanted from her,

Hareem was done with her. He sent the call to voicemail and put the phone down. Fifteen seconds later the phone rang again. He looked at the display; it was Gianna again.

"That your *other* other woman?"

Hareem nodded. "She was, but it's over."

"Oh, then she gots to go."

He handed Loonie the phone, and she happily answered the call before it went to voicemail. "Look, bitch, I don't know who the fuck you are, and I don't care! You're getting sent to voicemail for a reason. You seriously need to recognize, understand, and don't call this number anymore, because I'll be the one answering it," Loonie said and then ended the call.

Gianna looked at her phone. "Oh, no, this bitch didn't just hang up on me."

Since it had been days since she'd seen or heard from Hareem, and since she knew the reason was Cynthia, she had bought a burner and had sent Cynthia the image with the text to try to break them up.

"So this bitch wanna act all tough and play games with me? Fine," Gianna said aloud. Because she had more than just pictures to send; Gianna had videos. "You wanna play games with me, bitch? Well, let the games begin."

Chapter Twenty-five

For Imani and Brock, the past few weeks had been wonderful. Even though neither one had said it, they were in love. And when love was new, every day seemed like a new adventure to lovers, and every new discovery about the other thrilled them. It was a beautiful thing, because everything about every day together was so marvelous. Every minute Imani spent with Brock seemed so warm, so soft, and so tender. And they spent just about every minute of every day together.

They had sex each morning, when Imani woke up, which she did earlier and earlier each day. And once they caught themselves, they got in the shower, which always led to more sex. Once they were dressed, Brock would drive them to the house to work out and have breakfast with the family. And yes, Cynthia was there each morning. Then Brock would drive her to the office.

Some days her father would go, but most days he wouldn't. Each day she'd ask him if he was all right, and each day he'd tell her that he was fine. "I'm just a little tired, that's all. You worry too much," he kept saying. And it was true; she did worry too much. But Imani knew that something was wrong, and she planned to make an appointment with his doctor and make him go, even if she had to drag him there.

But other than that, Imani was happy. Instead of dropping her off each morning and leaving, now Brock stayed at the office with her all day. At first, it was that she didn't want him to go and he didn't want to leave. So each day, he stayed later and later, talking while she worked, until there was no point in him leaving at all. But by the end of the first week, it was like he worked there. And that was not simply because he was there all the time. He started contributing his expertise. Brock was very knowledgeable about the weapons business, so his involvement in business matters began with a simple question.

"Which do you think is the better semiautomatic rifle, the KelTec Sub2000 or the Ruger PC Carbine?" Imani asked him as she paced around her office one afternoon.

"The Ruger feels much more solid, but the KelTec has the advantage when you start talking about balance and handiness," he answered as he rocked back on the rear legs of the chair across from her desk.

That was how it began, and by the second week's end, Brock had some involvement in every aspect of their weapons business. And since he was knowledgeable about the charter business from his time working for Mr. O, he was helpful there as well. He had worked his way back in, just as Imani had said he would.

And when the workday was done, there was fine dining in all the best restaurants and long walks on the beach, followed by hours of fascinating conversation, sitting on her balcony, watching the waves rolling in and out. And then there was their sex. Oh, let's not forget the sex, because it was off the charts. They couldn't get enough of each other, because it was so damn good.

It was Friday afternoon, and Imani was in her office, where Brock was talking about a shipment of Hi-Point 9 mm carbines that she planned to buy, when Mr. O stopped in the doorway.

"Hey, Daddy. What's up?"

"I just got a call from Manny. He said that Moreno Fernandez was found murdered a week ago in a hotel room in Saint Augustine."

"Ferdie?" Imani asked.

"You remember him?" her father asked.

"Of course I do. He used to be one of your competitors, wasn't he?"

Brock and Mr. O looked at each other and then at Imani.

"What?" she asked.

"She needs to know," Brock said.

"Ferdie came to me over a month ago and wanted to borrow some money. He said that he was being pushed out by some of his own people, and he believed that some of them tried to kill him." He paused for a moment. "But I don't think any of that will blow back on us."

"You're right," Imani said. "We haven't done any business in years that would conflict with his."

"I agree," Brock said, because he had considered the ramifications when he and Mr. O were last at the Hyatt.

"I'm going to the funeral. It's tomorrow morning, so I need you to get me a ticket and a room," Mr. O announced.

"I'm going with you, so I'll get three tickets," Imani said, looking at Brock.

He nodded.

The following morning Mr. O, Imani, and Brock, all of them dressed in black and wearing hats and dark glasses, attended the funeral of Moreno Fernandez. To avoid being seen, they arrived just as the service started, sat in the back of the church, and left before the service ended.

"This week has been a living nightmare. We have to admit, even as we stand before an Almighty God, that the peace and comfort we so dearly wish and pray for you is beyond our power to give," the priest said to the Fernandez family. "In the face of this tragedy, there are no magic words to make your rage and despair disappear. We simply pray that our presence here gives you some comfort in knowing that you are not alone in your grief."

After the funeral, Mr. O wanted to visit some old friends, so after they dropped him off, Imani and Brock returned to their hotel and did what they did.

"Fuck me and make me cum," Imani said as she began rocking her hips back and forth. Then she brought it up and dropped it down on him slowly.

She loved the way that he filled her so completely. Each time they made love, she felt as if he took her to places she had never been and made her feel things she had never felt before. Brock leaned forward and teased her nipples with the tip of his tongue before taking one into his mouth to suck. All the while he was pounding his dick up in her.

"That's it. Fuck me and make me feel it!" she shouted and kept bringing it down on him as hard and as fast as she could.

When his whole body locked, Brock screamed, "Take it from me!"

Imani's head drifted back, her eyes and mouth opened wide, and she screamed, "Fill me up and make me drip!" when she felt him expand and explode inside her.

"What a rush," Imani sighed before she drifted off to that euphoric place where well-satisfied women went.

Since their flight had left Jacksonville so early that morning, other than grabbing something quick at the airport, they hadn't eaten all day, so they ordered room service.

After they ate and returned to bed, Imani made an observation. "You never talk about your family." She rolled into his arms, pressed her body against his, and kissed his chest. "I mean, my family is my life . . . and I consider you to be a part of that family. But I've never heard you mention your family."

He kissed her forehead. "That's because there's nothing to talk about. My father was a drunk who beat his wife. My mother was a drunk that took it."

"I'm sorry."

He kissed her forehead again. "So one day . . . I was fifteen . . . and I come home and he is slapping the shit out of her. He usually did his dirty shit while I was out, and I'd come home and find him gone and her crying. But that night I walk in, and the beating is in progress." Brock shook his head. "I beat his ass. I tried to hit him for every time he'd hit her." Brock paused. "You wanna know what my mother did?"

"What did she do?" Imani asked and braced herself for the answer. She could tell from the sound of his voice and the pained look in his eyes that this hurt Brock to talk about.

"She told me to get out and never come back. Then she ran out after him and brought him back to the house."

"I'm so sorry, Brock," Imani said, feeling his pain as if it were her own. Brock wiped away her single tear. "What did you do?"

"What she asked me to do. I packed my shit, and I never went back."

"Are they still alive?"

"I don't know."

"You should find out."

"Why?"

"They're your parents."

"No, Imani, they're not. Your mother and father are my parents," Brock said. He rolled on top of Imani and ended the discussion when he entered her and she wrapped her legs around his waist. This may have ended the discussion, but it lasted only until their amazing sex was done, and then Imani was right back on it.

"Okay, okay, we can roll by there," Brock said, and Imani clapped.

Later that afternoon, their driver drove them through Brock's old Overtown neighborhood. It was one of Miami's oldest historical black neighborhoods. Even with the active presence of the police, which at times seemed like an occupying army, crime, drug activity, shootings, and murder ran rampant here. Not much had changed since the last time Brock had rolled through these streets, and what had changed had gotten worst.

Their driver pulled up in front of a house and parked. It was as if his entire childhood flashed across Brock's mind in those few seconds. Brock felt nervous, and thinking that this was a bad idea, he started to tell Imani that he had changed his mind.

"It's going to be fine," Imani said, as if she could feel his anxiety. "I'm right here with you."

They got out of the car, she looped her arm in his, and they walked to the house and rang the bell.

"Hello, Ma," Brock said to the woman who opened the door.

She looked at him carefully. "Brock?" she questioned, because it had been more than twenty years since she'd seen her son.

"Yes, Ma, it's me."

"I thought you were locked up," she said through the screen door, and he was surprised that she knew. As far as he knew, she had turned her back on him and hadn't given him any more thought.

"I got out over a month ago." He paused and took a deep breath. "He here?"

"Who? Your father?" She shook her head. "He left outta here one morning about five years ago. Ain't seen or heard a word from him since."

Brock nodded his head. "Can we come in, Ma?" he asked, feeling a sense of relief that her nightmare was over.

She cut her eyes toward Imani, and then she unlocked the screen door to let them in. "Who that you got with you?" she asked as they came into the house.

"This is Imani Mosley," Brock said as his mother sat down on the couch and picked up her glass. "Imani, this is my mother, Ruth Whitehall."

"It's nice to meet you, ma'am," Imani said as she and Brock took a seat on the armchairs.

Ruth took a sip of her drink. "You Big O's little girl, ain't you?"

"Yes, ma'am."

"Heard you had gotten yourself hooked up with him," she said to Brock, and then she looked at Imani with contempt. "Heard it was 'cause of her daddy that you got yourself locked up."

"Yes, ma'am, it was." Brock was surprised that she had kept up with what he was doing.

Brock and Imani didn't stay there for very long, but both mother and son were happy that he had dropped in. Before they left, Brock told his mother he wanted to try to make up for the years they'd lost, and he offered to move her to Jacksonville, but she told him no.

"This my house now, free and clear. I even got his name off the deed. The only good thing that bastard ever did good was pay for this house," Ruth told them.

She did, however, agree to let him have the house renovated, and Imani promised that once the renovations were completed, she would come down and take Ruth shopping for new furniture. And once his mother promised not to drink herself to death with it, Brock gave her some cash, and he promised to be back on Monday morning to take her to the bank and open an account, which he would put money in.

"Thank you for making me do this, Imani," Brock said as he walked back to the limo, feeling relaxed and happy with his decision to reach out to his mother.

"You're welcome." She rested her head on his shoulder. "I told you that I was going to be everything to you. This was just a part of it."

"I really did need that more than I thought I did."

"Your mother is sweet."

"She always was. She didn't deserve the shit she took from him."

"She's feisty."

"Being feisty was what got her in trouble. She used to talk big shit," Brock said, thinking back on the arguments his parents had had.

"She still does. As much shit as she was talking to me." Imani laughed. "I like her."

"Yeah, she likes you too. That's why she was talking that shit to you," he said as the driver opened the door for her.

After they left there, Imani took Brock to see her mother. She was shocked to see them, and after she fussed at Imani for not calling before she came over, she fussed over Brock. Julia was so happy to see him, and seeing the two of them together warmed her heart. Like her ex-husband, Brock was the son she never had, so it was like having her children come home to see her. Julia insisted that she had to cook dinner for them. It was over fried chicken, mashed potatoes, and greens that she realized that they hadn't casually shown up together at her house.

"So, you two . . ." Julia laughed a little. "I'm not surprised, though, the way she used to drool over you."

"Mommy," Imani exclaimed, shocked that her mother would tell him that.

"Did she really?" Brock asked.

"She'd get that look in her eyes, and her mouth would open a little, and she'd say, 'Hi, Brock.'" Miss Julia laughed. "And you'd barely look at her and say, 'Hey, Imani,' and go back to what you was doing."

"You didn't have to tell him all that," an embarrassed Imani said.

They had a nice visit with Julia, and after sharing funny and embarrassing stories about Imani, they said good night. And then, instead of going back to their suite to do what they did, Imani and Brock did something that neither of them had done in years. Brock, because he'd been in prison, and Imani, because she'd given all that up when Brock went to prison. They hit the clubs.

Their night ended with sitting on the beach outside their hotel. He sat behind Imani, with his arms wrapped around her, and together they watched the sun come up.

Chapter Twenty-six

It was the morning of his twenty-first birthday, and Hareem woke up early. He looked over at Cynthia. She was asleep naked on top of the sheets, her face was buried in her pillow, and her ass was in the air. Hareem sat up slowly, took a look at that ass and the way it was perfectly positioned, probably wet too, closed his eyes, and shook his head before he eased out of her bed.

As quietly as he could, Hareem left the room and went into the dining room. He picked up his clothes and his shoes and went into the bathroom to get dressed, and then he got out of there. After stopping at his condo to shower and change his clothes, he called Loonie.

"Happy birthday!" she shouted.

"Thank you. You dressed?"

"Nope."

"Well, get you and Omeika dressed. I'm on my way to pick you up," he said as he walked out of the house and got in the car.

His girls, as he had become fond of calling them, were ready when he got there. Once they got Omeika in the car without waking her up, Hareem and Loonie set out. No matter how many times, how many ways, and how much she guessed, Hareem wouldn't tell Loonie where they were going. She had given up asking and had just settled into her seat when Hareem got off I-295 and got on Butler Boulevard, heading for the beach. Loonie got a little excited.

Is he taking me where I think he is? she asked herself. And then she convinced herself otherwise. *He's probably just going to the beach*, Loonie thought.

Even when he got off at Marsh Landing Parkway, she refused to believe it. After all, it was his birthday, he was having a party, and he had made it clear that she wasn't invited. When she saw the street sign and they turned onto Palm Forest Place, Loonie sat up straight.

"Oh, no, you did not bring me to meet your family and not tell me," she said and immediately pulled down the visor and looked in the mirror. "I look a hot mess," Loonie declared, even though she didn't.

"You look beautiful." Hareem looked over at her. "You are beautiful."

"If I knew you were bringing me here, I would have put on something a little nicer to wear. And I would have definitely done something better with my hair."

"You want me to turn around?"

"No," she said quickly. "This may not ever happen again."

Even though Hareem had been true to everything he'd said to her, Loonie still didn't completely trust him.

"Or you can wait out here in the car, and I'll take Omeika in to meet them?"

"Oh, hell no." Loonie shook her head. "They'll say, 'She's so cute. So where's her mama?' And you'll say, 'Oh, she looks a hot mess, so she's waiting in the car.' No, that is not gonna happen," Loonie said as Hareem turned into the long driveway. A moment later she saw the house. "Oh . . . my . . . God. This is where your family lives?" she asked as they drove around the fountain and parked in front of the house.

Once they got Omeika out of the car, Hareem walked proudly to the house and let them in.

"Wow. This house is amazing," Loonie said, looking around the entryway, which led to the great room.

"Yeah, it's okay," Hareem said, making faces at Omeika. "I'll be right back. Wander around like you own the place," he added and ran toward the stairs.

"No. We will be standing right here in this spot until you get back."

"Daddy! Imani!" he shouted before Loonie watched him disappear at the top of the stairs.

From where Loonie was standing, she could see the great room. She looked through the picture window. "Is that a waterfall?" she asked aloud as she stared at the grotto that flowed into the pool.

As she stood there, looking around, thinking about how she and Omeika could get used to living in a place like that, the front door opened, and Imani came in with Brock.

"Who the fuck are you?" Imani said loudly enough to frighten Omeika, and she started to cry. "And what the fuck are you doing in my house?"

"Hi. You must be Imani," Loonie said, trying to quiet Omeika. "My name is Lucinda Thompson, but everybody calls me Loonie. I'm a friend of Hareem."

"Imani!" Hareem said when he appeared at the top of the stairs with his father.

"I'm glad you're here," Imani said as he and Mr. O came down the stairs.

"What's this about, son?" Mr. O asked as Omeika's crying filled the air.

"I want you all to meet somebody," Hareem answered, going over to his girls. "This is Loonie." He took Omeika from her, and she quieted down in her father's arms. He walked up to his father. "And this is your granddaughter," he said and handed her to his father. "Her name is Omeika."

"My granddaughter?" Mr. O asked, fumbling a bit, as Imani rushed over to them. "Hey, pretty girl. I'm your grandfather."

Imani leaned in. "Hi, Omeika. I'm your auntie Imani," she cooed, and Mr. O handed the baby to her. "I am going to spoil you rotten."

Brock wandered over to Loonie, who was smiling but was understandably feeling a bit left out. He held out his hand.

"Brock Whitehall."

"Loonie Thompson," she said and shook his hand.

"Welcome to the family," Brock said.

"Thank you. It's good to be a part of a family."

Loonie was happy because now she knew for sure that she and Omeika wouldn't be Hareem's dirty little secret. The reception Omeika was receiving made her believe that over time, as the family got to know her, she would be treated with the respect she deserved.

Chapter Twenty-seven

A few hours later, the birthday party for Hareem was on and poppin'. Over a hundred people had come to celebrate with him. The party was being held outside the house, by the pool, and Imani had gone all out with the decorations. Tables with white tablecloths were decorated with blue roses laced with silver ribbons and garland. There were party favors and balloons everywhere.

With that many guests in attendance, Kimberly had hired Black Creek Food and Catering to provide the food for the event. The buffet table was laden with bowls of garden salad and Caesar salad, lemon-garlic shrimp kebobs, fried shrimp, Swedish meatballs, roasted chicken breast, smothered pork chops, steak, and ribs. Plenty of hot dogs and hamburgers were piled on large platters, and even blackened fish tacos were on the menu, as well as baked macaroni and cheese, Southern-style green beans, and corn bread. For dessert, there was fruit salad, watermelon, and as much cake and ice cream as you could stand. Everybody seemed to be having a good time.

Hareem was having a good time celebrating his birthday with Cynthia, but his mind was on Loonie and Omeika, whom he had driven home long before the party started. He wished that Loonie could be there to celebrate with him, but at the same time, Hareem knew what a bad idea that was. He was glad that he had decided to bring her and the baby to the house to meet his family earlier in the day. What made him happier was the way his father and his sister had responded to them. When Kimberly had got up, Hareem had introduced her to Loonie and Omeika, and she had cooked breakfast for the family. She then had sat down to join them, because she was a part of the family too. Everybody, especially Imani, had gone out of their way to make Loonie feel welcome. As they were getting ready to leave, Imani had pulled him aside. She had given him a big hug and then had put her hands on his shoulders and looked him in the eye.

"Whatever you need, I got you," she'd assured him.

Hareem smiled. "I know that. You always look out for me, even when I don't want you to or appreciate you doing it. I always know my big sister got me."

Imani shook her head. "I'm talking about Cynthia."

Hareem nodded.

"Whatever you need me to do, know that you just gotta ask, right?"

"Thank you, Imani," he said, surprised but not shocked that she had offered. Cynthia had never been Imani's favorite person, so it made sense. Hareem hugged her. "But I'm good for now."

He knew that "for now" was the correct way to look at it. Hareem having his proverbial cake and being able to eat it too was going to be more of a problem than he thought it was going to be. When he'd got back to Cynthia's house after dropping off his girls, he'd found her sitting in the living room, waiting for him to come in. Hareem had been able to tell by the look on her face that she was fuming.

"Where did you go first thing this morning?" she'd asked, with flaming darts shooting from her eyes, as soon as he shut the door.

He told her the truth; he just left out the Loonie and Omeika part. "I went to the house to have breakfast with

Daddy and Imani," Hareem said nonchalantly as he came and sat down next to her.

When Hareem tried to kiss her, Cynthia turned away, which was something that had never happened before. It was his birthday, and she had something special planned for them to do that morning. It infuriated her that Hareem could be that insensitive.

"Did you think to ask me if I wanted to go with you to breakfast or if maybe I had something else planned for us for this morning?"

"No. I didn't."

It was true. Hareem hadn't even stopped to think that Cynthia might plan something for his birthday morning, but he should have known that she would. Had he thought enough to ask her, he could have taken Loonie and Omeika to the house to meet the family the night before. Had he done that, he wouldn't be having this conversation now with Cynthia. All this did was make what he was trying to do that much harder.

"I'm sorry," he said meekly. "Did you have something planned?"

"Does it matter?" she barked.

"I'm sorry, but I wanted this morning to be, you know, a special kinda family thing." Hareem paused to look at her face, to gauge how his remark was going down. *Poorly.* "You know, for my twenty-first birthday and all."

"You could have told me that was what you were doing," Cynthia said, but she didn't believe a word he was saying, anyway, and there was a reason for that.

"You were asleep, and I didn't want to wake you."

"Whatever, Hareem," she said, bouncing up from the couch. She went into her bedroom and slammed the door behind her.

This made him realize that deception was not the way for him to go about this. Lying to Loonie was what had run her off. Hareem knew that he needed to learn from that mistake and tell Cynthia the truth, or he could lose her too.

Just not today.

The reason that it went so poorly was that after Hareem had left that morning, Cynthia had been awakened by her phone ringing. When she'd answered, the caller had hung up and had continued to call and hang up, and then she'd started getting text messages. When the constant vibration of her phone got annoying, Cynthia silenced her phone and went back to sleep. Cynthia checked the messages when she got up. Most of them were blank, one text said, Boo, there were a lot of texts that said, Bitch, and one said, Where's your man at, bitch? And there was another picture of Hareem asleep in her bed.

The last text said, I won't call his phone, but I will be blowing yours up, bitch. Count on it, bitch.

Gianna had plenty of pictures of Hareem, and she planned to send each one. But she would save for last the best shots—or the worst ones, depending on your perspective—and the video she'd shot without Hareem knowing it.

So Cynthia was there at the party for her man, sitting next to him at the main table with his family, laughing, smiling, and having a good time celebrating her man's birthday. But on the inside, she was hot. The fact that Mr. O, Imani, and even Kimberly had all told her that Hareem really had been there that morning made her feel better, but it didn't matter. Whoever it was who was sending her the texts was starting to get on her nerves. Therefore, she had taken steps to have this problem resolved.

Knowing that she really wasn't in the mood to be this phony, after the speeches were made, Cynthia planned to fake a headache. She'd then insist that Hareem should stay and enjoy his party with his family and friends. Then she would go to see her play toy to make her feel better.

"When you have a brother like you"—Imani shook her head—"you never know what to expect. But to this day, I gotta tell you, baby boy, it is always interesting." She paused for effect. "Yes, we'll say interesting. Interesting, because sometimes you were just weird."

Everybody, including Hareem, laughed, because Imani used to tell him that all the time.

Imani went on. "I mean seriously, with all that jumping around you used to do, sometimes I used to wonder . . . Did Daddy pick you up at the zoo?"

Once again laughter filled the air.

"But, Hareem, all bullshit aside, as your annoying older sister, I am blessed to have you as my brother. And I know that what you really want for your birthday is that one day I will finally stop annoying you, but that's not gonna happen. I love you too much, and I've been at it too long to stop annoying you now. Face it. You're stuck with me. I pray that all your other birthday wishes come true. Happy birthday, Hareem. Have a blast. This day belongs to you!"

As just about everyone rose to their feet to clap, a loud noise could be heard over the applause, and it was getting louder. Hareem stood up and hugged Imani. She handed him the microphone and then hugged him again. As the guests continued clapping, Imani curtsied and sat down between Brock and her father.

"Thank you, Imani. I have the best sister in the world. She is annoying as fuck, but there is no one in this world or any other like my sister," Hareem said over the loud noise.

Brock leaned close to Imani. "What is that noise?"

Imani shrugged. "I don't know, but it's getting louder."

Hareem shielded his eyes from the sun. "Looks like a motorcycle."

Mr. O chuckled. "Probably somebody trying to make a big entrance," he said as the motorcycle tore through the backyard and then approached the tables of partygoers.

When Imani and Brock stood up, they could see that there were two people on the motorcycle. As they got closer, the rider on the back pulled out an AK-47 and opened fire on the party guests. Chaos ensued as people dove desperately for the ground and under tables as the gunman sprayed the area with bullets. Some people ran away from the house, while others tried to run inside to get away from the barrage of shells.

Once they found cover behind some turned-over tables, Martel, Jaric, Devonte, and Jamarcus began shooting at the motorcycle, but they were too far away, and the damage had already been done.

Five people were dead, and many more were injured. The injured were taken to Baptist Beaches Emergency Room for treatment. Among them was Mr. O.

Chapter Twenty-eight

One of the hardest things in the world to do was to wait. And waiting to hear news of a loved one had to be the toughest of all. Each minute seemed to drag on endlessly. You couldn't ignore the excitement you felt each time somebody in a lab coat or scrubs walked by and the disappointment when they passed without a word. All there was to do was think. It didn't matter whether you sat, stood, or paced the floor aimlessly; you waited, and you thought.

You thought about what had happened and what you could have done to stop it. You thought about all the things you had felt but hadn't said, about the promises you had made but hadn't kept. You made a promise to yourself that you were going to do and say all those things if you got the chance.

Imani leaned against the wall and looked out the window. She was tired of sitting, and Hareem, who was thinking that this was all his fault, was doing enough pacing for both of them. So she stood, thinking. Her list of things that she could have done and said was long. All the things that she'd learned from him, not just about business, but about life. As the years had moved on, she and her father had got close to the point where at times he felt like her best friend. The idea that she may never see him again was unfathomable. Imani couldn't think of the last time she had told her father that she loved him.

As for Brock, he was used to waiting, to sitting around, with nothing to do but think. But that didn't make it any easier. He had come to love Mr. O. He'd looked up to him almost from the time they met. In that time, Mr. O had become the father that a young, wildly undisciplined, and arrogant Brock Whitehall needed. Everything important that he'd learned in life and about life, he'd learned from Mr. O.

When the doctor did finally come and talk to them, he said that in addition to being shot twice, once in the chest and once in the abdomen, Mr. O had also suffered a heart attack.

"Fatty deposits built up over time, which allowed plaque to form in his arteries. When a bit of that plaque ruptured, it caused a blood clot to form, and the clot blocked an artery, causing the heart attack."

"Can I see him?" Imani asked.

"He's resting now," the doctor said.

Later Imani and Hareem were allowed to see him, but they were encouraged to go home and get some rest, because there was nothing they could do at the hospital. But after seeing her father, Imani announced that she was going to stay for a while, so naturally, Brock was staying too.

"Go home, Hareem. I'll call you if anything changes," Imani urged her brother.

Hareem hugged Imani tightly. "I'm sorry," he said. He walked out of the hospital, leaving her to wonder what he was sorry about, though she knew that she would find out.

As Hareem sped away, the idea that Mr. O's suffering was his fault was inescapable. Hareem had been fucking with Cameron and Hedrick for weeks, so he should have been prepared for one of them, if not both of them, to come back at him. What better place and time to hit him than at his birthday party, while everybody was laid back and having a good time. Knowing the situation he'd created, the smart play would have been to have his crew spread out around the property as security during the party, instead of having them there as guests. If he had done that—or, better yet, if he had listened to what his father and his sister had told him about starting a war—none of this would be happening.

But that was then. Now they had shot his father, so whether it was good for business or not, Hareem knew that he had to hit back and hit back hard. He needed to make sure that everybody knew and understood that he was not the one to fuck with.

"But who?" Hareem asked himself on the way to the house.

The answer to that question came when he got a text from Loonie. Kevin knows about us and that the baby ain't his.

Hareem tried to call her back, but the call went straight to voicemail. Naturally, his first thought was that Hedrick had ordered the hit in retaliation. His next call was to Martel.

"What's up, Hareem? How's your pops?" Martel asked.

"He's gonna be all right. He's resting now. But I need you to do something for me, Marty-mar," Hareem said, so mad that his hands were shaking.

"Whatever you need. I got everybody here, and they ready to do whatever you need."

"It was Hedrick who shot my father. Pick one of his spots and make him pay."

"I know just the spot. I got you, Hareem. You be with your family, and I'll take care of this for you. Fucked up for a muthafucka to do this shit on your birthday." Martel paused. "I should have seen this shit coming, and I should have had some muscle there. I'm sorry for that."

"I should have thought of it too."

"I'ma make this right for you." Martel ended the call and looked around at his men. "Let's go."

"Where we going?" Chub asked as he put one in the chamber.

"Moncrief Street." Martel stood up. "Chub, Jaric, Devonte, Jamarcus, y'all with me. The rest of you niggas, stay here and wait for me to call," Martel said, and then he led the crew out of his house.

They went in three cars: Chub and Jaric were in one car, Devonte and Jamarcus in another, and Martel drove there by himself. When they got to the complex where Hedrick did business, Martel parked where he could see Hedrick's men going in and out of a building. There were more sitting around on cars. Chub and Jaric parked right next to Martel. Jaric took out two guns—each had a silencer on it—and waited for Martel to give them the signal.

Martel raised his hand in front of his rearview mirror, his signal to roll, and mouthed, "Go."

As two men came out of the building and approached their car, Chub stepped on the gas with his bright lights on and Jaric raised both weapons and opened fire through the passenger window as soon as he was close enough. He hit both men, delivering multiple shots in the chest to each one.

When Hedrick's men returned fire, Jamarcus and Devonte jumped out of their car and fired on them. They hit their targets with shots to the head and chest. Two men fired blindly as they tried to run, but they were met by Chub and Jaric, who left their car and killed them as they ran.

Two more men came out of the building firing and forced Jamarcus and Devonte to take cover. Chub shot one as he moved for cover. With one shooter remaining,

Jaric fired and hit him with three shots. With Hedrick's men taken care of, Jamarcus, Devonte, Chub, and Jaric rushed back to their cars and left the complex as quickly as possible.

Chapter Twenty-nine

De'Shane, Lucius, and some others who had attended the party hung around the house after the shooting, hoping to get news from the hospital about Mr. O's condition. Naturally, the topic of discussion was who could be responsible, and that discussion raged on for hours as they waited. Although nobody knew a thing about what had happened, just about everybody had a theory about who the perpetrator could be and what it was about. Some thought that it was somebody from the old Miami days who had caught up with Mr. O. There were also those, De'Shane and Lucius among them, who were sure that it had something to do with Hareem.

"Imani had me checking up on somebody called Diamond for him," Lucius said.

"Who's that?" De'Shane asked.

"She's the competition, but he doesn't know who she is. He's been fuckin' with her dealers, trying to get at her."

"What's the kid been doing?"

"He burned a couple of stash houses and killed some of her people," Lucius answered.

"Your right. This is the kid's shit," De'Shane said, and almost on cue, Hareem burst through the door and stormed into the great room, where everyone was waiting for information.

"How's your father, Hareem?" Alexis said as soon as she saw him. When the shooting had broken out, she had twisted her ankle when she'd tried to run. "Running in four-inch peep-toe pumps is not a good idea, trust me," was what she had told the paramedics while they treated her.

"He took two shots, one in the chest and one in the abdomen, but he had a heart attack too. The doctor said that he'll be fine. He's resting, and Imani is with him," Hareem announced.

"That's good news," Kimberly said, hoping that now that they had gotten the update they'd all been waiting for, they would leave, but nobody seemed to be moving.

"You got any idea who's responsible?" De'Shane asked.

"I know who's responsible," Hareem said. "And I swear to all of you, when I find him, I will make him pay. I promise you that."

De'Shane leaned toward Lucius. "Told you this was the kid's shit," he whispered.

"So I don't want anybody doing shit to retaliate unless I say so," Hareem said, appointing himself boss in his father's absence. He felt that since this was indeed his shit, and it had nothing to do with the weapons business, he was in charge.

"Right. You're in charge," Lucius said. *Until Imani comes through that door and your short reign ends.*

"I'm gonna go on and get outta here," Alexis said, standing up and trying not to put much weight on her ankle.

That seemed to open the floodgates. One by one, people began to extend well-wishes to Hareem as they called it a night and went home. Therefore, when Imani returned from the hospital with Brock, only Hareem, Kimberly, De'Shane, Lucius, and a few other people were still there. They all got up and headed into the foyer when Imani and Brock came into the house.

"Any change?" Hareem asked as he walked toward his sister.

"No change. I just came to shower and get a change of clothes, and then I'm gonna go back to the hospital," she said as she started for the stairs.

"Don't you think you should get some rest?" Brock said as he followed her to the stairs.

"I know, and I am tired, but . . ."

"Exactly my point. I'll go back. You need to rest," Brock said as De'Shane and Lucius looked on with jealous eyes.

"I know. But I need to be there when he wakes up," she said as they walked up the stairs together and disappeared at the top of the steps.

De'Shane leaned close to Lucius. "What's up with that?" he whispered.

"They fuckin'," Lucius spit out and walked toward the door.

"Since when?" De'Shane wanted to know as he followed him.

"Since you been gone. Fuck you care? She wasn't gonna give you none of that pussy either," Lucius said as they left the house. Hareem laughed at how pathetic they were.

When Imani and Brock came back downstairs later, everyone had gone, and Hareem was alone in the great room, on the phone with Cynthia. He told her that he was expecting her to be at the house when he got back. She told him that she expected to be asked to go with him to the hospital.

"But that didn't happen either," she said.

With new fuel for the fire, the argument they were having that morning continued, so Hareem was glad when Imani and Brock came into the room.

"I gotta talk to Imani before she goes back to the hospital. I'll talk to you later," Hareem said to dead air, because Cynthia had already hung up. "You getting ready to go back?"

"Yes." Imani knew her brother and knew that there was something that she needed to make clear before she left. "And I wanted to tell you not to do anything stupid before I get back."

"Stupid like what? Go hard at the muthafucka that did it?"

"How do you know who did it?"

"Trust me, I know, and I'm handling it."

"How do you know?" Imani asked again.

"Because them shooting Daddy was over the shit I been doing."

Hareem hadn't told her that Loonie was with Hedrick and that Hedrick thought he was Omeika's father. Hareem had thought that would be more information than Imani needed, and he had hoped that he wouldn't have to share it with her.

"I can't deal with this right now," Imani said and got in Hareem's face. "You don't do a fuckin' thing until I get back. You hear me?"

Hareem stepped back. "Yeah, Imani, I hear you," he said, nodding his head and taking a seat.

"Let's go, Brock," Imani said, and then she spun around and headed for the door.

"I'll be there in a minute," he said.

Brock had seen the look on Hareem's face and knew there was something he wasn't telling Imani. He waited until Imani had slammed the front door shut before he went and sat next to Hareem.

"What you do?" Brock asked him.

"What you mean?"

"I mean I know you ain't the one to just take this shit and not do anything about it. So tell me what you did."

"Why? So you can run out there and tell Imani?"

"No. I work for your father. I need you to tell me what you did so I can help you kill the person responsible."

Hareem knew that he needed to trust somebody, so he told Brock the short version of the muddle he was in with Loonie, Hedrick, and Omeika and revealed that he had sent Martel to hit one of Hedrick's spots.

"But you're not really sure Hedrick's responsible, are you?"

Hareem exhaled and shook his head. "Not a hundred percent sure, no."

"Okay. I gotta go," Brock said. "But before you do anything else, let me find out if this nigga really did it and if that was the reason why. Can you do that?"

"Yeah. I'll stand down. It'll give me time to beef up my soldiers. Because I'm gonna have to deal with whatever this nigga got coming back at me."

"I know you do. And you know I gotta tell Imani."

"I know you do."

Chapter Thirty

"What were you doing?" Imani asked when Brock got in the car.

"Talking to your brother." Brock started the car and headed back to the hospital.

"What were you talking to him about?"

Brock just looked at her.

"He did it, didn't he? He already hit back, didn't he?" Imana grumbled.

Brock just drove.

"Fuck!" she shouted. "The last thing we need is a drug war on our hands."

Brock continued to drive without comment.

"Damn it, Hareem." She took a breath to try to calm herself. "Did he tell you who he hit?"

"Hedrick."

"Why does he think it was Hedrick?" Imani asked.

Brock smiled.

"Why are you smiling?"

"Hareem thinks that Hedrick is behind it because Hedrick found out about Hareem and Loonie and that he isn't Omeika's father."

"Wait, what? I'm confused."

"It's simple, so stay with me."

"Okay."

"Loonie was with Hareem, they broke up, and she got with Hedrick, but she didn't know she was pregnant with Hareem's baby. But now Hedrick knows Omeika's not his daughter." Brock grinned. "Understand now?"

"Yes, Brock, I get it," Imani said, feeling frustrated. "But damn, really? My father is fighting for his life over some baby mama drama."

"Really, but it doesn't mean that we shouldn't take this seriously."

"I know," Imani said and frowned. "These niggas will start shooting over anything."

"And this is about his pride," Brock said, and Imani giggled. "To find out his baby ain't his baby . . . I guarantee you his whole set is talking behind his back. He had to do something."

"You know, Brock, I really do get all that, but the fact is that my father may die over this bullshit. But now we gotta deal with it," she replied as they got close to the hospital. "Take me home, Brock. I can't deal with the hospital right now."

"You'll get some sleep and feel better in the morning," Brock said and headed for Imani's condo.

"What about you?"

"I'm gonna watch over you," Brock said, just in case it wasn't about Omeika and Imani might still be in danger.

Imani laughed. "Watch over me?"

"Like a guardian angel."

Imani shook her head. "I think I need you to hold me tonight more than I need you to watch over me."

"Whatever you say, boss." *And then I'll watch you.*

"But we're not going to have sex."

"We're not?"

"I really do just need you to hold me tonight," Imani said when they arrived at her condo.

"I think I can do that for you."

Brock always wanted Imani; however, he also understood that she had a lot on her mind right now. Her father had been shot, and her brother had started a drug war. They got out and walked into the building hand in hand.

Since they always slept naked, holding Imani while she fell asleep was harder than Brock thought it would be in more ways than just the obvious. His mind was racing, continually replaying the shooting, because something about it didn't seem right to him. He thought that the first thing he should have done when he heard the motorcycle was move Mr. O indoors. He hadn't even had a gun on him, so he hadn't even been able to shoot back, much less defend himself or anybody else.

Brock tried to reason with himself that he wasn't security—he wasn't really even a driver—but he knew it was lame. His job or not, he should have been able to do something other than push Imani under the table as he watched Mr. O get shot. He thought about Imani, about her sleeping so peacefully in his arms, and wondered what he could have done to protect her better.

So between those thoughts and Imani's bare ass pressed up against his hard dick, which got a little harder each time she moved, it took him a while to fall asleep. His vow to arm himself in the morning settled his mind, and he was finally able to fall asleep.

Imani's vow that they weren't having sex that night had nothing at all to do with the morning. She didn't fall asleep all that easily either. She had so many things rolling around in her mind, all of them screaming to be heard. With the warmth of his body to calm her, his strong arms to soothe her, and his hard dick sandwiched between her cheeks, it was hard to quiet her mind and drift off to sleep. So she woke up wanting him.

Imani reached out for him. "Good morning, Brock."

"Morning," he said, and a slow smile crept over his lips as Imani stroked him while she tilted her hips so that he could slide his length into her.

She loved to be loved by him in the morning, loved the responsiveness of her walls opening up to accommodate his thickness. The sensation of it sliding into her wetness. And then she felt such contentment that his length filled her so completely, as if it was designed just to satisfy her.

It felt so good to her, and Imani had to have more. She thrust her hips back at him, the sounds of their bodies slapping against each other and their screams filling the room, until they had given each other all they had to give.

Therefore, when Imani and Brock arrived at the hospital, although still concerned about Mr. O's condition, they were in a better mood than they had been the night before. When they got to the coronary care unit, a specialized intensive care unit for heart patients, they were informed that Mr. O hadn't regained consciousness, but his vitals were strong. They were allowed a brief visit with him, and then they went to the waiting room.

It was over an hour later when the doctor arrived to check his chart and do some minor tests. When she came into the waiting room, she told Imani and Brock that Mr. O was doing fine, but with the added complication of the gunshot wounds, she felt it best to keep him under observation in the coronary unit.

"After a heart attack, some people have an increase in their blood sugar level, so those levels will also be closely monitored. After a couple of days, most patients' hearts will settle down, the risk of another heart attack lessens, and less intensive monitoring is needed," she explained to them.

"What happens then?" Imani asked.

"From there, he'll be transferred to a ward, and you'll be able to see him more." The doctor paused. "Have you been in to see him today?"

"Yes, when we first got here this morning," Imani said. What the doctor had said went a long way to easing her fear that her father was going to die.

"I don't think it will hurt if you have another very brief visit," the doctor said.

"Thank you, Doctor. We really appreciate that," Brock said and stood up.

Later that day, while Mr. O was recovering in the hospital, the war Hareem had started the night before escalated when two of Hedrick's men followed Jaric to the River City Marketplace. He was there shopping with his girl when they walked up on him. When she wasn't looking, they stuck a gun in his back and quietly walked him out of Bed Bath & Beyond.

"Where's your car?" one of the men growled.

Jaric pointed. The two men walked Jaric to his car and told him to get behind the wheel, while one of the men got in the back seat. The other man ran to his car, and Jaric was instructed where to drive. With the man following closely behind, Jaric drove until he got to a red light on Main Street. When Jaric stopped the car, his captor in the back seat shot him in the back of the head. The shooter got out, rushed to the other car, and the two men drove away, leaving Jaric with his head against the steering wheel as the car rolled into the intersection.

Chapter Thirty-one

Imani was in the waiting room with Brock when the nurse came and told them that Mr. O was awake and she was permitted to see him.

"Can he go with me?" she asked the nurse as she pointed at Brock.

"We try to confine visits to just the immediate family," the nurse said.

"He's my husband," Imani said and got a look from Brock before he put his arm around her to show that she was his.

"Oh. Then it's all right," the nurse said and led them to the coronary care unit.

They didn't stay long, because Mr. O was still very tired and weak. Although he was glad to see them, Imani could see that his breath was short, and he said that he felt lightheaded and a little nauseated. The doctor explained that this was perfectly normal and was a result of the immediate and sudden blockage of his artery. After the doctor promised that Mr. O's heart function would be monitored closely, he told them that once his condition improved, Mr. O would be transferred from the coronary care unit to a ward.

Over the days that followed, as Mr. O's health improved, the violence in the street got worse. It was all over the news. One afternoon Brock caught a report on the television in the hospital waiting room while Imani went to get coffee. "A Rodeway Inn on Division Street was the scene of the massive investigation. Witnesses tell Action News that a group of men broke into a room at the Rodeway Inn on Division Street, then shot and killed a man," said the reporter. "Police reported around eight p.m. that a twenty-three-year-old man had been shot inside the room and was pronounced dead at a local hospital. It was the latest in a string of at least six shootings in Jacksonville over the past week. All are believed to be drug related."

Worry lines creased Brock's forehead, but he said nothing to Imani when she returned with her coffee.

The morning after the Moncrief hit, Hareem moved Loonie and Omeika to a house in Amelia Island, a city thirty miles north of Jacksonville, for their safety. He couldn't run the risk of Hedrick coming after them or using them to get to him. Then he got Mayra, one of the women in his crew, to stay with them. Her job was to help Loonie with the baby and kill anybody other than him who came through the door.

Once his girls were safe, Hareem went to see Cynthia and tried to get her to go into hiding as well, but she refused.

"I have a business to run. I can't just pick up and go into hiding at the drop of a dime because some low-rent dope boys wanna go to war," Cynthia said.

She was still angry with Hareem, so she wanted her words to hurt. They accomplished their purpose, but since he was trying to get her to do what he wanted, Hareem ignored her hurtful words and pressed on.

"I know that you have to run the brokerage. But this thing may get serious, and I don't want anything to happen to you," he pleaded. "So please, Cynthia, at least let me put somebody with you for protection."

"No."

"You won't even know they're there."

"I said no."

"Okay," Hareem said, knowing he was going to put somebody on her whether she liked it or not. "Could you at least not stay at the house until this is over?"

"And when might that be?"

"Might what be?"

"When might this nonsense be over?"

"I can't tell you that. All I can tell you right now is that I want you to be safe, and you'd be safer if you didn't stay where people know you live. That's all I'm saying."

"I see." Cynthia took a deep breath and let it out slowly. "Okay, I will stay at one of the vacant long-term rentals. Would that satisfy you?"

"Yes, Cyn, that will satisfy me," he said, relieved that she was finally being reasonable. "Thank you for agreeing to at least do that. It's gonna get a lot worse out there before it gets any better."

Now that Hareem had taken care of the women in his life, he concentrated on fighting the war, which continued to intensify. Murderous tit-for-tat drive-bys and fire bombings became a daily occurrence, and there was even a shooting at the Jacksonville Beach Boardwalk in which civilians were killed. The escalation in the violence forced Hareem to move his crew into a house he had rented. They were going to the mattresses, as he'd heard them say in gangster movies. To protect themselves in times of war, Italian crime families were said to have rented apartments, where soldiers would sleep in shifts on the mattresses that were spread out on the floor.

Hareem left there and went home to pack some things. He had finished packing and had taken his bag to the car when he realized that he didn't have his phone. Hareem was about to go back for it and had just closed the trunk when he saw an old Ford Galaxie 500 coming at him fast. As he took a step toward the condo, a man with an AK stood up in the sunroof and began firing at him.

"Shit!" he shouted as he pulled his weapon and fired off a couple of shots and then dropped behind his car for cover.

When the Galaxie came to a screeching halt, two men got out and fired, pinning Hareem behind his car under heavy fire. He raised his weapon and tried to get a shot off, but Hareem was seriously outgunned and had to drop back behind the car. He crawled to the front of the car and fired three times at one of his ambushers and quickly dropped back for cover. Each shot hit the target in the chest, and he fell back on the hood of the car.

When the other ambusher stopped to reload, Hareem jumped up, fired shots until his gun was empty, and ran for the trees. The ambusher got the clip in and resumed firing until Hareem was out of sight.

Chapter Thirty-two

"Two people are dead following a shooting in downtown Jacksonville Saturday night, according to the Jacksonville Sheriff's Office," a police officer said in a televised statement. "Police were dispatched after several nine-one-one calls reported gunfire at the Hyatt Regency Jacksonville Riverfront. When police arrived, they found one person had been shot inside Morton's The Steakhouse. As additional officers arrived on the scene, they found a second victim dead at the intersection of Market and Bay Streets, according to the JSO. Although detectives have identified a possible suspect in the case, investigators are not sharing the suspect's name at this time, the JSO said. As soon as more information is releasable, we will put it out."

It was the day that Mr. O came home from the hospital. He was still weak after being shot and having a heart attack, but at least he was home resting comfortably. Imani was downstairs having a drink at the bar in the game room. Hareem had promised to meet her there, but he was a no-show. Although she was happy to have her father home, Imani still had a lot on her mind. There were arrangements that had to be made for him. She was sure that he wouldn't remember a lot of what the doctors and nurses had told him. She doubted if he had listened at all. Mr. O had just wanted to get out of there. Before he left the hospital, they'd all been given information about cardiac rehabilitation, and he'd received a supply of medicines. The nurse had explained how and when to take each of them and how to get refills, and all that was on Imani.

And then there was the war to talk about. Imani had decided not to tell her father what was going on while he was in the hospital. Seeing that Mr. O didn't watch the news—he was more of an ESPN and NFL Network channel kind of guy—it had been easy to keep news about the war from him. Hareem had no problem with that whatsoever. He was dreading the day when Imani made him tell his father what he'd done. The only one that had a problem with it was Brock. He felt like they were lying to Mr. O.

"We're not lying. We're just not telling him what he doesn't want to hear," Imani had argued, and Brock had told her it was the same thing.

Once again, Imani respected the position that he had taken, and although she found his integrity to be very sexy—and she would most certainly appreciate it more when his integrity was for her benefit—right then, Imani needed her man to have her back.

"You know I got you," Brock had promised.

The solution: he had never gone to the hospital without her, and since the television had always been on ESPN or the NFL Network channel, there hadn't been much talking going on. Although Mr. O was weak and hadn't said anything about it, he was not stupid, so he knew something was going on.

It's the look on his face every time I ask what's going on out there, and Imani answers whether I asked her or not, he'd thought more than once. So now he was waiting to get Brock alone.

Brock knew that too. Therefore, when he came into the game room, where Imani was doing her drinking, he walked up and stood next to her. He picked up the bottle of Jack and poured himself one. Then, with drink in hand, he turned to Imani.

"What is this? Your 'But I needed a drink first' moment?"

Imani nodded playfully. "I guess it is," she said and finished her drink.

"Well, now you've had your drink."

"And I'm gonna go upstairs and tell him."

Brock drained his glass, put it down on the bar, and held out his hand. "And I'll be right next to you."

Imani laughed. "Right next to me, keeping your mouth shut," she said, and they left the quiet calm of the game room to face Mr. O.

When Brock walked into the room, Mr. O turned off the television and smiled. Then he saw Imani come in behind him. The smile disappeared, and he turned the television back on.

"What's wrong, Daddy?" Imani asked when she saw the look on his face.

"Nothing's wrong. I just got excited when I saw Brock because I thought he was here to tell me what you've been keeping from me. But you're here, so that's not gonna happen," he said and folded his arms across his chest as if he were a pouty child.

Imani and Brock looked at one another. "I told you he knew," he said softly as Imani passed by him and sat down on the bed.

"Well, Daddy," she said timidly, "that's why we're here."

"Where's Hareem?" Mr. O asked and received blank faces in return. "I figured Hareem had something to do with whatever it is that you've been keeping from me."

"I don't know where he is. I called him, but he didn't answer," Imani said. Hareem had promised that she wouldn't have to do this alone, but he had disappointed her once again.

"No matter. Let's hear it."

"That night, after he left the hospital, Hareem got a text from Loonie," she began, and Mr. O smiled.

"Nice girl."

"She told him that a guy named Hedrick knew about her and Hareem, and he knew that Omeika wasn't his baby."

"I know all that," Mr. O said impatiently.

"You do?" a surprised Imani asked.

"Yeah, I know about it. Loonie and the baby came to see me last night at the hospital with that cute, gun-toting bodyguard he got her, and she told me all about that mess."

"Then you know?" Imani said.

"That your brother did something stupid? Of course I do. Hareem's a hothead. I knew that he'd want revenge and start shooting at whoever he thought did it." He looked at Imani and Brock and shook his head. "Don't just sit there looking stupid, like you're surprised that I know my own son," he said. *Because he's just like me.* "Tell me what he did."

Once Imani had detailed all that she knew of what was going on, Mr. O was furious. Although it was what he had expected, it was definitely not what he wanted, and he was astonished that it had gone that far. But it wasn't Hareem that he was mad at.

"Me?" a wide-eyed Imani asked, pointing to herself.

"Yes, you!" he shouted and pointed at Brock. "And you!"

"How is this our fault?" Imani asked.

"I expect Hareem to . . . to be himself. What I didn't expect you two to do was let it go on as long as it has."

"What were we supposed to do?" Imani asked.

"Stop him before it got to this point. That's what you were supposed to do. Not sit back and let this shit go on."

Imani dropped her head. "Yes, Daddy," she said, knowing that he was right.

Mr. O pointed at Imani. "You need to put a stop to this today!"

Imani hesitated, and then she said, "Yes, Daddy."

She was going to ask how he expected her to put a stop to it today, but she knew what his answer would be.

"I don't care. Just get it done!" he'd shout, and then he would throw them out of his room.

She didn't want to upset him any more than she already had.

"I'll get it done," Imani said and stood up.

"You're carrying power now, Imani," Mr. O said calmly. "I know you can do this."

"Yes, Daddy," she said and left the room with Brock.

Chapter Thirty-three

Imani shut the door, looked at Brock, and shook her head. "Right next to me, keeping your mouth shut," she said and started walking toward the stairs.

"I thought it was an order," he said, walking alongside her.

"So I'm sitting there, and I'm thinking, *He's gonna jump in any second.*" She shook her head and went down the stairs. "Not a peep."

"What did you want me to say?"

"Nothing, I guess," Imani said and went into her father's office and sat down behind her father's desk. "He's right. It was my responsibility to put a stop to it." She paused as Brock sat down. "But you know, there was a part of me that thought, Yeah, they shot my father, so they all need to die."

"Yeah, me too."

"But that wasn't what we should have done. War is bad for business." Imani laughed. "You know what's funny?"

"No, tell me. What's funny?"

"It was me trying to convince Hareem that war was bad for business, and now look at where we are."

"So what are we gonna do now, boss?"

Imani looked at him. "I don't know."

"You'll figure it out," Brock assured her, pointing. "Because that is your chair now."

"I know. I just don't know if I'm ready for it."

"You want me to handle this war for you, boss?"

"How?"

"You leave that to me."

"Handle it. I'll get Hareem to back off," Imani said, and Brock stood up.

"You might not see me for a couple of days, but I'll keep in touch."

"What are you going to do?"

"Whatever you need me to do," Brock said and left the office and Imani alone to think about how she was going to handle Hareem and end this war. She could have and should have done more to put a stop to it.

If only, she thought.

If only she hadn't sent Hareem away from the hospital that night after they spoke with the doctor. If he had been there with them when he got the text from Loonie, maybe she and Brock could have talked him down. And that was exactly what she should have done when she found out what he had done: talk him down before it escalated any further than it had. Imani had all but sanctioned his actions by her silence on the matter.

She was about to get up and go to the kitchen to see what Kimberly was cooking when her phone rang. Although she didn't recognize the number, Imani answered the call, anyway.

"Hello."

"It's Hareem."

"Thanks for being there to have my back, like you promised."

"I been shot, Imani."

As the shooter had kept firing, Hareem had run into the woods. Not knowing whether the shooter was following him or not, he'd kept running until he found his way out of the woods. It wasn't until then that he had felt the stinging pain in his right leg. When he'd touched the spot and looked at his hand, he'd seen blood. He had made it as best he could to a CVS, where he'd begged a woman to go in and get bandages and gauze while he used her phone.

"Oh my God! Are you all right?"

"I'm all right, but I need you to come get me."

Imani stood up. "Where are you?"

"The CVS on Saint Augustine Road, by my house."

"I'm on my way, Hareem. Are you safe where you are?"

"No, I'm hiding behind the dumpster, and I'm out of bullets," he said, signaling for the woman as she came out of the store, looking around for him.

"Hold on, Hareem. I'm coming for you." Imani grabbed her purse and dashed out the door.

Once Hareem handed the woman back her phone and thanked her, she helped bandage his wound and then offered to take him to a hospital.

"No, thank you. My sister is coming to get me," Hareem said, reaching in his pocket for his money. He handed it all to her. "Thank you again. Now you should go."

"You sure?"

"Yeah. The people that shot me may still be looking for me."

"Okay," she said and went back to her car, but she didn't drive away. After a while, she got out and came back to him. She handed him a piece of paper. "I'm Keisha."

He smiled. "Hareem."

"Call me, you know

. . . to let me know you're all right."

He took the paper. "I will. Now you need to go on and get out of here," Hareem said.

He watched her get in her car, and this time she drove away.

It was twenty minutes later when Imani arrived and took Hareem to their family doctor. Once the doctor had removed the bullet from his lower outer left thigh and cleaned and dressed the wound, Imani took her brother home. Which was the last place he wanted to go.

"How mad is Daddy?" he asked as she drove.

"He's not mad at you for retaliating."

"He's not?"

"No. He expected you to retaliate against whoever you thought did it."

Hareem smiled, feeling vindicated.

"But he's mad, all right."

"Who's he mad at?"

"Me," she said, and Hareem laughed. "It's not funny, Hareem."

"Yes, it is." He laughed some more. Why is he mad at you?"

"Because he expected me to stop you."

Hareem kept laughing. "Well, you are the responsible one. Me, I'm the shit starter."

"Shit for me to clean up," Imani said as they reached the house. She parked in the garage and helped Hareem hobble into the house.

"Come on," she said when they got inside, and then she started for the steps.

"Where we going?"

"You need to talk to Daddy."

"You mean listen to Daddy yell," he said and, leaning on the banister, he slowly followed her up the stairs to her father's room.

When Imani walked into the room, Mr. O was watching television. He smiled when he saw her. Then he saw Hareem come in behind her. The smile disappeared, and he turned the television off.

"About fuckin' time you showed up," he said, and then he laid into the two of them for the next fifteen minutes.

During that time, neither said a word, because they had learned a long time ago that the tongue-lashing didn't last as long if they just stood quietly, said, "Yes, Daddy," or "No, Daddy," whichever was appropriate, and walked away when it was over.

"What happened to your leg?" Mr. O finally asked.

"I got shot," Hareem said, and they were treated to another tongue-lashing. Hareem for being careless enough to go unprotected after he had started a war, and Imani for letting it happen.

After he was done, Imani said, "Yes, Daddy, it won't happen again."

Mr. O waved his hand. "Now, get out of here," he said and turned the television back on.

Chapter Thirty-four

For the second time that day, Imani was walking out of her father's room with her head hanging low. Although she had done nothing, she was responsible for everything.

Lesson learned. Stay on top of everything.

"Thank wasn't so bad," Hareem said as he limped alongside Imani.

"Maybe not for you, but as usual, what you do falls on me," she said when they got to his bedroom door. "You get some rest, but sometime today me and you are going to have a conversation about the way we're doing business. You and Daddy both got shot. Some things are going to have to change."

Hareem was about to say something, but Imani spoke first.

"And don't tell me that getting shot at is part of the game," she said, pointing in his face.

"I wasn't gonna say that."

"What were you gonna say?" she asked, almost apologetic.

"I was gonna say, 'Thanks for coming to get me and for taking the weight.' Like you always do." He paused as he reached for the doorknob. "But I gotta be honest with you. Sitting behind that dumpster, out of bullets, not knowing if he was still looking for me. I was scared that I'd look up and he'd be standing there and kill me. I ain't ready to die, Imani," Hareem said. Then he limped into his room.

He stretched out across his bed and called Loonie to check on her and Omeika, and he told her what happened. She told him that she would get Mayra to bring her and the baby over to see him, and he told her no. But Loonie persisted. Once he agreed that Mayra could bring them to the house the next morning, he ended the call with Loonie and called Cynthia at her office.

She picked up after several rings. "Hey, Hareem. I'm in the middle of something right now. What did you need?" she said, with the phone between her shoulder and ear as she signed the documents an agent had just placed before her.

He shook his head, but he was used to her playing him off that way. "Sorry to bother you at work, but I got shot today."

"Wait. Hold on." Cynthia placed her hand over the phone. "I'm gonna need the room." Once her office was empty and the last person had shut the door, she put the phone to her ear. "You got shot?"

"Yes, bae, I got shot."

"Are you all right?"

"I'm fine. Imani took me to the doctor, and she took out the bullet."

"Where are you?"

"I'm at my father's house."

Cynthia began gathering her things to leave. "I'm on my way."

"No. Finish what you're doing. I'll be all right until you get here," Hareem insisted. "Between Kimberly and Imani, they're taking good care of me. So finish what you're doing, and I'll see you when you get off."

"Uh-uh. I'm coming over right now. I'll see you when I get there," she said and left the office.

When she got there forty minutes later, Kimberly let her in the house, and Cynthia rushed up the stairs to

Hareem's bedroom. She suspected that part of Hareem's insistence that she not come right away was on account of the fact that he wasn't alone, so she expected to find another woman in there with him. With that thought in mind, Cynthia burst through the door, only to find Hareem in bed alone with the remote in one hand and the other hand on his thigh.

"I told you that you didn't have to rush over here," Hareem said and sat up.

She sat on the bed, put her arms around his neck, and kissed him passionately. When their lips slowly parted, Cynthia caressed his face. "I just needed to see that you were all right." *And alone.*

"I'm all right," he said, and then he told her what had happened. "I called Imani, and she picked me up. Like I said, the doctor took out the bullet, cleaned and stapled the wound. I'm fine, Cyn, really." He kissed her and rubbed his aching thigh.

"You should have called me right away. I would have come to pick you up."

"No, this was business, and that's Imani's job. You were working for us, making us money. That's your job—us."

"You still should have called me, Hareem. I know the mighty Imani is your sister, but I want to be there for you when you need me."

Cynthia never had liked that she always took second place to his family, despite that fact that she had always put his needs above everything. It would be nice if that went both ways.

"You're here now, when I need you," Hareem said before drawing her lips to his and kissing her lightly.

After that, Cynthia changed into something comfortable that she found among the clothes that she had there at the house, and then she cared for his wound. Once she had cleaned the wound, she put on a clean bandage.

Then she went to the kitchen to see if Kimberly had an ice pack and to see when dinner would be ready. When she returned with an ice pack and towels, Cynthia applied the ice to the wound, covered it with one of the towels, and elevated his leg on pillows.

"That will help decrease the swelling and the pain," she said and lay down next to him.

When dinner was ready, Cynthia went to get it, brought their food back upstairs, and then she all but fed it to him. After the meal, she sat patiently in the great room for an hour and a half while Hareem talked to Imani in his bedroom about her thoughts on the family's future, details of which he chose not to share with her. Then Cynthia watched television with Hareem until he passed out from the pain medication he had taken and the weed they had smoked. In the morning, while Hareem slept, Cynthia had breakfast with Imani. After trying without success to get Imani to talk about her thoughts on the family's future, Cynthia went to work.

After she left, Hareem called and had Mayra bring Loonie and Omeika to the house, and they spent the day there. As soon as they got there, Imani took Omeika from her stroller, and that gave Loonie a chance to check on Hareem. After a while, Loonie told him that she was going to go and say hello to his father.

"Mr. Mosley," Loonie called softly when she tapped lightly on his door. "It's Loonie," she said, sticking her head in the door. "Omeika's mom."

"Come in, come in," Mr. O said, waving her in and smiling brightly.

Loonie stepped into the room and smiled when she saw his smile. "I don't want to bother you." She took a small step toward the bed. "I just wanted to say hello."

"You're not bothering me," he said, and she smiled, because that was exactly what she wanted to hear. "Come and sit down for a minute. I'm glad for the company."

"Thank you," she said politely and sat down in the chair by the bed. "Me and Omeika came to see how Hareem was doing, and I wanted to, like I said, say hello and see how you're doing." She smiled again.

"Honestly, I feel terrible. But they tell me that's how I'm supposed to feel," he said, and they talked for almost half an hour before Hareem came and got her.

They were on their way back to his room when the parents heard Omeika crying, and they went to see about her. Her crying gave Imani her first chance to change Omeika's diaper.

"Might as well learn how it's done now," Imani said, knowing that it would be the first of many she would change.

After that, Loonie and Hareem hung out with Imani, who was enjoying playing with Omeika. Before she left, Loonie made it back upstairs so that Omeika could spend time with her grandfather. This time she didn't stay long, because Mr. O said that he wasn't feeling well and wanted to rest until the doctor came to see him later that afternoon. By the time Mayra took Loonie and Omeika back to Amelia Island, Loonie had an open invitation to come back anytime.

"You're part of the family now," Imani said and hugged her before she left.

Loonie may have made some bad choices, including falling for one drug dealer, getting pregnant by him, and then falling for another, but that was behind her now. She was a mother now, and she needed to make sure that her daughter was provided for.

Omeika being a part of Hareem's family gave Loonie the sense of security she felt Omeika needed. She needed to know that no matter how this arrangement worked out with Hareem, Omeika would always have some stability and consistency in her life.

Thirty minutes after Loonie and Omeika left the house, Cynthia arrived, and after spending a little time with Mr. O, she took Hareem to her house.

Chapter Thirty-five

Hareem was pretty quiet on the way to Cynthia's house. He blamed it on the pain meds he was taking, but the truth was that he'd had a good day with Loonie and Omeika, and he missed them. Hareem glanced over at Cynthia as she chatted away, and knew that he needed to tell her.

Seeing that he was tired, once she got Hareem settled, Cynthia went out and picked up beef brisket topped with grilled onions and jalapeños from a local restaurant for them to eat for dinner. After dinner, Cynthia set up pillows on the couch so that Hareem would be comfortable while they chilled and watched television. It had been a nice evening so far. Other than his phone not blowing up with Martel's calls for orders, it was no different than any other night that they'd spent at her house together. But that was about to change.

"I need to tell you something," he said during a silly insurance commercial.

"What's that?" she asked without looking over at him, as she was amused by the commercial.

"It's important, Cyn, and you're gonna be mad," he said, and that got her attention. When she turned her head, her look was intense.

"What?" she asked, thinking that he was going to tell her about Gianna.

Hareem looked at her for a while, thinking about how he was going to tell her. "Ain't no good way to say this, so

I'm just gonna drop it." He paused. "I have a six-month-old daughter," he said, and Cynthia went ballistic.

As Hareem continued repeating, "Calm down and let me explain," Cynthia cursed and cried and went back to cursing before she calmed down enough for him to tell her the whole story. And he was totally honest with her. Hareem did, however, leave out the part about him being in love with Loonie and certain details, in the interest of protecting her privacy, but other than that, he told her everything. Then he showed her an image of Loonie and Omeika on his cell phone.

Cynthia took the phone from him and looked at the image carefully and remembered that Loonie was the woman whom he was with when they first got together. Those days, Hareem was messing with her and two other women.

She's the one that moved out of town, Cynthia thought, and that made her more understanding when he delivered his next statement.

"I wasn't cheating on you. That happened before we got together. She didn't know that she was pregnant until after she moved back to Palatka. She got a DNA test, and I am Omeika's father."

Now that she was calmer—she had made herself another drink and had taken a few hits off a blunt—they talked about Hareem's relationship with Loonie. He wasn't lying to her when he told Cynthia that the relationship was not about sex. It was all about him being Omeika's father.

Despite him wanting to be inside Loonie each time he saw her, they'd had sex only that one time. She was serious when she'd said that she wasn't going to be the other woman, and she damn sure wasn't no side chick.

You wanna fuck, go fuck that skinny bitch you left me for.

He was her daughter's father, period, and to Loonie, that meant that they were not having sex. As far as she was concerned, any possibility of a sexual relationship had ended the day that he went to the doctor with her for Omeika's six-month checkup. Loonie had known right away that the reason that he was running late that day and couldn't take her calls was that he was with Cynthia.

Cynthia surprised Hareem by saying, "I want to meet her."

"Omeika?"

"Yes, of course. I want to meet her," Cynthia answered, smiling, while she looked at the image of Loonie and Omeika. "But I want to meet Loonie too. I need to know what type of woman is going to be raising our daughter."

"Our daughter?"

"Yes, Hareem, *our* daughter. We are one, right?"

For a number of reasons, Cynthia had never had any interest in getting pregnant and having children. She didn't feel like anything was missing from her life that a baby would fill, as she'd heard some of her girlfriends say before they'd struggled with the decision and a baby to take care of. At that point in her life, Cynthia's career was her priority, and she had so many options for the future she was so carefully crafting. The truth was that Cynthia had never seen herself as a mother and had absolutely no interest in the changes that pregnancy would make to her body.

"She is our daughter, right?" she asked.

"Right."

Hareem smiled because Cynthia was taking this way better than he had thought she would. Since she did have a tendency to be dramatic, he had expected Cynthia's cursing and crying to be followed by her yelling for him to get out and her screaming that she didn't care how he got home. Then she would storm to her room and slam the door behind her.

The truth? Who knew? Hareem thought, shrugged his shoulders, and went along.

"She's a pretty girl, bae," she said, handing him back his phone.

"She is."

"She looks like her mother," Cynthia said and watched Hareem's smile broaden as he looked at Loonie.

"I know."

Cynthia stood up.

"Where you going?"

"Going to set up a spot in bed for you to be comfortable," she said and went into the bedroom.

When she came back, Cynthia helped Hareem up from the couch and helped him walk to the bedroom. Once he was comfortable in bed, she cleaned and changed his wound before going back into the living room to straighten up. She was just about done when her phone rang.

"Hello," she answered.

"Turn on Action News." The caller hung up.

Cynthia picked up the TV remote, turned on the television, and turned to ABC Action News.

"Authorities are investigating a shooting in the Normandy area of Jacksonville. Around eleven thirty Wednesday night, emergency crews were called to a reported shooting near Truman Avenue," said the reporter on the TV screen. "Investigators say that Gianna Jennings was pronounced dead at the scene of what officials are calling a home invasion gone terribly wrong. The Jacksonville Sheriff's Office reports that, among other things, several televisions, a laptop, and the victim's phone appear to be missing from the home. No arrests have been made at this time."

"I know her," Hareem said when he appeared in the doorway.

He hadn't heard from Gianna since the day that Loonie had talked to her. He wondered if Cameron had found out about them, the way Hedrick had found out about him and Loonie, and had had her killed.

"Was she a friend of yours?" Cynthia asked, turning off the television and approaching him.

"That was one of Cameron's women," he said as he turned, made his way back to the bedroom, and gently got back in bed. Hareem was sad to hear Gianna was dead.

"Do you think he had her killed?" Cynthia said and began taking off her clothes before she got in the bed.

"Ain't no telling," Hareem said and tried to get comfortable.

If he was going to be totally honest with Cynthia, this would be the time to tell her about Gianna. He looked at her standing naked in front of him and decided that since Gianna was dead, the secret had died with her.

"Well, you just relax," she said and crawled closer to him. "Let me take good care of you," she added, freeing his dick from his shorts and running her tongue up and down it. She began to run circles around his head with her tongue.

After a while, Hareem reached for Cynthia and pulled her on top of him, and she positioned herself to ride his face. Hareem spread her lips and gently massaged her clit. Cynthia was dripping wet. His tongue slithered along her lips, making tight circles around her clit, as he moved his finger in and out of her.

"That feels amazing," she moaned as her body shuddered. Cynthia moved away from Hareem's tongue. "I need to feel you inside me."

"Just be careful with my leg."

"Don't worry. Mommy got this," she said, grabbing his dick and lowered herself slowly onto him.

Cynthia loved having him inside her. She closed her eyes and moved her body up and down on his dick slowly, savoring the feeling of her walls spasming and clenching his thick length violently. Hareem twisted her nipples, and she ground her hips into him so she could feel every stroke.

Cynthia leaned forward and kissed Hareem. He gripped her ass, pushing himself in her furiously. She sat straight up on him.

"Make me cum again," she demanded and a minute later she came, shaking, shuddering, and mumbling.

When they were done, Cynthia lay there next to the man she loved, curled in the fetal position. Her body felt magnificent. She would decide how she was going to deal with Loonie some other time.

Chapter Thirty-six

He had been following Hedrick's people for a couple of days, but Brock knew that sooner or later that they would lead him straight to Hedrick. Brock had been laying low since the Moncrief hit. When he had heard that Hareem had blamed him for his father's shooting, He'd gone underground. He had thought about reaching out to Hareem through Loonie, but she was nowhere to be found. So he had put the word out on the street: "I didn't have shit to do with it."

The word he'd got back: "You're gonna die for what you did."

At that point, he'd ordered the hit on Jaric, and it had been on ever since.

But since it had been quiet for a couple of days, Brock had decided to show his face and have some fun. It had been quiet for the past few days because between Mr. O and Imani, they had convinced Hareem to stand down. He had agreed only after Imani had told him what Brock was doing, and even though she had no idea exactly what he was doing, she had assured Hareem that Hedrick would be dealt with.

Knowing that his new Q60 would be easy to spot, Brock had bought a black 1995 Ford Thunderbird. One afternoon he followed Hedrick from a club on Kings Road. In his vehicle Hedrick had a woman whom he had come out of the club with and one man for security, who was behind the wheel.

"Easy peasy," Brock said and kept his distance until they reached the Ansley apartments on Harts Road.

Brock parked his car away from the apartment building and watched as Hedrick and the woman, who appeared to be a little drunk, went into the building. The man who had driven Hedrick there rolled down his window, turned the music up a little, and relaxed. Brock gave him some time to get comfortable, and then he got out and approached the car. Not wanting to be seen, Brock took the long way around and then stayed low until he was quite close to the driver's door. Then he stood up.

"What's up?" the man asked, startled, as Brock stood there.

"Where that good green at?"

"I don't know what's up around here," he said, reaching for his gun right before Brock put his silencer-clad nine millimeter to the man's eye and pulled the trigger. The man died instantly.

Brock put away his weapon and opened the car door, took the keys from the ignition, and opened the trunk. He went and pulled the man out of the car and put him in the trunk. With that out of the way, Brock went to move his car closer to the building and then waited for Hedrick to come back out. The wait wasn't long.

Thirty minutes later, Hedrick came out of the building and walked to his car. As he got closer, he noticed the no one was in the car.

"Now, where this nigga at?" he asked, then felt the feeling of steel in his back.

"He's dead, and unless you want to join him, you'll do exactly what I say. Understand?" Brock growled, and when Hedrick didn't answer right away, Brock hit him in the head with the barrel of his gun. "Understand?"

"Yeah, nigga, I got it," Hedrick muttered, and Brock hit him again.

"Take a step forward and turn around," he ordered.

Hedrick did as he was told and turned to see Brock with his gun pointed at him and a pair of handcuffs in his other hand.

Brock tossed him the cuffs. "Put them on."

Once again, Hedrick did what he was told.

"What now?" he asked once he was cuffed.

"We're going someplace we can talk privately. Now go," Brock said, motioning toward Hedrick's car with his gun. When Hedrick started to reach for the passenger-door handle, Brock hit his hand with the gun. "No, buddy. You're riding in the trunk with your boy."

Once he had Hedrick locked in the trunk, Brock got in the car and drove out of the complex. He took out his phone and called Mr. O.

"Hello," Mr. O answered groggily.

"Sorry to wake you up, boss, but I need a place to have a private conversation."

"You know where the Westside office is, right?"

"Yes, sir."

"Behind the main building is a storage shed." Mr. O smiled. "You'll find everything you need there." He chuckled. "I wish I could meet you there, but you know."

"Right, the whole 'You just got shot and had a heart attack' thing. I understand. I'll talk to you in the morning, boss," Brock said and swiped END on his phone.

When he got to the Westside office, Brock let Hedrick out of the trunk and walked him to the storage shed. Once inside, he hit Hedrick in the back of the head, and he went down. Brock turned on the light and had a look around until he saw a tow hook and a chain.

"Everything I need," he said aloud to himself.

He connected the tow hook to the chain and tossed the chain over a support beam in the shed. Once the chain was secure, he dragged Hedrick over. Brock attached the tow hook to the handcuffs and pulled Hedrick up until just the tips of his toes were touching the floor. Hedrick woke up when Brock threw a bucket of cold water on him.

"Shit!" he shouted. "That's fuckin' cold!"

"Yeah, that's the point," Brock said, putting on gloves. "I'm gonna ask you a couple of questions." He laughed. "Just not right away."

Brock put a gag in Hedrick's mouth and hit him in the face and then in his chest. He walked around to his side and hit him in his ribs. He walked around and punched him in his other ribs. Then Brock began punching him in the face with hard lefts and rights. After a while, both of Hedrick's eyes were swollen, and he was bleeding from his nose and mouth. Brock punched him in the stomach, and then he hit him twice in the face. He took a step back, wiped the sweat from his brow, and went back to work on his ribs.

Brock went back to hitting him with lefts and rights to his face, and then he stopped. Took the gag out of Hedrick's mouth and then Brock punched him in the stomach. That blow took all the wind out of him, and he spit blood.

"Let's talk," Brock said.

"Fuck you!"

"Look, I can keep beating you, or you can answer my questions and we call it a night."

Hedrick spit out more blood. "What you wanna know?"

"Did you try to kill Hareem and hit his father instead?"

"I didn't have shit to do with that," he said as Brock walked away.

"We'll see if you're still talking that 'I ain't have shit to do with it' shit in a minute," Brock said, wheeling over a cart with a battery and some cables on it.

"What the fuck!" Hedrick said when he saw it. "You're crazy!"

"Did you try to kill Hareem and hit his father instead?" Brock asked, connecting the cables to the battery.

"Look, man. It wasn't me. I didn't even know it was the nigga's birthday or where his Daddy lives. And even if I did wanna kill him, Diamond told us to back off."

That made Brock pause. "When did she do that?"

"Same day it happened."

Brock picked up the cables. "What did she say?"

"She asked me if it was me. I didn't know what the fuck she was talking about. She told me his Daddy got shot and for me not to do anything. But fuck that! I wasn't gonna be no pussy about it. He hit us, and we busted back."

"What about Loonie and the baby not being yours?"

"I knew that wasn't none of my baby the second I saw her. I didn't know it was that nigga's baby. I just knew it wasn't none of mine." He spit out some blood. "I told her I knew she wasn't my baby to get rid of her gobble-dollar ass."

Brock laughed.

"Serious, that bitch always got her hand out," Hedrick said and laughed.

Brock tapped the copper clamps together in front of Hedrick's face, and he stopped laughing. "You know what? I believe you," Brock said and wheeled the cart away.

"So we good?"

"Yeah, we're good," Brock said as he walked toward him. Then he put a bullet in his forehead. "All good."

After that, Brock took Hedrick's body down and put him back in the trunk. He went back into the storage shed and cleaned up. Once he was done, he drove the bodies back to the Ansley, parked the car, and took Hedrick's body from the trunk. Then Brock laid the body spread eagle on the hood of his car. With his work done, he walked back to the Thunderbird, got in, and went home.

Chapter Thirty-seven

The morning sun and a gentle breeze woke Imani up at her condo. She was alone and thinking about how much she'd missed Brock over the past two days. Although he said that he'd keep in touch, Brock had called her only once. It was a short call. It had been late, and she hadn't recognized the number, so she'd answered tentatively.

"Hello."

"It's Brock. I'm on Hedrick."

"Are you all right?"

"I'm fine, but I gotta go."

"I miss you." Imani might as well have said this to herself, because Brock was gone.

She sent a text: I miss you. Come by the condo if you can.

It went unanswered. All the same, she got out of her bed at her father's house and drove to the condo just in case he came by. Imani picked up her phone and tried calling Brock's number, but it went straight to voicemail, and she chose not to leave a message.

She lay there for a while, allowing her mind to drift from thought to thought. This was the second night she'd slept alone. Although it hadn't been all that long, she had gotten used to sleeping next to Brock. Which was something she hadn't liked to do before they started sleeping together. Imani had preferred to sleep alone and in her own bed. It was different with him. After they spent the night making love, he'd roll on his side, and Imani would snuggle up behind him, breathe in his scent, and fall into a blissful sleep.

But eventually, all of Imani's thoughts brought her back to her father's words.

You're carrying power now.

And hearing her father speak those words had scared her. Even though she'd been carrying that power for a long time, Imani had always had her father to guide her, to be her net as she walked the tightrope. But it wasn't his words that had scared her. It was why he had said them that scared her.

Is he sicker than he's telling me?

Since she really didn't want to think about that, Imani got out of bed and got in the shower. She planned to go to the house, check on her men, and work out before she started her day. As she showered, she thought how working out of the house while she took care of her father and brother was working out better than she had thought it would, and she planned to do more of it. While she was in the office, where there was always something going on, Imani always found a million and one things to do. Working from home, where there wasn't always something going on, allowed Imani time to think about and explore new opportunities to expand their businesses.

On the drive to the house, Imani thought about the family's businesses. Their core business was moving contraband in and out of the country: drugs, weapons, whatever. They were smugglers. Her father had taken them into and then out of the drug sales and distribution game. It was Hareem who had put them back in the game when they got to Jacksonville. Other than trying to tell him how to do things to advance his business, Imani was hands off. But the way she was feeling right then, she was thinking that maybe it was time for them to get out, leave the game alone, focus on their core business, and expand into other things that were legitimate, safer, and made more money.

"Hareem will not be trying to hear that," Imani said, laughing, as she turned into the driveway. She was surprised that Brock's car was parked in front of the garage. "He's here," she said excitedly, pressing the button for the garage.

She parked, rushed inside, and ran up the stairs, wondering why he hadn't come to the condo when he was done doing whatever he was doing. As she walked down the hall, her next thought was, *Maybe he's hurt, and that is why he came here.* Imani picked up her pace. She tapped on Brock's bedroom door lightly as she turned the handle. No answer. She went into the room.

"Brock," she called softly.

After not sleeping for two days, when he had got to the house earlier that morning, Brock had had just enough energy to step out of his shoes, take off his shirt, and fall on the bed. He was lying on top of the sheets now, snoring like a buzz saw.

"Brock," she giggled, and his snoring got louder. "He is out cold."

As she walked toward the bed, Imani picked up his shoes and the shirt he had tossed along the way. She put the shoes in the closet and the shirt with the rest of the dirty clothes. She went and sat on the edge of the bed.

"Brock." Imani nudged him.

Then she took off her top and bra, because she needed to feel his skin against hers. Imani lay down in the bed next to Brock and held him. She lay there caressing his back, and it seemed to stop the snoring. Imani got in rhythm with his breathing, and she drifted off to sleep.

She didn't sleep for long, thirty minutes or so maybe, but she awoke feeling wonderful. Whereas she had awakened this morning feeling restless, her mind racing, now she felt peace, a refreshing peace. She sat up. Brock was still dead to the world, so Imani got out of bed. She put her clothes back on and went downstairs to hit the gym. After she finished working out, which wasn't the same without him, Imani showered, got dressed, and then went to check on Brock.

"Still out," she said aloud as she peered at him.

She went to the kitchen, where Kimberly had prepared a heart-healthy breakfast of oatmeal sprinkled with chopped walnuts, cinnamon, and vanilla, with a banana and a cup of skim milk, especially for Mr. O.

"Oh, he is going to hate this," Imani said, putting the food on a tray.

She carried the tray upstairs to her father. "Morning, Daddy," Imani said brightly as she came in with the food.

"Good morning, Imani," he said and tried to sit up.

"Here," she said, putting down the tray. "Let me help you."

"I can manage," he said, but she ignored him. "Thank you."

"I brought your breakfast."

"If it's the same shit they called breakfast at the hospital, you can take it back."

"It is the same shit, and you're going to eat it, if I have to sit here and spoon-feed it to you." She giggled and put the tray on his lap. "Or I can send Kimberly up here and you can explain to her why you don't want to eat her food while *she* spoon-feeds it to you."

Mr. O picked up the banana and took a bite. "Happy?"

"Very."

"Just don't send that woman up here." He took another bite. "She really would spoon-feed me."

"What makes you so sure I won't?" When he said nothing, Imani sat down in the chair next to the bed. "Brock's here."

"He is? What did he say?"

"Nothing to me. I was hoping that he talked to you."

"No. I didn't even know he was here."

"He's asleep. I tried, but I couldn't wake him."

"He called me in the middle of the night. Said he needed somewhere to have a private conversation," he revealed and ate some oatmeal.

"He called me the night before and said he was on Hedrick."

"This ain't half bad," Mr. O said and ate some more oatmeal.

"Kimberly said she hooked it up just for you." Imani stood up. "I'm going to check on Brock again, and then I'm gonna eat. I'll be back to check on you."

"I'll be here. I don't seem to be going anywhere."

"You would if you could," Imani said on her way out the door.

"But I damn sure can't," he said, because he was too weak to even think about moving.

Imani checked on Brock periodically throughout the morning, desperate to know what had happened during his private conversation and whom it was with. Each time she checked on him, she found that he was still asleep, so after the third check, she settled on the couch in the great room to think. She sat back and thought that the three men in her life were all upstairs in bed. Two were recovering from gunshot wounds, and one was recovering from whatever he'd done the night before. Right then, they were safe, but Imani knew that things being the way they were, that may not last much past tomorrow.

Later that afternoon, Imani was in her father's office, on the phone confirming a deal she had made months ago to sell a shipment of 5.56 mm M855s, a green-tipped small-arms round used by the US military, when Brock walked in and sat down. Imani rushed to wrap up the call.

"Hi," he said when she hung up.

"Hi," she said, standing up and coming around the desk.

He stood up, and Imani drifted into his arms. "I missed you," they both said in unison, holding the other tightly.

It felt so good in his arms, warm, comfortable, and safe. And exhilarating. She was aroused. "I want you now," was what Imani wanted to say, buried in his chest that way, breathing in his scent. Knowing that if she kissed him, she would end up on the desk with her legs in the air, Imani forced herself to let her arms fall away and to step back.

Brock knew where it would end up too, but he didn't care. He pulled Imani back into his arms and kissed her like he had missed the fuck outta her. And when their lips parted, Brock let Imani go and took a small step back. She stood with her eyes closed, not moving for a second, before her eyes drifted open.

"I'm glad you're back," she said in a whisper and quickly went back behind the desk before she reached for his zipper. "Tell me about the private conversation you had last night."

Brock sat down and took Imani through his night with Hedrick step-by-step and then told her about what the man had said.

"And you believe him?"

"I do." He stood up. "Come on. There's something I want to show you."

Brock led Imani outside. "Since it happened, I've had this nagging feeling that something wasn't right about this."

"What's that?"

"I think that your father was the target, not Hareem, and everybody else was collateral damage."

"What makes you say that?" she asked as they reached the backyard, where Hareem's party had been held. He pointed at the bullet holes that had been left on the side of the house that day.

"I need to call somebody to take care of that," she said.

"Look at the pattern of the bullets." He pointed. "See how high they hit? Like they weren't trying to hit any-body."

Imani looked carefully at the pattern. "What do you think it means?"

"Those shots were to clear everybody out of the way of their real target."

"Daddy." Imani turned to Brock. "Daddy was the target all along."

Chapter Thirty-eight

Brock took Imani back inside the house, and they headed into the game room, where he showed her the video footage from the party. "See how the gunman shoots at the people as they approach? But when they get closer, the bullets hit the house," he said as Imani watched in slow motion. "Then they slow down long enough to aim and shoot your father."

Imani had Brock rerun the footage twice more before she sat back and told him to turn it off. "So this is more evidence that Daddy was the target all along," she noted and stood up. "We need to tell him." She walked quickly out of the office, Brock on her heels.

"First thing you need to do is get some men over here to protect him," Brock suggested as he followed her up the stairs.

"You're right. If I had known that he was the target, I'd have put somebody at the hospital."

"I know. But we were all so ready to believe that this was about Hareem that neither of us thought of it," he said as they walked into Mr. O's room without knocking first.

"Thought about what?" he asked, noticing the troubled expressions on both of their faces.

When Imani and Brock sat down, she looked at Brock and extended her hand, as if to say, "The floor is yours." Brock started at the beginning and told Mr. O first of his suspicions and of the video and the bullet pattern before he told him what Hedrick had said.

"And you believed him?" Mr. O asked.

"Yeah, I believed him. I killed him, anyway, but yeah, knowing what we know now, I don't think he had anything to do with it. What was interesting was that he said that even if he had wanted to go hard at Hareem, Diamond had told him to stand down."

"That is interesting," Mr. O said.

"Did you ask him who Diamond was?" Imani asked.

"No. He told me what I needed to know, so I killed him and took his body back where I picked him up," Brock answered.

"Where was that?" Imani wanted to know.

"Some apartments on Harts Road."

"Okay." Imani exhaled. "Any ideas on who might want to kill you, Daddy?"

"No. It could be some old shit from Miami, and that could be anybody," Mr. O said. "Other than that, I can't think of anybody I've had a problem with since we moved here."

"That was the point of the move. That's why it being about Hareem made perfect sense," Imani said as Hareem limped into the room.

"What 'being about Hareem' made perfect sense?"

"Daddy was the target, not you," Imani said and explained.

"You sure?" Hareem asked Brock.

"I'm sure he stuck to his story and died for it."

"He's dead?" Hareem asked.

Brock nodded.

"Thank you," Hareem said, taking out his phone to send Loonie a text with the news. "What we gonna do now?" Hareem asked, and all eyes turned to Imani.

"Find who did it," Imani said, though she had no idea how she was going to do that.

She had talked to the police only once since the birth-day party shooting. They had taken statements from her, Brock, and Hareem at the hospital, and she hadn't heard from them since. Not that Imani was expecting the police to be much help, but it would have been nice. She looked at Brock.

"I'll check with my contacts in Miami, see if anybody's heard anything," she said.

"I'll do the same," Brock promised. "Who were you hanging out with that night in Miami, boss?"

"Doc, Felix, Headly, and them."

"Check them out too," Imani said to Brock.

"What you want me to do?" Hareem asked.

"Nothing. Don't do anything. Even if Hedrick's crew wanna do something, you do nothing. Understood?" Imani said sternly.

"What if—"

"They won't," Imani said, stopping him. "For some rea-son—probably because she's smart—Diamond doesn't want to fight you. So stand down. If you wanna do some-thing, find the woman on the motorcycle. It's what we should have been doing in the first place. We find her, we find out who sent her."

"Yes, boss," Hareem said and limped out of the room.

For the remainder of the day, Imani, Brock, and Mr. O worked the phones, and Hareem put Martel on finding the woman on the motorcycle.

"What you want me to do when I find her?" Martel asked him.

"Don't kill her, Marty-mar. You bring her ass to me."

The day ended back in Mr. O's room, where Imani and Brock talked while he ate. For his dinner, Kimberly had prepared mixed salad with a low-fat salad dressing that she had made herself, salmon, and green beans with toasted almonds. Nobody had found out anything that would lead them to who wanted Mr. O dead. After he ate, Mr. O said that he was tired, and Imani and Brock left him to rest.

"You hungry?" Imani asked as they headed downstairs.

"Starving."

"What do you feel like eating?"

"Something different. All I've eaten for two days is fast food." He chuckled. "Your boy Hedrick loved him some Burger King."

"Let's go out. You like Mediterranean?"

"I do," he said and opened the front door for her.

"I know a place," Imani said, and she drove them to Beirut Restaurant & Spirits.

Over wine, spinach pie, grilled marinated rack of lamb served with grilled vegetables, a combination of keshek, onion, and paprika, and arugula and parmesan cheese, Imani and Brock got into an animated conversation that bounced back and forth between the topics of how much each missed the other, who was responsible for her father's shooting, and whether they would try again.

"I've been thinking about getting out and going completely legitimate," Imani said, and Brock kept eating as if she hadn't said it. She told him about a couple of businesses that she thought would be a good fit, and still, Brock said nothing. So she asked, "What do you think?"

"Have you talked to your father?"

"No. I'm talking, present tense, to you. I want to know what *you* think."

"I think that you should do whatever you think is best. I know you'll make the right decision." Brock held her hand. "All I know is I wanna be wherever you are, doing whatever you're doing."

"You need to take me home and fuck me," Imani said, and Brock signaled the waiter to bring the check.

As soon as they got to her condo, Brock was all over her. Imani swooned when Brock kissed her. His kisses made her legs feel weak, they made her very wet, and they made Imani want to feel him deep inside. His powerful hands eased the spaghetti straps off her shoulders, and then he reached under Imani's red Carolina Herrera dress, slid her panties to one side, and massaged her throbbing button.

"Undress me," she panted.

Brock smiled. "It would be my pleasure," he said and began removing Imani's dress slowly, as if it were the most important thing that he had ever done in his life. There was almost a reverence to the way he folded the dress and placed it gently on the bed, all the while staring into Imani's eyes. He casually strolled behind Imani and unhooked her bra, then eased it off her shoulders, allowing her full breasts to bounce free. He leaned in and slid his tongue over her hardening nipples. Her body trembled, and Imani hurriedly helped him out of his shirt. He unbuckled and unzipped his pants, removed them, and stepped out of his shorts as Imani peeled down her panties and stepped out of them.

Imani knelt in front of him and stroked his erection up and down as Brock's finger traced her quivering lip. Imani took him into her hot, wet, and wanting mouth. She sucked and then licked slowly, as if his dick were ice cream and she had to have it all. Brock grabbed her hair and guided her.

"I love watching you suck my dick," he said, moaning, and the sound of his voice only made Imani wetter and caused her to suck harder. When he could stand it no longer, he pulled Imani up and tossed her across the bed.

"Come get your pussy. It's been missing you," Imani said and spread her legs.

Brock practically dove between her thighs, because his dick did miss his pussy. In one furious thrust, Brock was inside of Imani, and then he was slamming his entire length in and out of her. Imani held on to his back and wrapped her legs around his waist as he thrust deeper inside her. Each slide in and out made Imani wetter as he pulled her hips back and forth against him.

Imani arched her back, bit her lip, and looked into his piercing eyes as his hands gripped her hips. He thrust into her swiftly, and Imani worked back against him, his chest brushing against her hardened nipples. Imani moaned as his mouth opened, and she felt him swell inside her. She tossed her hips in harmony with his thrusts, greedily milking the pleasure from him.

Chapter Thirty-nine

The next few months brought changes to the Mosley family as Imani began putting her visionary plan for the family's future into motion. Although she expected it, there was very little resistance to the direction she wanted to take them in. To be completely legitimate. Well, maybe not completely, but it certainly was the goal.

As time passed, and his wounds healed, Mr. O's health began to improve, and he felt stronger. He'd be the first to admit that he was nowhere near 100 percent, and there were still concerns about his heart, but he was out of bed and moving around. Imani had expected him to push back against her agenda, but he didn't.

It was the future that her grandparents used to talk to her about, like it was a pipe dream.

"That's why I handed you power," was what he told her. "My way of doing things is done. It's up to you to take us into the future."

What surprised Imani the most was that Hareem just said, "Okay. I'm in."

With Hedrick out of his way, she expected Hareem to ramp up what he was doing and take down Cameron. His elimination would take Hareem one step closer to Diamond and either push her out and bring her on board. But that didn't happen. Hareem did what nobody had expected: he stepped back. All the way back. He all but handed power to Martel so that he could spend the majority of his day being Omeika's father.

Imani's optimistic talk about a different future had a serious impact on him. He would sit there listening, massaging his thigh, as she talked about a future where nobody she loved ever got shot again. Therefore, with a new attitude, Hareem's focus became insuring that Omeika wouldn't grow up aspiring to run a criminal organization, as he and Imani had. His change of attitude made both Cynthia and Loonie happy.

Cynthia had always envisioned a legitimate future for them, so she had no problem with it. As long as Hareem didn't turn his back completely on the drug business and the drug money kept coming in to fuel her ambitions, Cynthia felt her plan was still viable, only now it came with a potential end date. So things were going well for Hareem. One Sunday afternoon, while Hareem was spending the day with Omeika, Cynthia met Loonie for lunch. It went as well as could be expected. The conversation, as expected, centered on Loonie's repeated insistence that she respected their relationship and had no interest in Hareem being anything other than a good father to her daughter.

Although the meeting eased Cynthia's concerns and she came away believing that Loonie would be a good mother and wouldn't not be a problem for her, Cynthia really didn't like her. Loonie didn't care one way or the other, because whether Cynthia liked her or not, by that time, she and Omeika were practically living at the house and were a part of the family. That was where she needed and wanted to be.

When Brock's condo was ready, he moved out of the house, so most nights it was just Loonie, Omeika, Kimberly, and Mr. O at the family house; and Mr. O was happy that she and the baby were there. The problem was that she was enjoying being with Hareem, and she delighted in the time that they were spending together as a family.

As for Imani, everything in her world was absolutely wonderful. Although the words had never escaped either of their mouths, she was in love with Brock, and he was in love with her.

Imani had promoted Ginger to general manager of their charter business, which left her free to focus her attention on other things. While she researched other opportunities, she invested in buying apartment communities to renovate and convert for sale with Alexis. Imani admired and fed off Alexis's drive and determination to accomplish her objectives. She did not allow anything, or anybody, for that matter, to keep her from getting what she wanted. "There is always a way," was what Alexis always said.

Imani had predicted that as time went on, Brock would decide what he wanted to do, and he'd work himself into it, and she was right. When Imani said that they weren't going completely legitimate, she meant that they were going back to focusing on their core business: moving contraband into and out of the country. Other than her father, there was nobody who knew their core business better than Brock.

Everybody concerned was satisfied with the direction that Imani was taking them. Well, almost everybody. De'Shane and Lucius were upset about the new direction. De'Shane had been Mr. O's big moneymaker, and Lucius had once been Mr. O and Imani's right-hand man, or at least he thought he had, but in her new world, they were reduced to little more than Imani's well-paid errand boys. And they didn't like that at all.

"Could you check on this for me? Could you drop this off for me?" De'Shane said, imitating Imani as he and Lucius sat around and talked. "Fuck that shit."

"I know what you mean. She does me the same way," Lucius cosigned.

"Muthafuckin' Brock thinks he ain't got no use for us. That's what the problem is. The nigga thinks he can do everything by his damn self," De'Shane said.

De'Shane saw himself running things and wanted Mr. O to see that he could handle it. De'Shane had been playing the long game, biding his time until he could put his plan into effect. He had always felt that he would use the relationship he planned on building with Imani to his advantage. De'Shane had thought that he could get close to Imani and eventually push her out. Now that fantasy future was dead. Both De'Shane and Lucius saw Brock's influence on Imani as their problem.

"That nigga gots to go," Lucius said.

And the conspiracy to kill Brock was born of that hate.

Chapter Forty

Ever since Hughbert Mosley met Saulo Lorencio, and Saulo took the Mosley family into the smuggling business, the Mosley family had attended an annual meeting hosted by their Venezuelan supplier. Although Mr. O's health wasn't anywhere near good, his gunshot wounds had healed nicely. However, there were still some lingering concerns about his heart. There were complications from the damage done to his heart, he often complained of feeling dizzy and having minor chest pains, and that made him fearful to exert himself. Therefore, the decision was made that he would not attend the annual meeting that year.

Knowing Imani's need to be on top of everything and her desire in years past to accompany her father, Mr. O was surprised that Imani didn't want to go herself.

"You know, Daddy, what you say is true, but I learned a new word recently."

"What's that?"

"Delegate." She smiled.

"A word you never knew before," Mr. O laughed.

"New world, new Imani."

Since he had accompanied Mr. O the past two years, De'Shane felt sure that Imani would tap him to go. However, Imani decided that she would send Brock to the meeting instead. Her decision proved only to intensify the hate that De'Shane had for Brock.

That year's meeting was being held in Noord, Aruba, at the Ritz-Carlton. Imani made reservations for a deluxe suite with a sweeping oceanfront view that could be enjoyed from the wraparound balcony.

"Aruba," Brock said unenthusiastically, not really looking forward to the trip, when she broke the news to him as they sat on the couch in the great room.

Since he had been to a few of these meetings and knew they were largely, if not entirely, ceremonial, he would have been perfectly content to let De'Shane or Lucius go and play the big man. And on top of that, he would miss her. But if it was what Imani wanted him to do, he was all about it.

"I've never been there before," Brock noted.

"I never have either. I think we'll enjoy ourselves there," Imani said matter-of-factly.

"Wait. You're coming with me?"

"I am. I'm just not going to the meeting." She leaned over and kissed him on the cheek. "You go to the meeting, and I'll shop, hit the spa, and go to the beach."

"I wanna go to the beach with you," Brock said, excited that she was going with him. It had gotten to the point where he didn't like being away from her for too long.

"And I'm sure you'll have plenty of time for that. But even though it's all ceremony, you need to be there to represent us." She shook her head. "That is why I will never send either De'Shane or Lucius. You are the image of continued strength and power that I want to project." She giggled. "I don't want people talking behind their backs about how Mr. O must be slipping if he had to send those two."

Aruba's five-star Ritz-Carlton's white sandy beaches sat on the edge of the Caribbean Sea. As promised, their wraparound balcony, with its outdoor dining area, faced the west and offered a breathtaking view of the

Caribbean. The deluxe suite itself was huge: a large living room, a bedroom separated by double doors from the rest of the suite, a fully stocked minibar, two bathrooms with marble vanities, deep soaking tubs, and separate showers.

"They even got the bomb terry-cloth robes and slippers," Brock said.

"Those are nice," Imani said, leaning against his chest and putting her arms around his neck. "I think we should try them on."

"We should shower first," he said, and their lips met.

"I agree, but I think we should work up a good sweat first. Don't you think so?" she said when the kiss ended. And Brock leaned in for a long, passionate kiss that drove them to the bed.

It was shaping up to be the perfect escape from their daily routine and an extraordinary opportunity to truly relax and enjoy each other.

After working up a sweat and showering, Imani and Brock donned their plush terry-cloth robes and slippers and hung out on the balcony before going to the hotel's Madero Pool & Beach Grill, which overlooked a breathtaking stretch of Palm Beach. That evening too was spent at the hotel, where they dined on steaks and fresh seafood at BLT Steak and visited the casino before returning to their suite to prepare for the meeting and make love until they passed out from exhaustion.

Imani's breath stacked up in her throat as he leaned over her and kissed her gently as they lay in bed.

"I'm glad you came along on this trip," Brock whispered and kissed her again with more passion.

"I wanted to share this time with you." *I love you*, she thought, but she still wasn't ready to say those words out loud.

Their lips and tongues intertwined as if they were one. Brock gently eased his hand between her thighs and touched her mound through her wet panties. She was ready for him to take her.

"Ah," she breathed out as he guided his finger into her.

Imani just stared into his eyes, her mouth open on a silent cry of passion.

"I wish this time would never end," he said, rolling her over and entering her slowly.

Inch by delicious inch, Imani thought as her warm, soft wetness enveloped his length. She wrapped her legs around his waist as Brock thrust in and out of her slow and deep.

His deep penetration encouraged Imani to lift her legs up toward her ears. Imani lay there, relishing the sensation, as Brock slid into her. His strokes were slow and long. Her toes curled, Imani screamed, and her walls rippled around his pounding length.

"Right there," Imani told him. She breathed out, receiving the pumps, which hit her spot every time. "Keep fucking me just like that."

Brock didn't stop.

"I'm coming!" she cried.

Brock pulled out, rolled Imani on her side, and slid in behind her. Once she caught her breath, Imani lifted her leg and guided him inside of her again.

Brock sucked on her earlobe, his palm holding her bouncing breast, his fingers tweaking her nipple. Imani took all of him, and her body felt as if it shattered as she rocked back against him until she thought she couldn't handle it anymore.

Imani screamed. "Shit!"

Her scream of passion pulled Brock in.

"I'm coming, I'm coming!" she moaned, feeling his length swell inside her.

And soon they were crying out together and shuddering while uttering each other's names.

Chapter Forty-one

The meeting was to take place at ten the next morning in the Ritz-Carlton ballroom. It was over breakfast on the balcony that Imani announced that she was going to the meeting with Brock.

"What a surprise," Brock said, feigning shock.

"What?" she asked shyly.

"Wasn't that your intention from the jump?"

"No," Imani said, choosing to stare out at the Caribbean instead of making eye contact.

"Come on, Imani. I knew you were going when you said you were going to spend the day shopping." He chuckled. "You're not a shopper. You go shop for what you need, and you get out of there. And since you don't need anything . . ."

"I was gonna do the spa and hit the beach too," she said meekly.

"I knew you intended to be there at the meeting."

"Guilty," she said with her hand in the air. "But it's *your* meeting. I'll just be there as Mr. O's daughter."

Brock looked at Imani curiously for a second or two. "I get it. The whole Latin machismo, patriarchal authority thing."

"Exactly. This is a boys' club. In my traditional role as a woman, I am expected to defer to your male authority. The women that are going to be there will be there strictly as eye candy, and you know that is not who I am."

"I get that too. Then be who you are." He smiled. "You run this."

"Because I don't need to. I know who I am, and that's all that matters."

"Understood, boss."

"Besides, I don't want to run the risk that my being a woman will interfere with business. You know, the Latin machismo thing." Imani smiled.

When Imani and Brock arrived at the ballroom, they were greeted at the doors by Romina del Valle Garcia, their host's personal assistant. "I was very sorry to hear that your father wouldn't be joining us this year," she said when Imani introduced herself.

"He was looking forward to being here, but his health issues wouldn't permit it."

"Please tell Mr. O that Rodrigo sends best wishes to your father and is praying for his recovery."

"I most certainly will," Imani said as Romina leaned close to her.

"With your father's issues, I imagine you will be assuming a much larger role than you have in the past."

"I imagine that I will," Imani said, wondering where that came from.

"Rodrigo has been aware of your role for some time now," she said and stepped back and looked at Brock. "Por favor, disfrute su día y todo lo que el evento tiene para ofrecer," Romina said, telling him to enjoy his day and all that the event had to offer.

"Gracias. Estoy seguro de que lo haré," Brock said, assuring her that he would, and then he escorted Imani into the ballroom. "What was that about?"

Imani leaned closer to Brock. "She was letting me know that she knows you're here strictly as my eye candy."

The entirely ceremonial meeting and the activities that surrounded it stretched from the morning till well into the evening. As would be expected at a gathering of that magnitude, the food was excellent; the alcohol flowed freely; and grandiose speeches, elaborate pledges of loyalty and respect, and outlandish boasts of money and power were plentiful and on display.

"You see why this wasn't me?" Imani said as they wandered around, making connections. She was satisfied with the recognition she had received from Romina del Valle Garcia. *Rodrigo has been aware of your role for some time now* would be the most important words she'd hear all day.

"You sure you don't wanna get drunk and make a speech?" Brock asked her as the day wore on.

"Nope. But you are more than welcome to get up there and pound your chest for the two of us."

Although the event would last well into the evening and a dinner banquet was planned, by late afternoon Imani and Brock had shaken hands with and spoken to as many people as she felt was necessary to accomplish her objectives, so it was time to go.

"We coming back for the banquet?" Brock asked as they left the ballroom to return to their suite.

"No. I made dinner plans."

"You said what now?"

She smiled, looped her arm in his, and rested her head on his shoulder. "I made plans to have a private dinner served on our balcony," Imani said as they walked to the elevator.

"Wow," he said, because he knew how spontaneous Imani liked to be.

"I know, right? Me, Ms. Let's Just Go Do It, actually planned a romantic dinner for us."

That night Imani and Brock enjoyed an enchanting and unforgettable evening. They dined on breaded chicken in a pomodoro sauce, grilled shrimp with white wine–garlic sauce, spaghetti with roasted tomatoes, and Mediterranean sea bass filet. Imani and Brock ended their night as they had the last, making love until they passed out from exhaustion.

The following afternoon they caught an Envoy Air flight to Miami, and following a three-hour layover, they were on their way home. Imani had called Luxury and arranged for them to be picked up at the airport when they arrived in Jacksonville after eleven o'clock. Although she had been promoted to general manager, Ginger had promised to come herself.

"It's my pleasure. After all, you are the very definition of VIP, Imani," she'd said.

Ginger was waiting for them in baggage claim. Once they had gathered their luggage, Imani and Brock followed Ginger to the hourly garage. Ten minutes later they were in the limo and on the road.

As Ginger got off at Butler Boulevard on the way to the house, she saw two cars in her rearview mirror with their bright lights on, and they were coming up on them fast. Thinking that it was just people in a hurry, she slowed down to let the cars pass. That was when the shooting started.

"They're shooting at us!" Brock said, hearing the shells bounce off the bullet-resistant glass.

Not knowing that Imani would be with him, De'Shane and Lucius had planned to ambush and kill Brock.

When the car De'Shane was driving rammed the back of the limousine, Ginger swerved, but she recovered quickly and kept going. Lucius pulled up alongside them in the other car and began firing out the window. Ginger stepped on the gas as the ambushers continued firing. De'Shane pulled up alongside the limousine and rammed it.

"I need a gun!" Brock said, and Imani pressed a spot on the door. A panel slid open, and behind it stood two guns.

"This limo comes fully stocked," Imani said, handing Brock a gun.

When De'Shane rammed them again from the back and Lucius hit them again from the side, the limousine fishtailed and crashed into a tree. Ginger hit her head against the steering wheel and then against the windshield. Both men brought their cars to a screeching halt and jumped out, firing.

While Brock pulled Ginger out of the car, Imani grabbed the other gun and got out, firing blindly into the bright lights but not hitting anything. Once Ginger was out of the line of fire, Brock joined the firefight. He aimed and shot out the headlights on one of the cars. Then he caught sight of a familiar figure.

"Lucius?" he questioned before he shot him twice in the chest.

When Brock began firing at Lucius, De'Shane kept shooting as he ran back to his car. He jumped in, slammed it in reverse, and sped away. Brock ran after him, firing, until De'Shane was out of sight.

"Brock!" Ginger yelled. "Imani's been shot!"

Chapter Forty-two

That night, it was Brock who leaning against the wall and looking out the same window that Imani had the day that Mr. O was shot. He had grown tired of sitting and had got up and paced for a while before ending up at the window. Although he was used to waiting, this was different, much different, because it was Imani who was badly hurt and he was in love with her.

"You should have told her when you had the chance," he said aloud.

"You say something, Brock?" Hareem asked.

"Just talking to myself."

Hareem nodded. "I understand."

After De'Shane had driven off, Brock had run to Imani. She was lying on the ground, holding her stomach. Ginger got the first-aid kit from the trunk, and Brock tended to Imani's wound. Then Ginger tried to get the limo started.

"Hold on, Imani," Brock urged, worry etched all over his face.

Once the limo started up, the decision was quickly made not to wait on an ambulance, and Brock carried Imani to the limo. Ginger drove like a streak and got to the hospital in minutes.

They hadn't been there for long when Ginger saw a nurse pointing at them, and two men began walking in their direction. "Here come the boys." Seeing how distraught Brock was, Ginger stood up. "I'll talk to them."

Brock sat there with his head hanging low as she told the police what had happened. When Ginger had answered all their questions, the detectives turned to Brock.

"Do you have a license to carry a firearm, sir?" one cop asked.

"No."

"Where'd you get the gun?" the other cop asked.

Ginger jumped in again as Brock's chin hit his chest. She explained that the weapon used was registered to the company, Luxury Private Charters, which was owned by the victim, and that both she and the victim were licensed to carry a firearm.

"But you don't have a license to carry a firearm, do you, sir?" asked the first cop.

"I was hurt, and she was shot. What did you expect him to do?" Ginger interjected.

"If we have any more questions, we'll be in touch," the second cop said, and then they left the waiting room.

As the police were leaving, they passed Hareem coming in with Cynthia. She stuck her tongue out, and he gave the officers the finger, and they continued on their way into the waiting room. Once Ginger had told them what had happened, and that nobody had come to talk to them about Imani's condition, they sat down to wait.

"You call Daddy?" Hareem asked.

"I did," Ginger answered, because Brock had said only one word since they'd arrived there. His heart hurt, and it was hard for him to breathe at times. He wanted to step outside to get some air, but he didn't want to miss any news from the doctor. And that was when the pacing began.

Brock had settled into a spot at a window when he looked up and saw Mr. O slowly making his way into the waiting room. Everybody looked up when he walked in, and then their eyes opened wide and mouths dropped when Loonie walked in right behind him, pushing Omeika in her stroller.

Cynthia glanced at Loonie and thought, *She is sucking up to Mr. O, trying to get in good with him.* She rolled her eyes as Hareem bounced up to help his father sit down. Then she smiled, because if the roles were reversed, she would be doing the same thing.

"How is she?" Mr. O asked.

"We haven't heard anything yet," Hareem said, and Mr. O pointed at Brock. He was still staring out the window and not speaking.

"He all right?"

Hareem shook his head. "Not good."

"Help me up," Mr. O said, and once Hareem had helped him get to his feet, Mr. O went and stood next to Brock.

"You okay?"

Brock shook his head. "No, sir."

Mr. O put his arm around Brock. "Come sit down, son."

"Yes, sir." The two men went and sat down.

Loonie saw the way Brock was looking, and it hurt her heart. Brock had been the first one to welcome her to the family, and as she spent more time at the house, they had developed a friendship of their own.

She approached Mr. O and Brock. "Can I get you anything, Brock?" she asked.

He looked up slowly. "Some water, please."

"I'll get you some," she said and went to get it.

The second Loonie left the area, Omeika started crying. Hareem started to get up to see about his daughter, but Cynthia touched his hand.

"I got her," she said, and she took the baby out of the stroller.

Even though she didn't want one of her own, Cynthia loved other people's babies, and she was good with them. Therefore, when Loonie got back with the water for Brock, Omeika had calmed down and was asleep in Cynthia's arms.

"You want me to take her?" Loonie asked.

"I got her," Cynthia said as a doctor walked into the waiting room and all eyes turned toward her.

"Your daughter was shot in the abdomen," she said, sitting down next to Mr. O. "And the bullet nipped the stomach. We were able to remove the bullet and repair the damage to the stomach. She's going to be fine in a couple of days. She just needs to rest."

"Can I see her?" Mr. O asked as the doctor stood.

"She is in recovery now, but once she's moved to a room, you'll be able to see her," the doctor said and walked away.

When Imani opened her eyes, the first person she saw was Brock. After the family was permitted to see her, the nurse sent them home. Seeing the way that he was looking at Imani when he asked if he could stay, the nurse felt compassion for Brock. They allowed him to stay and watch over her while they monitored her closely for any complications from surgery. He sat in the chair next to the bed and stayed awake, watching her chest rise and fall, knowing that she'd be fine but praying to God that she opened her eyes soon.

"Hi," Imani said softly hours later, and Brock looked over at her.

He squeezed her hand. "How do you feel?"

Imani coughed lightly, and it hurt. "Sleepy, and my throat hurts."

"The nurse said that's normal. You'll feel better once the anesthesia wears off completely."

She tried to sit up a little; it made her body ache. "I feel nauseated." She put her hand on her wound. "I guess this is how you feel when you get shot."

"Now imagine it without the anesthesia," he said, holding her hand tightly.

Now that he knew for sure that she was going to be all right, it was as if all the stress and worry melted away.

"What happened?" she asked him.

"What do you remember?" He yawned.

"I remember getting out of the car and shooting, but not much more after that."

"It was Lucius."

"Lucius Cunningham?" Imani asked, not wanting to believe that one of her own men had tried to kill her.

Brock nodded. "Lucius and another man. I want to say that it was De'Shane, but I didn't get a good look at him."

"Are you sure it was Lucius?" she asked, still refusing to believe it.

"I killed him, so yeah, Imani, I'm sure that it was Lucius."

She closed her eyes and turned her head away. "I don't understand." The thought of it made her mad.

"I don't understand either. But I'll find out what's really going on. I'm just glad that you're gonna be all right."

"If De'Shane was involved, kill him."

"That was my intention, but thanks for sanctioning it, boss," he said, and he kissed her lightly on the cheek. "You rest now, and I'll take care of it."

Imani closed her eyes, thinking that all this was going on and she still had no idea who was behind the hit on her father.

It was a couple of hours later when the family arrived at the hospital. It was Loonie that noticed how tired Brock looked, and offered to drive him home. At first, he refused, saying that he was fine, but after a while, he gave in and agreed to leave. He kissed Imani and promised to be back to see her in a couple of hours. She saw the look on his face.

"Get some rest, Brock. Please," she whispered.

"I will," he said and left with Loonie after she handed the baby over to the care of Cynthia. When she dropped him off, Brock waved and watched her drive away before he got in his car and went looking for De'Shane.

After leaving the scene of the failed ambush, De'Shane's first thought had been, What was she doing there? He'd driven away, checking his rearview mirror and wondering if Brock had recognized him. If he hadn't, maybe De'Shane could show up at the house in the morning and claim to know nothing about the incident. De'Shane stepped on the gas, knowing that was probably the stupidest thing he could possibly do. Whether Brock had seen him or not didn't matter. He had to get away from there and disappear. Mr. O's reach was long, and it extended to several countries. That meant he would need money and a lot of it. He headed for his house to pack and get the money that he had there, but De'Shane couldn't get access to the rest of money he'd need to survive until morning. All he could do then was hide and wait.

When Brock got to his house, he saw De'Shane coming out of his house, dragging a suitcase, with a duffel bag slung over his shoulder. He jumped out of his car as De'Shane walked to his car. He saw Brock coming.

"Hey, De'Shane!" Brock put up his hands. "I just want to talk to you."

Any chance of that happening ended when De'Shane dropped the bags and started shooting at Brock. Brock took cover, got his gun out, and fired back. De'Shane fired a couple of shots and then took off running. Brock got to his feet and ran behind him.

De'Shane wheeled around and shot at Brock. He was able to make it to cover and shoot again, and then he took off running and kept firing shots at Brock. Brock went after De'Shane again, reloading his gun as he ran.

Brock followed him down the street, firing shots all the way. When De'Shane turned and pulled the trigger, he found that his gun was empty. He threw the gun at Brock and kept running. Brock stopped, aimed, and fired; the bullet hit De'Shane in the leg, and he stumbled and fell.

Brock walked up to De'Shane and stood over him.

"Don't kill me!" De'Shane shouted, with his hands raised.

"Why'd you and Lucius try to kill Imani?"

"We weren't trying to kill Imani. We didn't know she was with you!"

Brock raised his gun, put three in the other man's chest and one in his head.

Chapter Forty-three

After spending a few days recovering from being shot by one of her own men, Imani was released from the hospital. While she lay in bed alone at night, recuperating, she tried to reconcile what had happened. Brock had told her what De'Shane had said before he killed him.

Now that they were dead, other people in her organization were talking. It seemed that everybody knew that De'Shane and Lucius had been dissatisfied with the new direction in which Imani was taking the business. They had been jealous of Brock and had thought that he was trying to push them out. Although Imani had always known that they were interested in her, she still had a problem believing that they were that jealous of her relationship with Brock to want to kill him.

It made her think, and it made her realize that it was her fault. Imani should have realized that she had taken away the very things that had defined them—position, access, power—and she had handed them all to Brock. She had expected pushback to her plan, but Imani had never expected pushback from *them*.

Lesson learned.

Over the weeks that followed, Imani's health improved, and things slowly returned to what they'd been before she got shot. She again focused on making her family legit. Her getting shot had only reinforced the need to make that happen. In addition to looking at apartment complexes to flip into condos and vacation rentals, she and Alexis put a 1.8-million-dollar bid on the Jacksonville Plaza Hotel & Suites near the airport.

Ginger introduced her to a woman who made her own lotions, cleansers, and skin-care products for women of color, and Imani invested in the woman's start-up skincare and beauty company. With Imani's backing, this budding entrepreneur planned to expand into makeup, artisanal soaps, dry shampoo, body butters, scrubs, and other natural beauty products. Imani was also looking into investing in a woman who was seeking to expand her virtual-assistant service.

As for Brock, Imani's plan fit right into what he had said he wanted. *No more penitentiary-type chances.* Well, since he'd been out of prison, he had gone back on that promise, but to him, each case had been warranted. When Brock had killed Sonny, it was revenge for the past ten years of his life. He had killed Lucius and De'Shane because they deserved to die for trying to kill him and Imani. However, the murder of Kevin Hedrick and Brock's involvement in the weapons business were harder to justify.

It's what Imani needed me to do, he thought, and that was enough justification for him.

He had found a place for himself in Imani's new world. With his knowledge of the weapons and shipping business, he was exploring the possibility of bidding on government defense contracts.

As for Hareem, he found himself living his best life. He had handed power to Martel, who turned out to be much better at running the operation than Hareem ever was. Therefore, even though he had told Martel that Cameron was hands off and had given up his pursuit of Diamond, his drug business was expanding.

Turns out war is *bad for business*, he thought, but he would never admit that to Imani.

With time on his hands, he was free to spend his days with Loonie and Omeika and handle whatever task Cynthia assigned him to further her objectives.

She and Hareem were out shopping at the St. Johns Town Center when Cynthia saw a woman with long, straight black hair come out of J. Jill and get on a motorcycle.

"Look at the woman," she said and pointed her out.

"What woman?"

"The one with the long black hair."

"I see her." He stared intently at her for a second or two. "Take a picture of her," Hareem said, and they both quickly got out their phones. While Cynthia captured images of the woman putting on her helmet, Hareem called Imani.

"I'm at Town Center, and I'm looking at a woman with long, straight black hair, and she just got on a motorcycle."

Imani looked at Brock as they sat across from each other in the great room at the house. "You think it's the same woman that shot Daddy?"

"I don't know. Cynthia took pictures of her." He paused. "You want me to step to her?"

"No. Follow her and send me the images."

"I'm on it," Hareem said. He and Cynthia ran to their car, which happened to be nearby, and a few minutes later they followed the woman when she drove away.

"What?" Brock asked when Imani hung up.

"Hareem said that he saw a woman with long, straight black hair getting on a motorcycle."

"Where?"

"Town Center. Cynthia's sending pictures," Imani said. Seconds later she received a text with images attached from Cynthia.

Imani looked at the images Cynthia had captured, and then she showed them to Brock.

"I know her." Brock paused when he saw the look on Imani's face. "At least we met."

"How do you know her?" Imani asked with just a tinge of jealousy in her voice.

Brock smiled. "I was with Mr. O one night when he had a meeting, and I met her at the hotel bar."

"And?" Imani said, all but demanding to know what else had happened at the bar with this woman.

"And we talked until your father was ready to go," he replied, thinking that her jealous look was cute.

Imani thought for a second about it. "That was the day that Daddy met with Ferdie at the hotel, isn't it?" The timeline was important for two reasons. Other than the obvious, it told Imani that Brock may have been at some hotel bar, flirting with another woman, but that had been before they got together. That made it a little better, but not much.

"Yeah, it was," Brock said, nodding his head, as he recalled the conversation he'd had with the woman. "She said that she was from Miami and that she was there to meet somebody who was staying at the hotel."

"You think she was there to meet Ferdie?"

"Maybe. I don't know," Brock said and got up from the chair.

"Where are you going?"

"To look at the security footage from that day. I want to compare her bike to the one the shooter was riding." He held out his hand to help Imani up. "You coming?"

"I sure am," she said.

They went into the game room, where the security system was housed. Once Brock cued up the footage, he and Imani ran it over and over again, slowing it down, capturing still images, and comparing them to the images that Cynthia had sent them. It looked like the same bike, but they couldn't be sure, since Cynthia's images were blurry.

It was right about then that Hareem called and said that he had lost the woman in traffic.

"What now?" Imani asked.

"I think I should talk to her to feel her out," Brock replied.

"How are you gonna do that?"

"I have her number."

Imani's eyes narrowed. "The two of you exchanged numbers?"

"I never called her." Brock paused to keep from laughing. "It was more to be polite."

"Right. You could have politely said no when she offered it," Imani said, and Brock just looked at her.

"That was so not the move," he chuckled. "So, you want me to call her or not?"

"Call her."

Brock dialed the number, and for Imani's comfort, he put the call on speaker.

"Brock Whitehall," Renata answered. "This is a surprise. How have you been?"

"I'm awesome, Renata," Brock said enthusiastically. "Everything seems to be going my way these days," he added, taking Imani's hand and bringing it to his lips.

"That's wonderful to hear."

"How about you, Renata? How have you been since the last time we spoke?"

"They're getting better. Things were a little helter-skelter in my world for a while, but they are getting better. I have to say, hearing from you has really put a smile on my face," Renata said, and Imani put her finger in her mouth.

"Well, then, I'm glad that I called," Brock said, and each of them laughed lightly.

"To what do I owe the pleasure?"

"I'm going to be in Miami in a day or two, and I'm hoping that we can get together . . . if you're free." He paused and then dropped his voice an octave. "See if we can't finish our conversation."

"I would love that, but I'm not in Miami. I'm actually in Jacksonville for a couple of days, tying up some loose ends."

"And you didn't call." Brock chuckled. "Should I be hurt?" he asked, sounding sincere, with his hand on his heart.

Imani folded her arms across her chest.

"And I apologize for that. I could lie and say that I was going to call you but just hadn't had the chance, but I'll just say that I am truly sorry and promise to make it up to you."

"Over cocktails and good conversation?"

"For starters," Renata said.

Imani sat up in her chair, shaking her head. *Oh . . . hell . . . no.*

"Sounds like a date," Brock said.

"Just tell me when and where you want me," Renata said flirtatiously.

"Do you know where the Bay Street Bar and Grill is downtown?"

"I do."

"Why don't you meet me there tonight? Does eight o'clock work for you?" Brock asked, enjoying the looks he was getting from Imani.

"That sounds perfect. I will meet you there at eight."

"Looking forward to it," Brock said, and he ended the call, put down the phone, and looked at Imani.

"I'm not sure I like sitting here listening to you mack another woman." She pouted. "And I'm going with you."

Chapter Forty-four

At 7:45 p.m. Imani walked into the Bay Street Bar and Grill, ordered a drink, and found a seat where she wouldn't be too conspicuous. As she sat there sipping her cocktail, she took a second or two to examine her motives for being there. Although it was true that they had a plan working and she was a part of that plan, her motives were a bit more basic. Renata was a beautiful woman, a beautiful woman who seemed very interested in getting together with her man. It wasn't that she didn't trust Brock with Renata, or at least that was what she was able to convince herself of, but she was very interested to see how he would interact with her. Or at least that was what she was able to convince herself of.

It was a little before eight when Imani saw Renata walk into the Bay Street Bar and Grill and be seated at a table. "Oh, no, this bitch don't got on her 'Fuck me' outfit," Imani grumbled as she squinted at the animal-print minidress with the zipper in the front, which was zipped down to her cleavage, and the woman's over-the-knee black leather boots.

Imani sucked her teeth, got out her phone, and called Brock. She knew that they wanted to observe Renata when she arrived, and that the plan was for him to wait outside until Renata was seated. This would give him a chance to check out the bike and Imani a chance to observe her. However, since Renata had arrived in an Uber, that plan had gone out the window.

"She's at a table," Imani spit into her phone when Brock picked up.

"On my way in," Brock said. He quickly got out of his car and headed inside.

Imani rolled her eyes and thought again about her motives for being there as Renata smiled brightly and waved enthusiastically as Brock walked in.

Look at her titties just bouncing, Imani thought and shook her head.

"Hello, Brock. It's good to see you again." Renata stood up and gave him a not so polite hug, which made Imani's fists ball.

"How are you, Renata?" He stepped back and took her hands in his. "You look amazing this evening."

"Thank you, Brock. You look very handsome yourself," Renata said, taking in the single-breasted gray-plaid silk suit that Imani had picked out for him to wear. Never in a million years had Imani thought she would ever dress her man for a date with another woman.

Imani looked on, wishing that she had invested in some kind of listening device so she could hear what Brock was saying to Renata that had her smiling and laughing.

Titties just bouncing. Imani shook her head.

The conversation was a little uncomfortable and forced at first, but after drinks were served, the conversation began to flow. As they had the last time they talked, they talked about Miami. But this time Brock moved the conversation away from places they'd both had been to people that they both knew. As he expected, they knew a lot of the same people, and both shared funny stories about them. But when he mentioned Mr. O's name, Renata's expression changed, and he could see the hate in her eyes as she mumbled, "We've met." Brock quickly moved on.

Now that he had gotten what he'd come for, Brock was ready to go. He looked at Imani and nodded. That meant that they had gotten to the part of the plan that Imani was looking forward to. When he gave her the signal, Imani quickly called his phone. The plan was to make it seem like there was an emergency, and so he would have to leave the restaurant right away.

His phone rang. "I need to take this," he said, looking at his phone's display. "I'm sorry."

"No problem," Renata giggled. "I promise not to eaves-drop too much."

Brock chuckled. "I'll only be a minute," he said, then turned slightly and swiped TALK on the little screen. "Hello."

"Having fun?"

"Not really. What's up?"

"I just assumed, given the way she keeps shaking her titties in your face, that you were having a ball."

"I haven't really been paying attention to that, but I see why that might create a problem for you. What do you need me to do?"

"I need you to say good night to Miss Bouncy Titties and leave. I'll take it from here."

"I'm on it," Brock said. He ended the call, faced Renata, explained the situation, and apologized for having to run out on her again. After they made a date for the following evening, Brock dropped a fifty on the table to cover the check and left.

Now that Brock was gone, Imani sat and watched Renata as she took out her phone and made a call. And then Renata sat there for another twenty minutes, sip-ping her drink and periodically checking her phone, before she signaled for the check. That was Imani's cue to head for her car and wait for Renata to come out of the restaurant. When Renata did and then got in her car and drove away, Imani followed her.

When Imani got to the house, Brock was already there waiting for her. Imani told Brock that she had followed Renata to the Hyatt downtown.

"You know what room she's in?"

"No. But I have a girlfriend that works in security there. I'm sure that she'll be more than happy to tell me what room she's in for a couple hundred dollars."

"So what you wanna do?"

"Go down there and kill her."

Brock took a deep breath. "I think it's time we tell the old man what's going on."

"I do too," Imani said and held out her hand. "But wouldn't you rather just go down there and kill her?"

"First things first."

They walked up the stairs hand in hand and went to Mr. O's bedroom. The door was closed when they got there. Imani tapped on it lightly.

"It's not locked," Loonie called.

When they walked in, Omeika was asleep on the bed next to Mr. O, and Loonie was sitting in the chair next to the bed, watching television.

"We need to talk to you for a minute, Daddy," Imani said, and without having to be asked, Loonie stood up and picked up Omeika.

"Careful not to wake her," Imani said and then stood quiet as mother and daughter left the room.

Mr. O turned off the television. "What's up?" he asked when Loonie had shut the door behind her.

"We think we might know who shot you," Imani began, and they both took a seat and told Mr. O what they knew and suspected at that point.

"Do you know if Ferdie had any children?" Brock asked.

Mr. O laughed. "Ferdie had many children. The man never met a woman that he didn't want to fuck and get pregnant. But there was one, the youngest one, a daughter. She was his favorite. I can't remember her name, but I remember that she was very close to him."

Imani showed him the images of Renata that Cynthia had sent. "That her?"

"I don't know. I haven't seen her since she was a little girl." He looked at Brock. "Pretty woman, though."

"Very," Brock cosigned, and Imani just looked between the two of them.

"I think I know somebody that can tell us if that's his daughter or not," Mr. O said, taking his phone from under his pillow, where he had hidden it from Omeika, who loved playing with phones. He dialed a number, and someone picked up. "Manny, Big O here. What's going on, partner?"

"How's it hanging, *mi amigo*?"

"A little to the left today, and that's why I'm calling."

"This sounds serious, my friend. What's up?"

"You ever meet Ferdie's youngest daughter?"

"Renata, yes," he said, and Mr. O could hear the smile in his voice. "Many times."

"Then if I sent you a picture, you'd recognize her, right?"

"Of course I would. Some women are unforgettable."

"Hold on," Mr. O said, and then he gave Imani the number to send the image.

"That's her," Manny said when he received it. "That is Renata Antonella Fernandez-Cano. Ferdie's pride and joy." He paused. "Now, if I may, why do you ask?"

"Just curious," Mr. O said and quickly ended the call before Manny asked too many more questions. "That's her, all right." He paused. "You know, I thought about the possibility that it was about Ferdie. You know, thinking that whoever tried to kill me believed that I was responsible for Ferdie getting murdered."

Imani and Brock both looked at each other and then at Mr. O.

"How come you never said anything about this before?" Imani asked.

"Because we all agreed at the time that we hadn't done any business that would conflict with his in years." He shrugged his shoulders. "I didn't even think about it."

Chapter Forty-five

Imani was about to ask her father what he wanted her to do, but before she could get the words out, Mr. O saved her the trouble.

"What are you gonna do?" he asked.

She thought for a second about Hareem going after Hedrick without being sure that he was responsible.

"Find out if we're right about her. She may be Ferdie's daughter and have black hair, but that doesn't mean she's the one that tried to have you killed."

Mr. O nodded from satisfaction with her answer. He was so proud of how Imani had stepped up and wielded the power he had handed her. He picked up the TV remote.

"Then why you still standing here?" he said and turned the television back on.

Brock stood up.

"No reason," Imani said and stood up too.

They left the room and went back downstairs to what was slowly becoming her office, as the space had been taking on more of Imani's personality and less of her father's. She was the boss now; Imani held absolute power over their business. So, now that she had constructed the plan, all she needed to do now was outline how it was gonna get done. She sat down at her desk.

"I think we need to talk to Renata. Lay it all out for her and see what she says," she offered.

"I agree with you except for one thing," Brock said.

"What's that?"

"I think that I should go without you."

"Why?"

"Because if we're right, she already tried to kill your father. There is no way I'm going to take the chance of her killing you. So, no, Imani, I don't think you should go, for your own protection."

"But . . . ," Imani said quickly, because she really wanted to get in Renata's face, but she knew he was right. She exhaled. "Okay. Let's hear your plan, because I know that you have one."

"I do." Brock smiled. "And there is a part in my plan for you to do what you really wanna do."

Imani smiled coyly. "What do I really wanna do?"

"Kill her."

"You fuckin' right I do," Imani spit, allowing her anger to surge to the surface.

"I know you do. So here's the plan," Brock said, and when he was done laying it out, Imani was happy with it.

The Hyatt Regency Riverfront, located adjacent to the bright blue lights of Jacksonville's iconic Main Street Bridge, was Brock's destination. As he drove across the bridge, Brock looked out at the panoramic view of the St. Johns River on his way into downtown. When he arrived at the Hyatt, he parked, went straight to the suite that Imani's contact at the hotel had said Renata was in, and knocked on the door.

"Brock!" a surprised Renata exclaimed when she flung open the door after gazing through the peephole. She had taken off her animal-print minidress and was wearing a silk leopard-print robe.

"Hello, Renata."

"What are you doing here? And how did you find me?"

"I'm here because I work for Orpheus Mosley, and I came to ask you a question. Can I come in?"

Renata looked at Brock; now that he had mentioned Orpheus Mosley, she knew exactly why he was there. The man that she had had drinks with a few hours ago and had thought about sleeping with was there to kill her. Renata stepped aside and allowed Brock into her suite, thinking about how she was going to get to her gun. But she hoped that wouldn't be necessary.

"I know what you want to ask me, and the answer is yes. I'm the one that was on the motorcycle that day."

Brock took out his gun and pointed it at Renata. She put her hands up. "Mr. O didn't have your father killed. He came to Mr. O for help. Ferdie said some of his people were trying to push him out."

"I know."

"You do?"

"I do now. Please, Brock, before you kill me, give me a chance to explain."

He cocked the hammer. "Let's hear it."

"Can I sit?" she asked, lowering her hands slowly by running them along her sides and then down her hips. "You can see that I don't have a gun."

He looked around the room. "Go ahead," Brock said, motioning with his gun toward the chair by the window. "Have a seat, but remember, even though I just came to talk, I will kill you."

"I'm sure you will. And I am very sorry this happened. But I was sure that Orpheus Mosley was responsible for my father's death," Renata said as she sat down and seductively crossed her legs. "I was in Spain when my father called and told me about his problems. That's why he was in Jacksonville. He said that he was here to make a deal with the men who were trying to push him out. That's when I saw Mr. O at the hotel the day that we met. I was certain that he was the one, and when my father wouldn't give in, Mr. O had him killed."

"Ferdie asked Mr. O for money, but when we came to give it to him, he was gone," Brock explained. "Mr. O didn't have him killed."

"The men responsible for my father's death made that clear to me after his funeral."

"Then you know who these men are?"

Renata nodded. "Vicente Pedicini, Alejandro Vega, and Emerico Martinez. That is why I am here. I found where these animals are hiding, and I came here to kill them."

"Need help?" Brock lowered his weapon. There was nothing that Renata had said that surprised him. It was almost exactly what he had expected her to say. In fact, it was part of his plan.

Renata looked at Brock curiously. "You came here to kill me. Why would you help me kill them?"

"These are the men who are responsible for Mr. O's shooting. They have to die."

Renata smiled. "That is a very enlightened attitude for you to have about the matter."

"But it does make sense. So, do you want to go kill the people responsible for your father's death, or should I just shoot you now and call it a night?" Brock said and raised his weapon.

Renata smiled seductively. "Now that we've worked out our differences, I can think of some *other things* we could do, but . . ." She stood up as Brock looked at her and imagined what those *other things* would feel like. "Let's go kill those animals."

Once Renata had changed into something a little more appropriate to hunt down her father's killers and had got her gun, she and Brock left her suite and climbed in his car. He had an idea where they would find the three men. Twenty minutes later he parked the car again and checked his weapon; then he and Renata walked toward Mojitos Libre Bar. Brock opened the door, and then he followed Renata inside, with their guns drawn.

"Do you see them?" Brock asked, looking around the small spot.

"No, but they're here. We passed their car on the way in," she said as they put their guns away and moved deeper into the bar.

When Alejandro and Emerico came out of the back room, they saw Renata and immediately drew their guns and began shooting at her. Brock grabbed Renata's hand and pulled her under a table for cover. Some people inside the bar ran outside, and others dove under the tables for cover and stayed there with their hands covering their heads while the shooting continued.

"I guess I don't have to tell you that's them," Renata said, and she pulled her gun.

He took out his guns. "I figured that out."

As the music continued to play, Brock got off a couple of shots at the two men. Alejandro fired blindly at them as he ran for the exit. Brock stood up, fired at him. Once he made it to cover, Alejandro fired at Brock. Brock returned fire and hit Alejandro three times in the chest.

When Renata stuck her head out to take a look around, she was immediately fired upon, and she hit the floor for cover. When the shooting stopped, she rose slowly from the floor and then saw Emerico with his weapon raised. He fired at her and dropped back behind a table for cover. She fired back, dropped to the floor again, and then watched Emerico run to the back of the club. Renata scrambled to her feet and went after him.

He ran into an office, flipped over a desk, took cover, and waited for Renata to come running through the door. When Renata reached the door, she fired twice, and Emerico shot at the doorway until his gun was empty. When she heard his empty gun clicking, Renata entered the office and walked up to him, smiling.

"Where's Pedicini?" she snarled.

"He's at our place," Emerico said, and Renata shot him twice in the head just as Brock ran in the room.

"You know where the other one is?" Brock asked, and Renata spit in Emerico's face.

"Yes." Renata reloaded her gun. "I followed them there yesterday," she said as they made their way through the stunned crowd of patrons at Mojitos Libre.

Brock and Renata ran to his car, and Renata gave him directions as he sped through the streets of Jacksonville. When they got to the apartments that Renata had followed the men to the day before, she pointed out the man in front of the building who was standing sentry.

"Wait here," she said and got out of the car.

Brock watched the smile on the man's face broaden as the beautiful Renata walked right up to him. Then she put her gun to the man's head and pulled the trigger. When he went down, Brock got out of the car and moved the body out of sight as she headed for the breezeway.

"I don't see anybody else," he whispered when he caught up with her.

They moved quickly through the breezeway, up the stairs to the second floor, and down the passage to the fourth apartment on the right, where she believed Pedicini had set up his operation. The operation that he had stolen from her father. She paced back and forth like a nervous cat in front of the door while Brock went to work on the lock. When he was done, he checked his weapons; Renata opened the door, and they stepped inside.

"Look out!" Brock yelled when he saw Pedicini.

Pedicini fired a few shots at them and ran to the back of the apartment. Brock and Renata moved quickly but carefully through the darkened apartment, and they got to the bedroom in time to see Pedicini jump off his balcony. As Renata turned and ran out of the apartment,

Brock went over the balcony after him. When he got to his feet down below, he saw Pedicini running along the wall in the back of the building. He stopped, fired at Brock, and then he ran.

Brock went after him and stopped at the edge of the building as Pedicini reached the parking lot. When he saw Renata come out of the building, Pedicini fired and tried to make it to cover on the other side of the wall. Brock stepped up and fired at him. While Pedicini exchanged fire with Brock, he didn't see that Renata was working her way to get behind him. Once she was set, Renata raised her gun and shot Pedicini in the back three times. The impact of the bullets forced his body onto the hood of a car. As his lifeless body slowly slid to the ground, Renata walked up and stood over him.

"This is for my father." Renata spit on his body and then emptied her clip.

Brock dashed over to where she stood. "We need to go."

Brock and Renata ran back to his car, and he drove away from there as quickly as possible. They headed back to the Hyatt, parked, dashed inside, and made a beeline for the elevators. When they reached her suite, Renata opened the door and stepped over the threshold, envisioning how the rest of her night with Brock would be, and turned on the lights. Imani was waiting there, with a gun in her hand.

"What's this about?" Renata asked as Brock closed the door behind him.

"You tried to kill my father," Imani said.

And then she shot Renata in the head.

Chapter Forty-six

Alexis Fox woke up when her alarm went off at eight the following morning, but she didn't get up. She swiped the SNOOZE button. Alexis had been out late the night before and hadn't got to sleep until almost four, so she was tired. Knowing that she had another long day ahead of her, after the third snooze, Alexis checked for new listings that would fit her clients' criteria, and then she got up and went to get in the shower. Forty-five minutes later, dressed in a gray and black Alexander McQueen "Prince of Wales" virgin wool suit and Gucci "Silvie" chain-heel sandals, Alexis Fox got in her Avalon hybrid and headed out for another long day at work.

That morning she had two clients to show properties to and a final walk-through with a buying client, and then she would rush back to her office to attend closings with other clients. Later that afternoon, Alexis had to go to The Park at Atlantic Beach, the property that she owned with Imani. She had to negotiate contracts, set up repairs for newly vacated units, and schedule a meeting with the service technicians. And then Alexis had a meeting with Imani. And that evening they were going to present their final offer for the Jacksonville Plaza Hotel & Suites.

Nothing went the way she had planned it that morning: her first client of the day was late, and then he was indecisive about what he was looking for. That pushed everything back, and Alexis had to be rescheduled her afternoon meeting with Imani.

"I'm not going to be able to make our strategy session, Imani. It's has been a crazy day."

Imani was at home, in her office with Brock, talking about the events of the previous evening and how those events may affect them in the future.

"No problem. I was going to call and tell you that I was tied up with something too," Imani said.

"But we are still on for tonight, right?"

"Most definitely."

"Great."

"See you tonight," Imani said and ended the call and looked at Brock.

"Who was that?"

"Alexis. We're closing on the hotel tonight, and I think she's a little nervous. This is a big deal for her."

"For you too. Unless you own another hotel you haven't told me about."

"Okay, okay, it's a big deal for me too. I'm not as nervous about it as she is. That's all I was saying." Imani paused. "Now, you were saying . . ."

"I was saying that this thing may not be over," Brock said.

After she had put a bullet between Renata's eyes, Imani had placed the gun on Renata's chest and had left the Hyatt with Brock. On her way home, Imani had called her friend who worked security at the hotel. For a couple of thousand dollars, she was more than happy to manipulate the security footage so neither Imani nor Brock would be seen on tape in the hotel that night.

"Why do you think that?" Imani asked now. As far as she was concerned, her putting a bullet in Renata's brain was pretty final.

"Because there were two people on that bike. Renata and the one that did the shooting."

"You're right. I didn't even think about that," Imani said, and she thought that she needed to get better at seeing the bigger picture. She looked over at Brock, and for so many reasons, she was glad that she had him.

"Either the shooter was hired, or it was personal to them."

"Like it was for Renata."

"There are two ways that could go. Hired gun moves on to the next job."

"But if it's personal, they'll be back."

"Especially if they tie Renata's murder to us."

"Which they won't," Imani added quickly.

"Whoever it is will be after us."

"And we'll be ready for them." Imani looked intently at Brock. "Right?"

"Right. But I don't think that we have anything to worry about."

"Why do you think that?"

"Because Renata was alone. If it were personal for the shooter, they would have been right there with Renata."

"I agree." Imani paused to think. "But I think we need to be proactive about this and find out who the shooter was. I think that makes more sense than waiting for her to blindside us."

"Her?"

Imani had watched the video countless times, and that was always the impression it had left her with. Two women on the bike. "It was a woman. Or at least I think it was a woman." She stood up.

"Where you going?"

"To get ready for my meeting tonight."

"So early?"

"I'm going with Alexis, and I need to pick out something to wear," Imani said. Even though it wasn't a competition, it was a competition that Alexis was winning, because she always dressed like she just had walked off a magazine cover.

When Alexis arrived at The Park and met with the service technicians, she was still running late. After she apologized for being late, the meeting got started, and it ran an hour longer than scheduled. After the meeting, Alexis made calls and waited while the technicians inspected the units and wrote up price quotes. Therefore, when she was getting up to leave, it was almost seven o'clock.

She drove as fast as safely possible to pick up Imani for their eight o'clock meeting, wondering why she hadn't arranged for Imani to meet her at the lawyer's office. When she got to the house and rang the bell, Hareem opened the door and told her that Imani would be right down. He then led Alexis into the great room, where Omeika was standing up in her playpen.

"And who is this adorable little lady?" Alexis asked as she went over to the playpen.

"She's my daughter," Hareem said proudly and plopped down on the couch in front of her.

"Your daughter? Why didn't you tell me you had a daughter?"

Hareem shrugged his shoulders. "You ain't been around in a minute."

"She's so cute. Can I pick her up?"

"Go ahead. She doesn't bite."

Alexis picked her up. "What's her name?"

"Her name is Omeika."

"That's pretty."

"Her mother named her."

"Where is her mother?"

"Upstairs, asleep."

Alexis glanced at Hareem. Knowing that Cynthia was pregnant the last time she saw her, Alexis wondered how to ask her next question delicately. "Do I know her?"

"No, you two have never met."

"We have got to do better than this. You know you're like a brother to me. You could have called and said, 'Hey, Alexis, I got a daughter,' or something."

Once again, Hareem shrugged his shoulders and wondered, *Why do all the really fine women always see me as their brother?* "I thought Imani would have told you."

"And me and Miss Imani are going to have to talk about that," Alexis said just as Imani came into the room.

"Talk about what?"

"Hareem's daughter," Alexis said and put Omeika back in her playpen.

"I thought he told you," Imani said, and then she started for the front door.

"The three of us are going to have to work on our communication," Alexis said and followed Imani out.

After their offer on the hotel was accepted, Alexis took Imani back to her house and then went home. For real estate agent and investor Alexis Fox, the day was over. As soon as she got home, she kicked off her Gucci sandals, came out of that virgin wool suit, ran a hot bath, and sank into it with a glass of wine. When the water began to get cold, she got out, dried herself, and laid out her clothes and shoes for the evening: an Alice + Olivia "Avelina" vegan leather wide-leg jumpsuit, a Devonte embroidered leather moto jacket, and Giuseppe Zanotti mock-croc zip combat booties.

Then she selected her jewelry: limited edition Syna abalone drop earrings, a Nikos Koulis "Oui" eighteen-karat white gold and enamel teardrop pendant necklace encrusted with diamonds, an eighteen-karat white gold diamond coil bracelet with three rows, an eternity band with diamonds, a three-stone diamond ring for her left hand, an onyx and diamond ring because it matched her outfit, and a crossover wide diamond ring because it was her favorite.

When she was dressed, she grabbed her black Serpui "Laila" floral straw bag with the wooden top handle, put on a pair of oversized, round, light-adaptive acetate sunglasses, got in her Jaguar F-Type coupe, and headed out for the night. When she arrived at her destination, she parked and walked to the door and rang the bell.

Cameron opened the door.

"What's up, Diamond? Come on in."